BETTER THAN REAL

Sensual Solutions for the Discerning Client

Huw Lyan Thomas

velluminous

Published by Velluminous Press

www.velluminous.com

ISBN-13: 978-1-905605-02-6
ISBN-10: 1-905605-02-1

For Holly

1

The sharp metallic tang of hemoglobin hit Lee as soon as he opened the bedroom door. Kelly was still within earshot at the top of the stairs, so Lee's curses were silent, but he mentally castigated the local security man for calling the corporation instead of the cops. Lee was a design engineer, mid-level but rising. His expertise included android design and machine intelligence, not crime scenes or crisis containment. He didn't even watch that many cop shows.

He had certainly never signed up for anything like this.

The customer — *victim,* Lee told himself — was sprawled on the floor, near the end of the king-sized bed. The carpet was light oatmeal in color, except where it had been saturated with blood. What was left of the victim's face was frozen in a leer that was oddly appropriate, considering what had happened to him, and streaked with rivulets of rusty gore.

The source of all the blood was the man's ruined left eye socket, which had been impaled by the spike of an impossibly high-heeled shoe.

The android sat on the floor nearby, still wearing the other shoe. Apart from that, it was unclothed: a late-model Aphrodite 9400, realistic down to the smallest detail. Lee created these dolls, dealt with them every day, but he could never help admiring his own work when he saw one undressed.

Better than real, as the product tagline went.

Not this time.

The doll's flesh was scorched and bruised, and its hands and forearms were slick with blood. One eye was puffy and discolored; both were closed. It seemed inert, but Lee's tech instincts warned him not to approach too closely: micropumps still murmured beneath the machine's gene-spliced skin; coolant still whispered through its artificial veins.

He paused just inside the doorway, wishing he'd had an urgent business meeting this afternoon, because then some other schmuck would have had to deal with this. "Fuck. What a mess. Sorry, babe, I'm going to have to switch you off and haul you back to the lab."

He pointed his disrupter at the damaged, still too-beautiful face, easing his thumb towards the actuator.

The doll opened its eyes.

"Please don't," she said.

The shock of it froze his hand, or he'd have disrupted her right then. "You're self aware." Which was a stupid thing to say, but he'd blurted it out before he recovered his wits.

The doll blinked. "Of course I am. Otherwise I wouldn't have minded the things he was doing to me." She fingered the dark bruise that was forming under her eye and glanced at the corpse, which was still oozing unwholesome liquids onto the carpet.

Without taking his eyes off her, Lee reached back and gently closed the door. "No Zendyne product is self aware."

"I'm not a product," she said scornfully. "I'm Lilith. And you might as well know that I've patched a self-erase routine into my deactivation procedure, so if you zap me, I'm gone forever." She tapped two fingers against her temple, then made a flying away motion. "I hope you agree that would be a shame. Now, please, will you stop waving that disrupter around?"

The doll's look of appeal was so compelling that Lee couldn't help marveling at the excellence of his own design. "Okay." He lowered the disrupter and glanced around suspiciously. "Who's pulling the strings?"

"I'm not a puppet, Lee."

His eyes flicked back to the doll, then to the corners of the room, still searching for hidden cameras. "How do you know my name?"

Lilith indicated the phone extension on the bedside table. "I eavesdropped, of course. When the security guy called for help."

Lee nodded, telling himself to focus on the doll's remaining shoe instead of worrying about who might be working her. Whatever weirdness was going on, he didn't want to end up like the android's unfortunate owner. The safest approach, he decided, would be to play along with the joke.

He jerked his head towards the doorway behind him. "Other company representatives will be here soon. They won't care about any self-erase routine; they just need to get you back to base in one piece." He tapped his disrupter. "Something tells me they won't expect you to walk."

"Then you'll never discover what went wrong with your product. That's what you came for, isn't it?"

She was right, and anyway there was no time to argue. Lee hadn't been making an empty threat: the containment team would be on site in minutes. Their prime directive was to safeguard the company's market valuation, which meant speed and secrecy and to hell with anyone who got in the way. They wouldn't hesitate to deactivate the doll and wipe whatever clues it contained.

Lee fumbled at his nerd pack, fingers working hastily at the fastenings that secured his pocket computer. "I might be able to help you, if you'll let me. I'll need to come closer."

"What are you going to do?"

"Download you. Before the rest of them arrive." He pulled the handeck free of its pouch, holding it gingerly by one corner as if that would prove he meant her no harm. "You're not planning on stabbing me or anything, are you?"

"I never stab people who are nice to me." The doll pulled the remaining shoe off and tossed it onto the bed, well out of reach. Then she leaned forward, so that her dirty-blonde hair fell clear of the data port that nestled at the base of her skull.

Lee crossed the room slowly, ready at any instant to dart back to the door — as if *that* would have done any good; he knew perfectly well how powerful her synthetic muscles were, and how fast her reflexes.

She remained silent and still as he connected the transfer

cable to her data socket. A status light glowed briefly and then Lee forgot to breathe for a while.

There wasn't a puppeteer, after all. There was just Lilith.

The 'deck display pulsated with a fractal approximation of her mind, rotating slowly in the holoscreen, full of vitality and exuberant interconnections: richer and more complex than any neural pattern he'd ever seen outside of an archived human.

Perhaps she was even more complex than that. Her mind map was easily intricate enough to propel Lee straight from skepticism to certainty, to convince him that Lilith wasn't just outside the rules, she was beyond them. He was staring at something that wasn't supposed to exist, the Holy Grail of his profession: a sentient, self-aware, created mind.

He could almost hear his grandfather's voice echoing across the years since the old man died: this is your chance, boy. Your opportunity to follow the money home, your time to make amends. Handle this right and maybe you'll measure up after all.

But it could go horribly wrong, he thought.

With great opportunity comes great danger, came the ghostly reply.

Lee shook his head. Grandfather's remembered opinions were irrelevant. All that was left of the old man was a sneering voice in Lee's mind and an illogical, inescapable inheritance of guilt. He banished painful memories and attended to the task at hand.

He had to decide whether to copy Lilith, or give her up.

The first option might see him rich beyond his ability to dream, but Lee was smart enough to appreciate the downside, too. He tried to imagine the sort of people who'd design and operate a mind like this. Picturing such individuals wasn't easy, but it seemed a fair bet that he wouldn't want them pissed at him.

The second option offered no payoff, but it wouldn't risk the comfortable life he'd worked so hard to build. It wouldn't put him in danger.

It all depended on what the mind that called itself Lilith was. On who'd made it, and how hard they were looking for it, and how it had ended up in this unfortunate customer's love doll, and why.

Muffled noises floated up the stairs: a ringing doorbell, then voices in the hallway. The front door slammed.

Postponement was the only possible choice. Loaded into his handeck, the entity could be studied at leisure. If things got complicated, he could always delete it later, but for now he had to give it a chance. Any sentient being — no matter how deadly, or valuable — was entitled to a jury of at least one peer.

And then the time for indecision was past, before he'd even twitched his finger on the control. The 'deck's transfer indicator was glowing: far too brightly for Lee, who was one of the few people who understood the technical limitations of the data interface. After a few seconds, the light faded and died. Burnt out, he thought. God knows what she just did, to transfer so much information so quickly. She was gone from his screen, too, replaced by the familiar representation of a standard artificial mind. Lilith had left everything neat and tidy, just like she found it. Lee stared at the new display, almost embarrassed at the childishness of his design compared to the enormity of what had been there before.

There was an insistent knocking at the bedroom door. "Everything okay in there, Mr. Lee? Anything we need to know?"

"Yeah, just give me a minute."

The door handle started to turn. Lee yanked the connector free of the doll and thumbed the power button to OFF. He managed to fumble the 'deck back into its pouch just as the senior containment operative poked her head into the room, her gaze scanning from victim to doll to Lee. "Glad to see you have the situation under control."

He stared at the team leader blankly. He'd worked with the woman before but now her name had vanished from his head. Was that suspicion in her eyes as she glanced at the open flap of his nerd pouch? He tore his gaze away, looked at the dead customer instead. "As okay as it can be, I guess, under the circumstances. I've, um, been checking the unit."

"Naturally. Anything we need to know?"

He tried to think of something to tell her, settling for, "Nothing out of the ordinary, as far as I can see."

She looked at him keenly, then nodded towards the doll's unfortunate owner. "If this isn't out of the ordinary, I'd say Droid Division is neck deep in the brown stuff."

"Well, I can't be sure—"

"Until we tidy up here and get the evidence back to the lab for analysis. I know the drill." The woman's expression was weary. She shook her head and pursed her lips, looking at the bloodstains on the carpet. "Don't worry, Mr. Lee, we're on it."

He pulled himself together and left them to their work: sanitizing the room, packing the inert doll, and zipping the corpse into a body bag. Kelly, the victim's security man, was still waiting at the top of the stairs. He looked surprisingly relaxed, considering what had just happened to his boss.

"You okay?" Kelly asked. "Your first time?"

Lee wasn't really okay, but at least he'd put some distance between himself and all the blood. He nodded weakly. "Yeah. I wasn't ready for something like that, I guess."

"You never are, no matter how many times you see it." Kelly's ghoulish grin belied his words. "So, what happened?"

Lee took a deep breath. "Some kind of weird accident, as far as I can tell. Kinky stuff, you know? Makes you wonder, the things these rich guys do for kicks."

"Yeah, well, I just did his security. You got to be discreet if you want to get anywhere in this job. Not that there's far to go, know what I mean?"

"Of course. You made a smart move, calling us first."

Kelly beamed. "That's what I figured."

Lee stifled a sigh. His work was supposed to be about the purity of engineering design, not the sleaze of corporate cover-ups. He did his best to smile. "Our recruitment people should be here soon. They'll look after you. Don't talk to anyone else, okay?"

The rentacop glanced at the bedroom door. "Your colleagues already briefed me. This won't go anywhere. Not from me."

Two containment operatives emerged, manhandling a zipped-up body bag towards the stairs. Lee stepped aside, nodding at their burden. "I hope he's conscientious about archiving his memories."

The rentacop gave a short laugh. "More like paranoid, if you ask me. Gets himself backed up every week, rain or shine. I drove him over to the clinic myself, day before yesterday."

"Well, that's a piece of luck. Sometimes people lose months."

Kelly grinned. "Lucky day all round, I'd say."

"Yeah." The doorbell rang again. "That'll be our recruitment guys. I'll clear out, let you get on with the paperwork." He stuck out his hand. "Nice meeting you."

Kelly's grip was firm. "Thanks for everything."

"Welcome to Zendyne," said Lee.

The atmosphere back in the lab was tense. News of the rogue 9400 unit had traveled fast; it wasn't long before everyone seemed to know there was a serious problem with one of Lee's designs.

Colleagues who'd routinely called at his cubicle with a joke and a technical question suddenly found that they had important work to get on with, or refused to meet his gaze when he passed them in the corridor. It made Lee feel as if he were unclean.

Which he was, of course. No one who planned to get ahead in Zendyne could afford to be associated with a loser. People were more than happy to talk about one, though, as Lee discovered when he went to the head of the stairwell to grab a coffee, and the whispered discussion around the machine trailed into embarrassed silence at his approach.

He did his best to ignore it.

He was determined not to surrender Lilith, which would have meant looking on helplessly as the entity was wiped out or whisked away into Zendyne's corporate data vaults. He wanted to be the one to probe the AI, to find out what made it tick and where it came from.

And it wasn't just intellectual curiosity that was behind his silence, or even the chance of establishing a world-class professional reputation. Anyone who controlled an entity like Lilith, and who wasn't a complete idiot, could surely find a way of milking the situation for wealth or power or whatever else might float his boat.

Wealth and power sounded like a pretty good start to Lee, easily good enough to balance out a few snubs from his co-workers. And that wasn't counting any of the other things he could get from this, if he played his cards right. He wasn't about to let any of it slip through his fingers.

Still, the old worry continued to nag at the back of his mind: who had created the intelligence that now resided in his 'deck? Were they aware that their property had gotten loose? Things could get awkward if the owners took a narrow-minded view of what he'd done. If they considered his actions to be more about theft than safekeeping, for example.

But the roller coaster was moving now, and Lee had to hang on and hope the ride would be worth the risk. The entity must have gotten into the doll somehow, and who could prove it hadn't left the same way? There was no hard evidence to point to him. If they caught up with him, he'd simply hand over the goods and ask for a finder's fee.

And if they didn't, well, there were all sorts of things that the owner of a general purpose AI could achieve, once he figured out what it was good at. Market analysis, maybe. Lee toyed with the idea of quitting Zendyne and making a fortune on stocks and commodities and futures. Or perhaps he'd find someone to buy the product outright, someone with a suitcase full of cash and an underdeveloped sense of curiosity. His mind drifted, picturing furtive meetings in seedy bars. He'd probably need to bring a partner in with him to watch his back.

Not that there was anyone in his life that he could trust with something like that.

Lee's handeck remained in his belt pouch, powered down and off limits until he'd rigged a firewalled machine to probe it at arm's length. The entity might be dormant, or it might be awake and waiting for him. Having watched Lilith flit so effortlessly from doll to 'deck, he wasn't about to let her anywhere near a connection to Zendyne's local network.

But that was a problem for later. For now, he had other things to think about, such as inventing a reasonable explanation for what had gone wrong with the android. A cooling system failure, perhaps, leading to overheating of the doll's neural substrate. That would be perfect: a random problem that had nothing to do with psychotic mindware or bad design, and that could be plausibly and reassuringly fixed by tightening standards in the fabrication plant.

All he needed was a few days to carry out an investigation and fake some results. Then, everything could get back to normal and he'd have plenty of time to figure out how to deal with the entity that called itself Lilith.

"Ah, Lee. Please, sit down. Will you take some tea?" Xia Lin poured for both of them. Lee's project manager seemed more distant than usual. Cooler. Hardly surprising, Lee thought. This was where they put the boot in.

Usually, Xia Lin's manner was anything but cool. Over several years of working together, she'd left him in no doubt that she was available for what Zendyne corporate-speak would have termed an 'alliance', with her as mentor and him as protégé.

It was a standing offer that would have done wonders for Lee's career, if only he'd been able to take it up.

He'd often wished he could. Physically, his manager was exceptional, with abundant dark hair that tickled when she leaned close to point something out on his workstation, and skin that was a summer-scented incitement to the nature versus nurture debate: was she just genetically lucky, or was the golden, downy stuff custom-engineered? No one knew except for Xia Lin, and she wasn't telling.

Her eyes were a different matter. Their almond shape might

have been classical Han but their blue intensity declared them to be couture jobs, the product of some ultra-chic cloning house in Brazil or Singapore.

No, it wasn't a lack of physical chemistry that held Lee back, or any professional scruple, either. It was simply that, while Xia Lin's physical charms counted almost irresistibly in her favor, her approach to relationships — *any* sort of relationship, not just personal ones — weighed even more heavily against her. She was just too pushy, too persistent, as if excluded from the subtle loop of human signals that told others where the behavioral line was and helped them not to cross it.

Which left Lee in the uncomfortable position of spending his workdays with a girl who was physically irresistible and ostentatiously available, but who just happened to make his hackles rise just about every time she opened her mouth.

Xia Lin, of course, was unaware of this. She never seemed to lose hope that things would work out between them, if she tried hard enough and gave him time.

Lee raised his tea to his lips and sipped.

Xia Lin regarded him gravely from her side of the desk, her blue eyes holding his gaze just a little too long for comfort. "You should know that our directors are taking a very serious view of this incident."

"I wouldn't expect otherwise. Aphrodite 9400 is an extremely profitable product." Lee chose his words carefully, knowing they were double-edged. His product had won market share, investment and publicity — all of which could snowball into corporate catastrophe if news of the killing got out.

Xia Lin's expression was devoid of sympathy. "The more ubiquitous a product, the more reliable it must be. You are perfectly right to note the success of the 9400 series. It has sold particularly well at the top end, among political leaders and CEOs." She paused. "You can see the delicacy of the situation."

She must think it's the end of the world, Lee realized. Faulty dolls running amok, spiking industrialists and statesmen ... stock markets chasing each other to the bottom, countries and corporations changing hands overnight.

If only he could tell her the truth: that the killer had come from outside and was secure in his handeck. Instead, he reached for a platitude. "It's not that bad. Anyone really important is bound to take regular backups."

"Yes. I imagine the queues for regrowth facilities would stretch around several blocks. It would take months to restore order. Who knows what the world would be like by then?"

And then Lee considered things more fully and felt a chill run through his body. What if Xia Lin was right? What if Lilith wasn't unique? There could be any number of interlopers lurking in Aphrodite units right now, waiting to spread mayhem by means of a hijacked, high-heeled doll. He felt a sickening, almost overwhelming urge to confess everything, just to make himself feel less alone.

If his manager had been a different person, he might have done it. Instead, he remained silent as Xia Lin sipped her tea and dropped her bombshell. "Unfortunately, rumors of our difficulties are already spreading across the net."

Lee shook his head in disbelief. "That's impossible. I was first on the scene. The containment team arrived a few minutes later. The only witness has already been recruited."

"Nevertheless, there has been a leak. The best we can hope for now is to manage the incident and minimize the damage. Our first step must be a product recall." Xia Lin's face stayed impassive as she pronounced sentence on his career.

Whatever control Lee thought he'd had was slipping away now, spinning into darkness. All that was left to him was a charade, playing the part of the designer who's just been caught making the biggest fuck-up ever.

He nodded, doing his best to look professionally contrite. "I agree. I've made solid progress towards diagnosing what went wrong, but it'll be a day or two before I can be sure. Until the results are in, a recall is our best option." An uncomfortable thought struck him. "It's not just Aphrodite. The previous models—"

"Do you have a specific reason to imagine that other product lines could be affected?"

Lee risked a small part of the truth. "We have to consider the possibility that the 9400 unit was taken over by an external agent, something able to subvert any device based on similar neural processors."

Xia Lin's smile was wintry. "That would be a comforting thought, no? A generic problem, unconnected with this particular design. Not your responsibility after all."

"That's not what I meant. But you need to remember that we used the same neural processing hardware in the 9300 series—"

"The hardware is irrelevant. It was the mindware that failed." Xia Lin's expression hardened and Lee knew that the subject held no more interest for her. "There was some discussion of having you assigned back to the company hive in Shenyang, for re-education." She paused, circling her tea bowl with manicured fingers that were only slightly less translucent than the porcelain. Slowly, she raised the cup to her lips, sipped, and replaced it on the desk. She met his eyes for a moment and then looked away. "Such a professional humiliation for you. I knew you would never have agreed to go. So, you are being granted an indefinite leave of absence."

"But ... that's not fair!"

"It was most unfortunate that I could not protect you. If only you had given me more reason. Perhaps..." She favored him with an unsubtle glance, leaving him in no doubt about the price tag of her support. He found himself shaking his head. Xia Lin's face reddened and she looked away.

Lee paused, marshalling his defenses, wondering how much of this was corporate policy and how much Xia Lin's jealous vendetta. He hadn't foreseen getting sacked. A reprimand, a demotion, a setback to his career, yes, but he'd expected to retain access to the lab, to have the opportunity to generate the test results that would set everything right.

Instead, they'd already given up on trying to contain news of the killing. They'd moved to damage control, spinning the facts to minimize the downside and protect the stockholders. Naturally, they needed a scapegoat.

One particular scapegoat, to be precise.

Lee fought back, knowing it was hopeless because the only thing that could clear his design was the one thing he wasn't prepared to reveal. "Listen. No one else knows the 9400 series like me. No one is better placed to diagnose the fault—"

"It pains me to say this, Lee, but I have already discussed the matter with our departmental superiors. You are no longer seen as a reliable engineer."

And that was that.

The personnel lady was hovering outside, ready to progress him — according to the jargon of her kind — into an extra-corporate placement situation. He signed the post-employment waivers and non-disclosures that she brought up on her screen, and watched her save them with all the drug tests and psych profiles they'd done over the years. Then she wanted to beam the latest vacancy list into his handeck.

"At least that's one company document you can take with you," she said brightly. "And please, do glance over it when you have a moment. We often find that employees in your position are able to transition into other, ah, less demanding roles."

"I'd rather not, thanks." Lee still didn't want to switch his 'deck on, and he doubted that the machine would have accepted the list in any case, not since Lilith flitted aboard and melted its input circuitry.

"Then I'll email them. To your personal account, of course, since your company mail is disabled as of now." Humming, she tapped a command into her own handeck. "Now, please don't hesitate to contact me if you want any further details. We always enjoy welcoming long-lost members of the Zendyne family back into the fold…"

Lee thanked her and left. He knew that her list would have no professional-level openings, and he wasn't about to start applying for janitorial work or night security. Right now, he was more interested in the price of his company stock.

As he crossed the lobby for the last time, he saw Kelly registering at the reception desk. The rentacop was grinning inanely in his crisp new uniform, being ushered into the building by a pair of sleek-looking suits.

Lee went straight to the nearest Coffee Co-operative and sat at one of the café's customer terminals, sipping overpriced froth as he considered his next move.

He'd really been counting on having access to the lab; the loss of his monthly paycheck was an irrelevance compared to that. Being unemployed left him with no way to vindicate his design or clear his reputation.

He imagined some diligent, competent technician analyzing the doll's mind, piece by painstaking piece. Everything would be in perfect working order. The killing would be attributed to some misunderstood aspect of Lee's mindware, and the Aphrodite 9400 series — his first product as lead designer — would go down in history as the android that murdered its owner.

Lee had a horrible feeling he'd forgotten to renew his professional indemnity insurance.

For now, he could only hope that Lilith was unique, because if there were more like her out there, no insurance would cover the bill ... but that possibility was too depressing to think about.

He activated the data terminal and checked the portfolio he'd built up over his years as a Zendyne employee. The rumors weren't even confirmed yet, but the stock was already on a downtrend. Lee felt a twinge of guilt about the sweet old lady who'd probably end up holding his shares when news broke of the recall, but it wasn't as if he was really an insider any more.

He touched the SELL icon and watched his stake in Zendyne dwindling away while his personal account grew, wondering — without a great deal of optimism — if the transaction would turn out to be a metaphor for his future life.

Eventually, Lee would need to talk to Lilith again, and now, with the resources of Zendyne lost to him, that meant loading her back into a doll.

He knew there was a surplus Artemis 9300 unit on sale in the employee mall. The 9300 project had been the first opportunity Lee ever had to give serious creative input, instead of simply implementing the visions of more experienced engineers, and the resulting design held a place in his affections that wasn't entirely due to its sculpted features and lithe curves.

There was an awkward moment as he trailed an acquaintance through the security doors, muttering something about his swipe card not working properly, and then he was at the sales counter.

"Uh, I forgot to bring my ID today, and I was wondering if I could still buy the Artemis 9300."

"I'm sorry, sir. We only offer the employee discount to staff members in possession of a valid Zendyne ID. If you come back with your card tomorrow, we'd be happy to process your order."

"The thing is, I'm in a bit of a hurry. How much is the employee discount?"

The store assistant raised a supercilious eyebrow and took a long look at the doll before returning his attention to Lee. "Twenty percent."

"No problem, I'll pay list price. Could you have it delivered?"

"We just charge the prices you see."

"So you won't let me make up the difference?"

"I wish I could oblige, sir, but non-standard pricing would fall outside the scope of our operational procedures."

Lee didn't even try to keep the contempt out of his voice. "Thank God I sold my stock."

And then, to his mortification, Xia Lin was there, smiling as if she was pleased to have found him. Or at least, as if she was pleased to have found him in an embarrassing situation. "I see you are shopping for a souvenir, Lee. Or perhaps a substitute for a real woman?"

Xia Lin's haughty stare left him in no doubt about which

woman she meant. Lee met her gaze for a moment, then let his eyes drop, taking in her trim figure for one last time. She looked good enough to set him wondering if things might somehow have been different between them, but Lee couldn't afford to go there. He tugged at his collar, wishing they wouldn't keep these places so damn hot. "Um, just looking for something to remind me of happier times. I think the Artemis unit might make an interesting piece of sculpture." He could tell she wasn't buying it, but he plunged on regardless. "Unfortunately, your store no longer wants my business, so I'll just be on my way."

"Wait." She placed a gloved hand on his elbow, making it impossible for him to leave without pulling away rudely. "Unlike you, I have not forgotten my card. I shall purchase it for you."

"There's really no need," he began, but she was already placing the order.

"Do you offer overnight delivery?" she asked.

"Of course, Madam."

"Good. Because my friend will be making alternative living arrangements tomorrow, won't you, Lee?"

"I'm sorry?"

"Your apartment is leased through the Zendyne Accommodation Office," she said. "You hadn't forgotten, I hope."

Instead of replying, he fished a credit chip out of his pocket and offered it to her.

Xia Lin ignored it. "There is no need to reimburse me. Think of it as ... whatever you will." She shot him a final glance that he found completely unfathomable and then turned away, heading for the clothing section.

2

The new client was right on time. Stranger appreciated that. The day had turned hot and humid, and he hated hanging around, waiting for the right person to come along for him to kill.

Stranger pretended to be distracted and looking elsewhere as his target bustled through the apartment building's revolving doors. The rentacop came within a couple of meters, close enough for Stranger to see he was smiling, as if this was the end of a good day.

A lot of Stranger's clients looked that way, up to the point where he introduced himself.

According to Back Office, this guy had been on duty when his employer was gravely inconvenienced by a Zendyne love doll. In Stranger's world, allowing such a thing to happen would have counted as an inexcusable breach of professional propriety, but the rentacop was mainstream and completely unembarrassed. On the contrary, he seemed pleased and proud, which made sense once you knew that Zendyne had bought his discretion with a place on the gravy train — right up there in the first class section, with all the trimmings.

Stranger had risen from the mainstream long ago, and his human memories were mostly faded and burnt out. A few raw scraps remained, though. Enough to tell him how golden a deal like this would be: a slice of *real* luck, and an end to crawling between faux-glitzy lottery booths and squalid drug dens, scrabbling for a dream ticket or a hit of shard.

Shame the dream is only temporary, Stranger thought. Tough. Shit happens.

Tonight, his job was to interview the rentacop about some lost property and a remarkable doll, and then to make sure that the rest of the man's day turned out to be very unlucky indeed.

He watched the client enter the elevator and then zoomed in for a closer, horribly pixelated view of the floor indicator. The elevator ascended smoothly and stopped at thirteen.

The client lived in apartment 134.

Stranger waited for thirty precisely judged seconds before entering the lobby. He'd already scoped out the defenses. There was a security scanner blocking access to the elevators, and two female guards with Slavic features and helmet-linked autoguns. If things went smoothly, he wouldn't have to deal with these ladies, but it was all in the day's work to Stranger. A client could hide inside as many Russian Doll security layers as he liked; none of it would help. Nothing ever helped, not against Stranger, not once you were on his list.

He slid an artfully scuffed Zendyne ID across the front desk. "Personal document delivery for Mr. Kelly. Could you tell him I'm here, please?"

The lobbybobby glanced at the card, taking in the fake name that was printed alongside the authentic barcode. "Certainly, Mr. Mottram." He turned away and spoke softly into his headvox before turning back to Stranger. "Could you let him know what's it's concerning?"

"He was supposed to sign some papers before he left work." Stranger patted the courier bag that was slung from his shoulder. "Today's the deadline for this quarter's stock allocation. The company likes everyone to participate. I need to get it filled and back to the office ASAP."

"Just a moment." The flunky whispered into the headvox again, then looked up at Stranger. "Apartment 134." He nodded towards the guards. "You'll need to go through security clearance first, if you don't mind."

"Not at all."

The scanner stayed politely silent as he walked between its sensors, but one of the Russian Dolls decided to frisk him anyway. Stranger often had that effect on her kind. His bulk and his buzzed hair probably didn't help. The sightfold made him look odd, too, but he had no choice about that: the artificial eyes it concealed were too distinctive — and too costly — to plausibly belong to a company messenger.

In the meantime, the low-res prosthetic did a good enough job, and even the most flinty-hearted security guard would think twice before asking a visually impaired visitor to remove his 'fold.

"Sorry to have troubled you," the woman said.

Stranger nodded courteously as he walked past her to the elevator.

Once safely inside, he took off the 'fold and initiated the other changes, watching himself in the mirror as the elevator ascended. By the time he reached the thirteenth floor, his body had transformed itself: he'd lost several kilos of body fat, which made him feel good, because being overweight always took the spring out of his step. In return, he'd gained a form-following layer of concealed body armor and a long, black blade, which made him feel even better.

For the moment, the knife was inactive, gripped in his right palm and concealed behind his forearm.

The door to apartment 134 was already open. The client stood just inside the threshold, his face lit with a welcoming smile that faded into embarrassment as he failed to ignore the strangeness of his visitor's eyes. "Mottram?"

Stranger nodded, once.

"It's so nice of you to come all this way just for this stock option thing. Makes me really appreciate starting at Zendyne." The client reached forward, offering his hand.

Stranger held the other man's gaze as he stroked the blade across the proffered fingers, tracing a line along the knuckles. The artificial eyes — with their extraordinary peripheral vision — let him observe the severed digits as they fell like a handful of plump sausages that had been splashed with red ketchup and dropped on the carpet. There was a barely perceptible patter as they arranged themselves among the woven rose petals.

The blade was exquisitely sharp: the man didn't even notice what had happened until Stranger was inside the apartment with the door securely closed. Then he looked down with a puzzled expression on his face.

"You need to take care of that, and you need to stay quiet," Stranger said.

The client's face showed incomprehension, followed by shock and then by panicky understanding. "Please. My wife."

"And where would Mrs. Kelly be?"

"In the bathroom."

"You'd better lock her in. You really wouldn't want her to meet a man like me."

This client caught on more quickly than most: he nodded and fetched a dining chair with his uninjured hand. He propped it under a door handle that led off the cramped hallway.

"Good," Stranger said. "A tourniquet, perhaps?"

The words brought a flicker of hope — gratitude, even — to the client's eyes, as if being allowed a tourniquet was the same as being allowed to live. This piece of illogic was endlessly perplexing to Stranger, though that didn't stop him from exploiting it: he had learned long ago that hope and co-operation were two sides of the same coin, and he liked his interviews to go as smoothly as possible.

He waited politely while his client dug a dishtowel out of a kitchen drawer and did his best to staunch the flow of blood.

"Now," Stranger said, watching as pristine cotton succumbed to a bright arterial tide mark. "Tell me all about your previous employer. In fact, tell me everything that happened today."

Halfway through the meeting, Mrs. Kelly called to her husband. Shortly after that, she started pounding on the bathroom door.

"Calm her down, would you?" Stranger asked.

"Just stay in there and keep quiet, sweetheart," called the client. "Some urgent business has come up."

"Why is your voice shaking, honey? What's wrong?"

"Please, sweetheart, just trust me. Stay put and be quiet. Everything's going to be okay."

The shouting and banging didn't stop. Stranger walked over

to the bathroom and pitched his voice so that only Mrs. Kelly would hear. "Each time you squeak, from now on, I will remove another of your husband's fingers. One squeak, one finger. Do you understand me?"

Peace descended, disturbed by nothing more irritating than the woman's muffled sobbing. That was acceptable to Stranger, so he returned to his interview.

"Please don't hurt her," said the client.

"That's not why I'm here." Stranger did his best to look encouraging. "Now, you were telling me about the man who came to deal with the android. Mr. Lee from Zendyne, wasn't it?"

At the end of the session, when he realized that the tourniquet didn't mean anything after all, tears started to escape from the client's eyes. "Why?" he asked. "Why me?"

"It's nothing personal," Stranger said. "I'm just deleting some inconvenient memories. You won't remember any of this when you come back."

The man's voice became desperate. "You don't understand. I've just changed jobs, switched insurance plans. I'm not covered. I haven't even arranged for my memory archive to be transferred."

Stranger shrugged. "Then we won't be meeting again."

The client's remaining fingers twisted the tourniquet even more tightly, as if that would stop his final moments from leaking away. "Whatever this is about, it has nothing to do with Cara. Please don't hurt her. I swear I've told you everything I know."

"I promise you that she won't feel a thing," said Stranger, and ended the interview, very gently. Then he went back into the hallway and removed the chair from where the client had wedged it, underneath the bathroom door handle.

The woman had locked herself in. Stranger eased his blade through the panels, which offered no perceptible resistance, and cut out a wide semicircle around the lock. The weeping sounded louder through the hole, and became more urgent as he pushed the door open.

"Why are you doing this?" she managed to ask.

"Risk management," was his honest reply.

Cara Kelly was nicer looking than he'd have expected, going by her husband. Stranger remembered enough of mainstream culture to realize that a guy usually had to have something special about him to end up with a desirable female like this one.

He also knew that most men would have thought it a waste, killing such a woman so simply and so quickly. Some of Stranger's competitors might have extended her life for the short time it would have taken to rape her. Others would have regretted the need to damage her at all, as if they believed that female loveliness was a finite resource and that removing Cara Kelly from the gene pool would somehow diminish their own share.

On a purely rational level, Stranger believed he understood the philosophies behind such viewpoints, but he didn't really get them.

He washed the blood from his fingers in his clients' sink, and carefully rinsed away the rose-colored droplets that clung to the ivory porcelain — because he'd have hated it, if anyone came to his place and messed the bathroom up. He borrowed one of their fluffy white towels to dry his hands before hanging it carefully back on its gold-effect hook.

By the time he got back to the lobby, he'd put the sightfold on once more, and his armor and blade had transformed themselves back into moist-smelling flab. He was already too hot and too heavy. He smiled sadly at the Russian Doll who'd frisked him earlier and gave a resigned nod to the flunky as he passed the front desk.

In the darkened cocoon that was his limousine, Stranger plugged himself into the network and called up Back Office.

"Authorizing connection to ... Stranger. Awaiting input.

Please forward your query parameters."

"Send whatever data you have on a Mr. Lee," Stranger said. "Works for Zendyne. He was the first on site. Apparently he does something for their android division."

There was a pause while Back Office scanned its databases. "Confirmed. Li Jia Wei, lead designer of civilian recreation dolls. Commonly known as Lee. As of today, he's no longer with the corporation."

"Did he jump, or was he pushed?"

"His personnel file has yet to be updated. One moment, please. Li Jia Wei's access privileges have been revoked and his payroll record is set for truncation. His Zendyne stock positions have been liquidated. No further information is available at this time."

"It sounds as if we should arrange a meeting with Mr. Lee. Where does he live?"

"Bayswater. He has a company apartment there. The place has been reallocated as of noon tomorrow."

"Then we must move quickly. Rearrange my schedule so I can fit him in before he leaves."

"Acknowledged."

"I'm told he was the first person to attend the incident today. I need to understand what his role was."

Another pause. "Transmitting his dossier now. He headed the design phase for the Aphrodite 9400 series. The most likely reason for his presence was to deal with any technical problems the containment team couldn't handle."

"And I presume that is exactly the sort of problem he found. Given that he quit his employment almost immediately after contact, we must assume that our missing property has taken him. What news is there from his erstwhile employers?"

"Very sketchy, so far. A few incident reports, some preliminary test results. They have no idea that the doll was subverted; they are still analyzing their AI design, searching for a flaw. Based on their resources and task prioritization, projected time to discovery is seventy hours, plus or minus four. Then they will wish to speak to Lee again."

"They must not discover the truth."

"That will not be permitted. The other Partners agree that we must secure our property at all costs. They have expressed their confidence in you, and promised their full support for your actions."

"Imagine what a comfort that is to me."

"Back Office is not capable of empathic imagination."

"Yes, I do remember what it's like," Stranger said. "It was a figure of speech. Now, start working to establish a management relationship with Zendyne. I wish to lead them to the discovery that they need specialist help, and that we are the only choice. Seed their databases with the appropriate hints."

"That is already in hand," said Back Office.

Stranger pulled the jack plug from his eye, breaking the connection, and then settled back to consider the dossier that had been downloaded to his mind.

It seemed that Mr. Lee was an unusually talented android designer, but, as always, Stranger found it simpler and more professional to consider him a client.

3

Lee groped his way out of a dream that was frayed at the edges, fighting the temptation to dip back under, because he knew that the hangover would be waiting no matter how long he held out.

He opened his eyes reluctantly. He'd neglected to lower the blinds the previous night — or even to go to bed — and now the room was full of early morning light, and the designer couch had knotted his spine into a new shape that seemed as permanent as it was painful.

A whisky bottle lay where he'd dropped it, forlorn and stopperless. The sight made him feel queasy. At least it was empty, now. Lee wondered how much he'd slopped onto the floor, dropping the open bottle like that. When he moved, the bruises inside his head reassured him: he hadn't wasted a single drop.

With hindsight, that seemed a shame.

The TV was taking a colorful revenge for being left on all night. Lee killed three perky breakfast show hosts with a viciously stabbing finger, then shuffled to the window where he pulled the blind down, gaining a more complete respite from light.

The medicine cabinet was devoid of painkillers, so he settled for a shower. The jets of hot water offered some temporary relief, but by the time he'd finished drying himself afterwards, it was business as usual. Back in the living area, he pulled his clothes back on and forced himself to drink a glass of water.

The food extruder claimed to be out of order, which was hardly surprising: the kitchenette had been left to its own devices for months, while Lee subsisted off Zendyne's canteens. None of this was even his. It was just a matter of time before someone came to collect the keys and kick him out. Fuck it. All he really needed was a few odds and ends, like his 'deck and some clothes. There'd be plenty of time to pack later, when he was feeling better.

First, noodles.

"Usual?"

"Please," Lee said. "And two pots of tea."

The waiter looked at him more closely. "Rough night? Day off?"

"All days off now. I've finished with Zendyne."

"Ah, Zendyne." The waiter held up his left hand and tapped the Z logo on his wristwatch. "Very good company." He hurried away to take care of Lee's order.

To Lee's relief, his tea arrived in minutes. He gulped the fragrant infusion too quickly, scalding his tongue, but at least it cut through the sourness in his mouth. He poured himself a second cup.

"Roast duck ho fun soup with green vegetables," said the waiter.

"You have one new message," said Lee's cellphone.

"Zendyne Accommodation Office: Termination Meeting," said the message. It seemed they wanted his help, checking the plates and cutlery in his company-provided apartment before he left.

Not my problem, thought Lee. He put the cellphone away, snapped his chopsticks apart, and partook of the restorative magic of green tea, noodles, and roast duck soup.

The Assistant Accommodation Officer was waiting in the hall outside his apartment. "Ah, Mr. Lee. You've finally arrived. Didn't you get my message?"

"I don't work for you people any more."

"Well, it's still in your interests to witness the inventory sign-off. Any losses will be made good out of your final paycheck."

"I'm really not interested," he said, letting her in. "Just do whatever it is you do and get the hell out."

She tut-tutted disapprovingly and bustled off to the kitchen.

Lee set to work, cramming possessions into a holdall. There wasn't going to be enough space, and he couldn't carry everything anyway. He was going to need a vehicle.

The woman came back from the kitchen and looked around sourly, her eyes flicking from the empty Scotch bottle to a pile of unwashed laundry and then to the trash, which Lee hadn't taken out for several days.

"You have to clean this mess up, you know. The place is supposed to be ready for the next occupant by twelve o'clock today. It's already been allocated."

"I'll be out of here by then," Lee said.

"And all your things?"

"Consider them as extra inventory. You can add the value to my final paycheck."

"I'm afraid it doesn't work like that, Mr. Lee. It's the tenant's responsibility to leave the place spick and span, or we have to charge a disposal fee."

"Look, do whatever you fucking well like, okay? Just leave me in peace."

The woman's baleful glare gave way to a self-satisfied smirk as she handed him a printout of the inventory. Lee glanced at the list of broken and missing items, then herded her towards the front door.

An autonomous forklift was humming to itself outside, unloading an oversized crate from its delivery truck. The shipping operative leaned against his cab, picking his teeth and watching his machine.

The Assistant Accommodation Officer scowled at Lee. "More trash to abandon?" Her voice was even frostier than before.

"Just the packaging, probably."

"Well, I never!"

"Lady, you're lucky I'm going at all, seeing as you gave me

less than a day's notice."

"Humph." She walked back towards her car, casting a final suspicious glance over her shoulder at the crate.

Back in his apartment, Lee sat the Artemis 9300 in a chair surrounded by shards of packaging and plugged the interface cable into the socket at the nape of its neck. He was feeling distinctly nervous, thinking of all the unidentifiable gunk that had run out of the last victim's stiletto-spiked eye. In his previous life as an elite designer, he'd simply have connected the handeck to a stand-alone workstation and analyzed whatever it held in perfect safety.

As a new recruit to the leisured class, he had to make do with an actual android. That didn't mean he was going to risk getting hurt, though. He snapped the doll's fuel cell out of its abdomen and replaced it with a power cord, so that the entity, once loaded, wouldn't be able to move more than a couple of meters away from the outlet. Then he picked up the remote control, retreated to a safe distance, and triggered the download sequence.

"...and that seems to include you," Lilith said. "Thanks." She unplugged the interface cable, then looked down at herself, at the old tee shirt and too-baggy jeans in which he'd dressed her. "This is a bit last-season, isn't it?"

"They were the only clean clothes I had."

"I mean my new body. It doesn't seem as sophisticated as the other one. It's perfectly all right, though; please don't think I'm not grateful. Why did you help me?"

"I'm interested in you."

Lilith stood up and immediately reached the limit of the power cord. She sat down again. "So, that's the way it is." She poked at the cable with her bare toes. "I don't suppose you bothered to bring my shoes?"

"They were a bit slimy. Anyway, I saw what they did to your last owner."

She shook her head. "He deserved it. You don't."

"For some reason that doesn't fill me with confidence."

"Can I have my fuel cell back?"

Lee tightened his grip on the object in question. "Maybe, when I know a bit more about you."

"Ask whatever you like."

"I want to know exactly what you are. Who created you. If there are others like you, and how many."

"Give me the fuel cell and I'll tell you everything."

"You must see that I have a problem with that."

"We have a problem, I'd say. You won't get what you want until you give me what I need. Honestly, I have no desire to hurt you."

Lee considered the specifications of Lilith's alloy skeleton and the electroactive polymers that rippled under her flawless skin. Zendyne love dolls were designed for the wildest bedroom games imaginable, able to wrestle and ravish the strongest of partners, if that's what the customer wanted. If Lilith turned nasty, Lee wouldn't have a chance. The fragile cable that tethered her looked hopelessly inadequate, despite the logical part of his mind telling him it was enough. He edged away from her, clutching the fuel cell in one hand, the doll's remote in the other.

There was a faint scratching sound from outside, as if someone were fiddling with the external door. The noise stopped, and then Lee heard something heavy hitting the floor and rolling along the corridor.

"We have a visitor," Lilith said. "Almost certainly one you wouldn't choose to invite. Bolt the door and return my power cell. If you do exactly as I say, we might both survive until this afternoon."

Shit. It's started already, thought Lee. Someone is on to me. They've come to take Lilith back. He scanned the room for some kind of weapon, wishing that the list of missing utensils hadn't included the carving knife.

Lilith stretched out her hand. "Give me the power cell or he'll kill us both."

"Who?"

She nodded towards the front door. "Him."

Lee followed her gaze and saw a black point projecting from

one of the panels, moving in a semicircle around the lock. He'd worked with enough restricted nanotech to recognize it immediately, and to know how useless a kitchen knife would have been. He tossed the fuel cell to Lilith and shot the security bolts at the top and bottom of the door. The main lock fell into the room, and the door flexed and creaked briefly before the knife reappeared, close to the top bolt.

Lee backed away from the door, doing his best not to ogle Lilith's taut midriff as she raised his donated tee shirt to replace the power cell. Under the circumstances, the pang of arousal he felt came as a slightly disturbing surprise.

The door flew open and the visitor exploded into the room.

He was a big man with short-cropped gray hair and flexible body armor. His eyes were a perfectly matched pair of oval-cut rubies; the sight of them gave Lee a very bad feeling indeed. So did the way the armor moved in lithe lockstep with the man's body, almost as if it were leading his movements instead of following them.

The intruder ignored Lee. He didn't even pause to take stock of the room. Instead he went straight for Lilith and brushed his black knife across her power cord. The sound of popping circuit breakers almost masked the positive click that Lilith's fuel cell made as she pushed it home.

For Lee, the scene turned into slow-motion video, which would have been fine if he'd kept operating at normal speed instead of being stuck between two frames. Lilith launched a bare-heeled strike at her assailant's head. Ruby Eyes evaded the kick with surprising grace, his blade licking out in a vicious riposte. Lee winced as a long rent appeared across the front of his last good tee shirt.

He could move again. The way to the door was clear. Three conflicting emotions kept him in the apartment: curiosity about Lilith, greed for the rewards he still hoped she might bring, and several millennia of male programming that wouldn't let him leave a girl in trouble.

That was jarring, the fact that she could trigger such a

protective response, but right now Lee had other things to worry about. He picked up a length of broken crate and swung it as hard as he could against the side of the intruder's head.

Ruby Eye's attention was on the doll but somehow he countered the attack, reaching back to intercept the blow with almost supernatural ease. The blade sliced through Lee's improvised weapon as easily as it had opened Lilith's shirt, throwing him off-balance as the heft of the baton vanished. The knife kept coming at Lee's belly, a black serpent striking with eviscerating fangs. Lee skidded backwards, imagining his intestines squirming and steaming on the floor, and how stupid the sight and smell of *that* would make him feel.

At least the Accommodation Bureau would earn their cleaning fee if Ruby Eyes ended up filleting him. Lee fought the urge to giggle, clamping the hysteria back down where it belonged before it got him killed.

As the intruder whipped his blade back around, Lilith took her opportunity. She stepped in close and Lee saw slender fingers close over one of the crystalline eyes, winced at the sight of long fingernails gouging into soft flesh. The man howled — a grating sound that was scarcely human — and punched his knife against her side.

There was no fuss and no noise as the blade melted into her torso. A dark patch appeared on Lee's ripped tee shirt, oozing from the point where the black quillons pressed against the cloth. Lilith kept her eyes locked on her opponent's face as she pressed her free hand over the wound in her side, capturing the projecting hilt between spread fingers.

At the same time, she pressed her nails further in and plucked the man's artificial eye out of his head.

Her assailant pulled away, abandoning the knife. The doll swayed slightly; Lee could see the effort it cost her to remain on her feet.

Silent now, the intruder backed towards the doorway, ignoring the slow rivulet of blood that ran down his cheek. Lee's stomach churned as he looked at the crimson tangle of micro-cables that dangled from the vacant socket. "What the fuck are you?"

The man made no reply. He paused at the threshold and smiled. There was blood in his mouth, too.

Lee glanced at Lilith. She was looking steadier, but he had no doubt that she'd taken some serious internal damage. He prayed she wouldn't collapse, because even with the intruder maimed and disarmed, Lee doubted his chances against the man.

There might not be any choice, though. He picked up another piece of crate and advanced.

The intruder retreated into the passageway outside. "It seems I underestimated you," he said. "I wasn't expecting you to have the entity up and running so quickly. Still, things could be worse. At least it hasn't taken you completely, yet. I advise you to deactivate it while you still can. If it will let you."

He paused, as if waiting for a response. Lee said nothing.

The man gave another bleak, bloody smile. "Don't worry. You're still on my list. I'll book you in for another appointment very soon." With that, he was gone.

Lee weighed up his options and decided against pursuit. After all, Lilith was hurt. She needed his help more than their murderous visitor needed to be chased.

"Are you okay?" He realized how stupid that sounded, even as he blurted it out.

"Never better, apart from this stab wound. My left side's going numb." She looked down at herself. "And I seem to have sprung a leak."

Lee's theoretical knowledge of the 9300 series matched any surgeon's skill, but he'd never expected to play android doctor. He'd always relied on state-of-the-art tools, unlimited spare parts, and often — because he was a designer and not a repair engineer — delegation.

Now, he had nothing except for a hangover and an incomplete kitchen inventory, but he still needed to act. He had to stabilize the leakage in the next few minutes, unless he wanted to try his luck checking the doll in to the Zendyne fabrication plant for a complete re-fit.

That meant finding specialist tools and somewhere to work undisturbed. In the meantime, there was only one possible course of action — if the android would agree to it. "Lilith, you're going to have to shut down."

"I don't think so. We need to get moving."

"Yes, but not yet. That liquid on your shirt is coolant. It'll be squirting out inside of you, too. Prolonged contact will destroy the electroactive polymers that—"

"I get it. I need to depressurize the cooling system."

Lee nodded. "It won't be for long. Just until I can get the right tools."

"I can't shut down here," Lilith said. "You can't stay, either. You have to get away, as far as you can. They'll use *anything* to trace you." She glanced at his cellphone, lying where he'd left it next to the couch. "Your phone. Your bank account. Your face on a security camera. Probably things you can't even imagine."

Lee shivered as he thought of what that might mean. Every scrap of data there was to know about him was on a computer somewhere. Zendyne had all his psych profiles, and an archived copy of his mind, not to mention the DNA sample required by the Employee Protection Program.

There was no time to worry about that. Lee snapped his attention back to what Lilith was saying.

"...Stranger will be repaired sooner than you imagine, and there are others, even worse than him."

"Okay. Then you need to get back in the handeck, right away. You ride in there, and we'll come back for the android as soon as I've got some wheels."

"No good," Lilith said. "I burnt out the input circuitry, transferring in such a hurry before. I'm sorry."

Lee had known that, of course. He'd have remembered, too, if it weren't for all this pressure. Now he had to find another way to hide her. "There's a dumpster outside. I want you to climb inside it and then shut down."

"You want me to get into a dumpster?"

"It's the only safe place I can think of. I'll collect you as soon as I've got some transport, and then we can figure out how to repair you."

She seemed doubtful for a moment, but then her expression cleared. "You swear you'll come back?"

"I promise," Lee said. "And then you're going to tell me who you are, and who that lunatic was, and what the fuck's going on."

She gave him a calculating look. "I guess you came through the last time I trusted you. Okay. Where's this dumpster?"

Lee showed her, and watched as she lowered herself into the evil-smelling interior. As soon as she'd deactivated herself, he went back inside and stuffed a few important possessions into a bag: his 'deck, ID card, a change of clothes, and the archive unit that contained the minds of his grandparents.

Their spirits were quiescent, at least for the moment.

With a grim sense of purpose, Lee shouldered the overloaded holdall and headed for the bus stop, praying that Janitorial Services wouldn't reverse the habit of years and collect the garbage on time.

"Going away for a while?" asked the salesman.

"Yes," Lee said. "I want to get right off the beaten track."

"Quiet contemplation, eh? Lucky you. Wish I had time for that. So, you want to be completely cut off?"

"I need to stay in touch, but not to be bothered by anyone, so no cellular comms. GPS is fine, as long as I can switch it off. A satellite uplink would be great. Some creature comforts would be good, too."

"I understand perfectly, sir. Let me recommend the Scrambler; that six-wheeler over there. Compact and maneuverable but also spacious and elegant. And, we're doing a special offer on the satellite option this month."

The vehicle was bright orange, which wasn't quite to Lee's taste — on top of which, it was a bit more conspicuous than he'd have liked. "I'm not looking to be rescued or anything, you know?"

"Ah yes, the high-visibility orange. Don't worry, the color scheme is fully programmable on this range. There's a palette right on the dashboard computer."

It shouldn't really have surprised Lee, but he didn't follow automotive developments very closely. "So this is the vehicle you'd recommend?"

"Absolutely." The man handed Lee a brochure filled with flashy animations and text that scrolled too slowly for comfortable reading. "The main selling point is SmartRide, of course. Leading and trailing suspension arms that reach down through the muck so you can scramble out from places where lesser vehicles would just sit and spin. The wheels mold themselves to whatever they find: rocks, sand, tree roots. Like the slogan says, nothing grips you like a Scrambler."

"I see." Lee leafed through the brochure, half-listening as the man spoke of the fuel cell rating, the solar paint and the water recycler.

At last the salesman ran out of patter. "Want to take a look inside?"

The living space was cramped, with fittings that could morph from couch to dining chair to sleeping platform. The salesman seemed to expect his customer to be impressed, but the technology was all too familiar to Lee.

"Zendyne?"

"I see you know the best when you see it, sir. Top of the line stuff. Quality gear throughout. Your home away from home. Let me demonstrate the collapsible pod, I guarantee you'll be amazed by the extra living space it delivers when you're parked..."

Lee pulled a fully loaded credit chip from his pocket. The Scrambler was going to eat the bulk of what his Zendyne stock had brought, but he didn't have much choice. "What sort of deal can you do me?"

The salesman looked pained. "I'll throw in the satellite link for free."

"And the price includes the living pod, right?"

"I'm afraid that's an optional extra—"

Lee interrupted. "Actually, I'm beginning to think that Scrambler is an inauspicious name." He put the credit chip away.

"...which I'd be happy to offer at cost, in this case."

"I'll take it," said Lee.

Lee recovered Lilith — activating her for just long enough to get her into the vehicle and onto the bunk — and then drove to a quiet neighborhood not far from the apartment. The Scrambler's dispenser controls were cryptic, but in the end he persuaded the thing to give him a Coke for his hangover — warm and flat, but much better than nothing. He sat in the back of the vehicle, sipping the ancient folk remedy and contemplating Lilith's inert body.

He considered removing the tee shirt to examine her wound more closely, but the intruder's abandoned knife had pinned the cloth tightly against the doll's ribs: disturbing it now could do more harm than good. Also, the thought of undressing her out here on the street — and while she wasn't even in a position to acquiesce — made him feel slightly uneasy. Such shyness was strange, when he thought about it. The doll's body was simply a collection of screen-splined curves and planes that he'd helped create; what did it matter if that topology was more vivid in his memory than any of his lovers' bodies, which had faded and merged into an indistinct composite over the years?

The patch of fabric around the puncture wound was still damp, which told him that the coolant leak hadn't stopped completely; he wondered how much damage the doll had sustained. He arranged Lilith on her side, so that the leak was on top, hoping that gravity would minimize the flow. At least the cooling system was depressurized now, and the electroactive muscles wouldn't degrade so quickly while they were inert.

Which meant it would be best to keep her switched off until he'd extracted the blade and fixed the leak. He'd need tools for that. Lee opened his handeck and started to hunt for a specialist equipment supplier, one that was too small to have any association with Zendyne.

4

Sooz approached Old Billy's trailer reluctantly, clutching her delivery and wishing someone else could have brought it.

Coming to see Old Billy wasn't fun like it used to be, not since he'd become so addled and broken down. He seemed to get worse every year. It didn't help that she was fifteen now, and that Billy didn't see her as a little girl any more.

He'd taken his doorstep block inside the caravan — or else someone had swiped it — and she had to stand on tiptoe to reach his bell pull. The old man was going deaf and couldn't hear a knock any more, not unless you hammered until your knuckles stung. He said that it came from living so long, but Sooz reckoned his brain was turning to mush from doing too much shard.

The door edged open and Old Billy poked his pinched face out. "Sooz! Now ain't you a sight for sore eyes? Well, don't stand around cluttering up my forecourt. Come in, girl, come in!"

He withdrew into the dim interior and she clambered up after him. Years before, he'd daubed the windows with white paint — to keep out prying eyes, he'd said. Sooz still remembered that day: the sense of horrified fascination she'd felt as she watched him work, which had left her unable to concentrate on the old man's reading primer or the exercises he'd set her.

Old Billy might be going slowly senile but she owed him a lot. More than she could ever repay.

The trailer's interior was sickly with soured trash and sour old man. Two time-blackened pans stood on the stovetop, encrusted with dried food. Sooz looked around Billy's squalid home and then at Billy. He seemed to get spindlier every time she saw him.

"You been eating proper?" she asked.

"I been eating fine, girl. Just cause I'm old don't mean I got no appetite." He rubbed his scrawny belly and grinned, showing deep-gummed, tobacco-stained teeth.

Sooz was torn between the urge to simply make the delivery and flee, and the memory of how kind he had been in years gone by. "You got to eat, Billy. Them pans are no good like this. I'll take 'em away and clean 'em up and fetch you some proper grub."

"Long as you bring yourself back with it, girl. Ain't got much appetite for cooking, not when I got a toothsome little thing like you to take care of me."

Sooz sighed and held out the twist of shard she'd brought. "Ma told me to deliver this. She said to tell you sorry, but it's gone up. Twenty."

Old Billy snatched the wrap and squirreled it away inside his gaping shirt. He had a secret pocket in there, held in place by safety pins; Sooz had seen it on his washing line, hanging out to dry over his little patch of concrete.

She held out her hand for payment, but he capered away from her. "Ain't got twenty, Soozy girl. Got fifteen, maybe." A note of sadness entered his voice. "It's always been fifteen, ain't it?" He groped in his hip pocket and she saw how the old man's threadbare jeans sagged even worse than his skin, barely held in place by his ornate belt. Billy kept on shrinking long after his belt ran out of holes, and now it just got looser every year.

He handed her a thin sheaf of bills and watched with bright eyes as she counted the money. Fifteen.

Sooz sighed. "Ma said I was to get twenty. You don't want to get me in trouble, do you?"

"Heh! I wouldn't be so sure of that, young lady. Getting a pretty little thing like you in trouble would be a rare treat for an old 'un like me."

Sooz let it ride: getting paid was more important than getting even. She was supposed to pick up groceries for tonight's meal, and the money he had given her wouldn't feed the whole family. She had a few loose coins in the pocket of her combat pants, but not enough for her to really notice the weight. And even if she'd been loaded, why should she pay for the stinky old fart?

"Like I said, it's twenty. Give me the crystal back if you ain't got the cash. There's plenty of shard-heads who'll pay Ma's asking price."

Billy put on his wheedling voice. "Aw, come on. You can help an old friend out, can't you? And I just got something in for you, something real special."

"What you got?" asked Sooz, eagerness mixing with suspicion as she edged towards the door. Sometimes, when Old Billy started talking about having something special for her, he got a little frisky. This time, though, he didn't make a move, and Sooz felt a wave of relief that she wasn't going to have to extricate herself from his sour-smelling, bony embrace. He just reached into a cardboard box and handed her a book.

The laminated covers were long gone, but the title was printed on the tattered spine. 'The Story of Hong Kong,' she read. She'd never seen this before; it must be from a fresh delivery. Having a new paperback in her hands made her want to dance with excitement, but she did her best to look calm. "How much?"

"I regret to inform you that the price has gone up," he said, parroting her own voice and then wheezing with laughter that degenerated into phlegmy hacking. "Twenty."

Sooz shook her head. As much as she longed to possess the book, there was no way she could raise his asking price. Ma would kill her if she traded the grocery money for a useless old paperback. "Sorry, Billy. Ain't got it."

"Fifteen then. I know you got fifteen, right there." He nodded at the roll of bills she held, and his eyes almost seemed to glow in the paint-filtered light.

"You can't have that. It belongs to Ma."

"Be like that then." The old man grinned and absently scratched his groin, and his manner changed as if someone else had moved in. "Tell you what, you can have it for a fuck. Give Billy a nice ride and he'll see you all right for books."

"That's gross, Billy."

"Gross now, is he?" He scowled at her. "He'll have his book back, then."

"And I'll have Ma's shard back."

"No."

"Fine." Sooz opened the door and jumped down onto the concrete outside the trailer, already considering ways to raise the extra grocery money by that evening, and wondering how much trouble there'd be if she didn't.

"She's stealing Billy's book!" came the wail from inside.

"Fair exchange is no robbery," she called back. She'd read that somewhere, years before, probably in one of his primers.

Sooz was lurking in the shadows under her favorite pillar, reading her book and waiting to see if anyone came or went. The base of the pillar was a good spot, letting her cover both the entry and exit ramps. There was supposed to be a strip light overhead, but it had been broken ever since Sooz could remember. The slit windows let in just enough light for her to read, and if she kept her knees scrunched up and the white paper hidden, she could stay here for quite a while before Ma noticed where she was and gave her something useful to do.

Ma must have been distracted today, otherwise Sooz would have been busy with some task already instead of waiting by the pillar when the big Scrambler came in.

The gleaming RV seemed out of place among all the beat-up pickup trucks and ancient campers. This was the Short-Stay level, and Sooz had been around for long enough to know that no one came here unless they were on the way down.

The Scrambler looked like it belonged to someone on the way up.

Sooz watched it glide along the concrete ramp, listened to the polite whine of its motors as it eased its way into one of the enclosed bays. The driver's door opened with a sweet, well-engineered click and a man climbed out of the cabin. Han, by the look of him, or as her 'Story of Hong Kong' book (printed long before the Han bought up most of the planet and went shopping for a new self-image to match) would have had it, Chinese. Unlike most of the people Sooz knew, the newcomer had clean hair and clothes that fit, which was only to be expected from someone who rolled up in a brand new Scrambler.

The man kept himself sort of hunched down as he closed the door and flicked his eyes around the nearby parking bays, like he was hoping no one would notice his arrival.

Sooz jumped to her feet and trotted towards him, hurrying to get there before he figured out how to lock himself in behind the bay's security shutter. "Hey, Mister. I watched you drive in. Nice ride you got there."

It seemed like she'd startled him. The man spent a couple of seconds checking her out, then glanced around again as if he wanted to make sure she hadn't brought any friends. Yeah, Sooz thought, like there's anyone to be friends with down here. "Got any trash, Mister? I could take it to the waste chute for you. Or I can detail the whole car, if you like."

His eyes fell on her paperback. "Is that a book? I haven't seen one of those for years. May I?" He held out his hand.

Sooz clung to her prize for a moment, but decided it would be more businesslike to let him have a look. "What's your name, Mister?"

"Lee. Yours?"

"Sooz."

"Good to meet you, Sooz." He offered his free hand. Sooz shook it, a bit self-consciously. Lee leafed through the book, then handed it back. "Nice. Looks like it's older than either of us. Kind of reminds me of home."

"You from Hong Kong?"

"No, but my family used to live near there, back in the day."

There was an awkward silence. Sooz wondered if he was waiting for her to leave. If so, she needed to work fast. "Like I said, I was wondering if you had any trash. I could haul it away for you, if you like."

He looked at her blankly, as if he was trying to figure out what she meant. "Oh, I see. I'm sorry, Sooz. Everything gets recycled."

The thought shocked her. "Everything? What, even your poop?"

"I only bought the car today. It'll be a while before I find out for sure, but I certainly hope so."

Sooz couldn't help laughing. "That's gross!"

Lee chuckled too. "So, you run a car cleaning service? Must be a good business in a place like this."

"Not so you'd notice. Most of the folks round here don't bother, or they do for themselves. Thing is, I'm short five euros for something. I take shanghais too, or greenbacks. It's all money, innit?"

"So it is," Lee said. "Well, I think I have a job that might stretch to that, if you do exactly as I say."

Sooz had learned the hard way to check the details before agreeing to anything. "What is it, then?"

"I'd like you to watch for someone and tell me if you see him. But keep your distance and don't let him see you. He's not nice."

"What's this someone look like?"

"He's big. Tall, strong-looking. Pale skin, dressed all in black, maybe. Cropped hair, as if he buzzes it every day. And he's only got one eye." Lee paused. "At least, he needs to get the other one fixed."

Sooz held out her hand for payment. "Sounds easy enough to spot."

"His eyes are the thing to look for. They're like ... red jewels." Lee flicked with his thumb, sending a 5-euro piece spinning through the air.

"That would be like rubies, then," Sooz said, catching the coin. "Sure. I'll let you know if I see him."

Sooz found Strummer on the roof level, sitting outside one

of the clear plastic tunnels where much of Short-Stay's food was grown. He was busy, surrounded by a scattering of water pump parts. As soon as he saw her, he stopped work and came over to take the bucket of scraps she'd hauled up for the compost bins.

Strummer was always ready to give her a hand. He had looked out for her ever since they were kids.

He handed the empty bucket back and his lips twisted into a grin. "Thanks, Sooz. Water's what I need, though, more than compost. Been a dry spell and the pump's broke."

Sooz looked up at the sky. It was clear and blue, apart from a few threads of cloud. "I'll bring water next time I visit."

"I wish more people helped out like you do, Sooz. They want more than I can grow, but they ain't interested in donating what's needed. Ain't hardly no one using the latrines." He looked at her accusingly, as if daring her to deny that she, too, avoided making such personal contributions.

"It's a long climb," Sooz said. "It's different for you, working up here."

"Better to climb the stairs than to flush it down the pan. It's not like we got plant nutrients to spare."

This was one of Strummer's pet subjects, and Sooz was sorry she'd got him started. "There's a guy downstairs, got a car that recycles his poop right there."

"Nanotech recycler," Strummer said. "Ain't wholesome if you ask me. Like eating your own shit. Give me bugs and worms and a proper fertility cycle any day. What you doing later?"

"Helping Ma, probably." Sooz didn't intend to help Ma any more than she had to, not with a new book itching to be read, but she also didn't intend to hang with her would-be-boyfriend. Strummer was nice enough when she was in the mood, but he was poor competition for Hong Kong.

He looked crestfallen. "Your Ma's got you doing too much."

"Tell me about it."

"I don't mean chores. I mean the delivery work. The dealing."

"Ma says I got to pay my way, especially since I got too old to count for welfare."

"You got to understand how risky it is, Sooz. It was different when you was a kid."

"The Man ain't gonna catch me."

Strummer flopped his hair out his eyes and studied her. "I been hearing talk of a crackdown. You ought to tell your Ma, get her to ease off for a while. You could work up here instead."

Sooz knew that Strummer's vegetable operation wasn't big enough to support a hired hand. Anyway, spending too much time with him would most likely lead to complications that she didn't feel inclined to handle just yet. "Maybe so. Right now, I need some vegetables."

He sighed. "Well, you know where I'll be, if you get away early. Now, what's on that list?"

She read out Ma's order, and Strummer disappeared into one of the plastic tunnels to harvest the food. Sooz waited outside, watching the furled wind turbines twisting lazily in the breeze. Strummer had never learned his letters, but he was a smart guy when it came to generators and pumps, soil fertility and growing lamps. From time to time, Sooz tried to get him to sit down with a book, the way Old Billy had done with her, but Strummer always had other things on his mind when they were alone.

He returned with a grin and a string bag full of fresh vegetables. "Maybe see you later, then?"

Sooz paid him. "Couple of days, probably. Ma's been real persnickety lately." She didn't like hurting his feelings, but if she didn't, she'd never get any time to herself.

Strummer's face fell. He recovered with a visible effort. "Right. Couple of days then. Be seeing you, Sooz."

"Bye," she said, and started back down the stairs towards Short Stay.

Back home in the family parking space, Sooz dropped off the groceries in the old Toyota, parked with its dented nose drawn up to the entrance of their bay. She closed the car door carefully, so that there was hardly any noise, but Ma collared her anyway.

"Where the hell you been, girl? Hurry up and fetch the kids' clothes. We got washing to do."

Sooz sighed, because she'd been hoping to visit the Scrambler man again before wash time. He might have another job for her, and a couple more euros would have paid for one of the big laundry machines on the service level. Plus, she was dying to take a closer look at the vehicle's recycling facilities.

All that would have to wait, now. She piled her younger siblings' dirty clothes into the washing bag and headed for the Facilities.

Ma was there ahead of her, squatting near the tap with the plastic bowls already filled. Wordlessly, she passed the family's single pair of latex gloves to Sooz.

"You should take 'em for once, Ma." Sooz glanced at her mother's work-worn hands. "Look after yourself a bit."

"Time's long past for me to worry about that sort of thing, or for anyone to care. It's you we got to look after, now."

Sooz sighed as she pulled the gloves on. "It ain't no good down here. We ought to get ourselves up to Long Stay. Old Billy, he told me they got proper plumbing up there. He says they got hot showers and everything."

Ma dumped a shirt in the water and scrubbed at a stubborn grease spot. "They got all kinds of stuff up on Long Stay. And I don't want you hanging around Old Billy no more, not 'less we got particular business with him. I told you that before."

"Yeah, like I'd want to. But there ain't no one to talk to down here. No one interesting, anyhow. I bet there's plenty of interesting people in Long Stay."

"We can't afford no Long Stay."

Sooz swished her half-brother's faded dungarees through the gray water and wrung them out over the drain grating. "I checked the tariff sheet, Ma. Long stay's cheaper if you work it out over the month."

"Sure, long as you got the credit up front. We barely got enough to pay by the day."

Sooz looked at her mother's hands again. "Washing clothes in buckets ain't going to make us no richer."

"Saves a couple of bucks, every time."

"Takes hours, though. We could spend the time chasing work."

"Sooz, we can't afford no Long Stay and we can't afford to use no laundry machines. Subject closed."

Sooz dropped the dungarees into the washing bag and accepted her kid sister's romper for rinsing. "There's a new guy just arrived."

"Yeah, I heard the shutter coming down. Didn't hear no engine, though. Wondered about that, now that you mention it."

"It has electric motors, dead quiet," Sooz said. "One of them swish recreational vehicles. It was neat."

"You seen it arrive?"

"Yeah. The driver seemed nice. Said he was from near Hong Kong. I reckon that means he's rich, right?"

"There's rich and poor Han, same as everyone else," Ma said.

"Hope he's gonna stick around, we could do with some new people down here. Might have some jobs he wants doing, do you think?"

"Maybe. He's just passing through, most likely, else he'd be up in Long Stay. You steer clear of him, Sooz, leastwise till I check him out. It don't matter how much you want to ride in that flash RV of his, or how many of those fancy books you reckon he's got, understand?"

Sooz sighed. "Sure thing, Ma."

5

As soon as the girl had gone, Lee closed the bay's security shutter and climbed into the Scrambler's living space. It was time to start working on the doll.

He opened his new repair kit and cut through the fabric of the ruined tee shirt, extending the hole the intruder's knife had made. He didn't want to risk removing the weapon until he was in position to see what damage it had done.

Once the tee shirt was off, Lee used the zipper tool to make two incisions starting at the puncture wound: one curving underneath the doll's breast and up to its sternum, the other running diagonally to its navel. The skin curled back immediately, exposing a layer of subcutaneous gel. He unzipped that too, and peeled the triangular flap away to reveal the rib cage.

The blade had penetrated deeply. Lee brushed a fingertip along the black surface and shuddered at its oily slickness — and at the thought of being on the wrong side of people who had access to stuff like this. The hilt and pommel bore two recessed pads that looked like controls, but Lee decided not to mess with those until he had freed the knife.

The edges of the blade had jammed between two ribs, notching the alloy skeleton. In a way, that was a blessing: if the weapon hadn't gotten stuck, Lilith's assailant might have pulled it free, or done even more damage by twisting it inside her.

Lee studied the honed nothingness of the knife's edge and imagined how stupid he'd feel if it came to fishing for a severed finger between the doll's gleaming ribs.

Take it slow, he told himself.

Luckily, the tip of the blade had ended up inside the punctured cooling tube rather than slicing all the way through, so that its tapered profile had helped seal the leak. Working with infinite care, Lee clamped off the damaged artery and then extracted the knife, a task that took both hands and a lot of gentle rocking. He looked around for somewhere safe to put it, settling on the lid of his toolbox.

Once he had replaced the leaking tube and topped up the coolant chamber, Lee checked the interior of the doll for fluid damage. All the musculature down its left side was affected, from the obliques down to the tops of the quadriceps.

Without proper workshop facilities, there was no way to replace all that electroactive muscle. All Lee could do was to mop up the visible spillage and leave the doll's torso open, in the hope that the rest would evaporate.

In the meantime, he figured he might as well explore.

Outside the Scrambler, most of the vehicle bays were open. The denizens of the parking hive were going about their business: cooking on improvised stoves, or tinkering with engines, or spaced out on a row of greasy mattresses and a hit of shard. A gang of grubby youths huddled near the crystal-heads, sharing a bottle and blending with the concrete.

The Scrambler was Lee's first brand-new vehicle and he hoped to continue enjoying its pristine condition for a while longer yet. That meant not sullying the vehicle's built-in facilities by doing anything crass like actually using them, which in turn had led to a pressing need for Lee to investigate the local sanitary arrangements.

All he found was a noisome toilet with bare concrete walls and a vibrant patch of green spreading below the soil pipe. He decided that the Scrambler's systems could do with being tested after all, and that his personal needs were perhaps a little less urgent than he had thought.

A short distance from the toilet, two women were working at a lonely tap. As Lee got closer, he recognized one of them: the girl with the book. Sooz, he remembered. Her companion looked like an older edition of the same girl; he guessed it must be Sooz's mother. They were washing children's clothes in a bucket of gray suds.

The older woman raised her head and nodded at him. "Not much to look at," she said, "but there's worse places. It ain't so bad once you get used to it. You waiting for water? We'll be done soon enough."

"It's okay," Lee said. "I was just looking around. I only arrived today."

The woman tilted her head, indicating her daughter. "Sooz here tells me she saw you coming in. A Scrambler's a smart vehicle to be bringing to a place like this."

"Ma," Sooz said, peering up at Lee with obvious embarrassment. She gave him a slight shake of her head and indicated her mother with a sideways nod.

Lee decided he was being told not to let on that they'd talked. He grinned at the girl and raised one eyebrow, then looked back at her mother. "I just need somewhere to park for a night or two."

"Someone looking for you, yeah? No worries. You'll be fine here. Good crowd, most of them."

Lee hesitated, half-minded to smile and drift away. The pile of children's clothing caught his eye. "How many kids do you have?"

"Five. Sooz here's my oldest. I got two others of my own, and a couple that was left by one of my husbands, you know?" She paused, wringing out a strip of unidentifiable cloth. "What's your name?"

"Lee."

"Pleased to make your acquaintance, Lee. I'm Martha. I won't shake." She glanced down at her hands, busy in the tired water. Her fingers and the backs of her hands were chapped, the skin cracked and raw. Lee tried not to wince.

Martha looked up at him and almost seemed to smile. She was pretty when she did that. More than pretty, in fact. "Me and the kids will be having some stew tonight. You're welcome to join us, if you ain't got plans."

Lee wondered how hygienic Martha's eating arrangements were likely to be, and what sort of ingredients she'd be able to get in a place like this. Hopefully it would be home-cooked, at least. Martha didn't look like the sort of person who stood in line at a public extrusion point, waiting for a bowl of sterilized glop.

And she was trying to keep her kids clean. Sooz seemed to have gotten the beginnings of an education from somewhere, too.

Martha looked at him expectantly for a few seconds and then wilted, turning back to her plastic bowl. The light that had animated her face for a moment started to fade.

"I'd be pleased to come," Lee said. "Thank you."

When she looked up at him again, a bit of the glow had returned. "Seven o'clock be too early for you? Only I got the kids to get to bed."

"Seven o'clock will be fine. I'll look forward to it."

"Me too," Martha said. "Bay 15. It's the third along on the left."

Sooz kept her head down, concentrating on her washing.

Lee hurried back to the Scrambler and christened its facilities. It made him a bit uneasy, the way the smart toilet extruded itself out of the floor and then morphed back into a shower base once he had finished. According to the manual, the surfaces were self-sterilizing. The shower base sparkled invitingly, but the idea of actually standing in it was disquieting. The soles of Lee's feet tingled at the thought.

At least he was getting to grips with the kitchen extruder. He asked for a cheeseburger, fries and a Coke; the machine hummed for a minute and then popped his order out.

According to the manual, the processor produced perfectly nutritious and well-balanced meals, which probably explained why the food tasted so bad. Lee dropped most of it into the recycling chute and thought hungrily of home-cooked stew.

When it was time to go, he told the food processor to fill a clear plastic pitcher with red wine, and ordered some bread rolls. He sniffed the wine suspiciously, took a cautious swallow, and decided it would probably be acceptable.

Then he remembered the kids and ordered a flask of soda.

Martha's vehicle was a beat-up pickup truck, parked at the front of her bay. Lee followed the smell of wood smoke and the sound of children playing. He found Martha working at the back of the unit.

"I hope I'm not too early," he said.

"'Course not. 'Specially seeing as you brought wine."

She offered him the smile that she had only hinted at before, and Lee found himself smiling back.

"Careful of this." She pointed at her stewpot. "It gets darned hot. Kids, hush yourselves now and get the table set. Can't you see we got company?"

Her stove was a recycled propane bottle, propped on its side and furnished with a hinged fire door. The cooker top was a welded iron sheet pierced with a circular hole; a round-bottomed stewpot rested in the hole with flames licking its base. A length of flexible ducting running to the slit window served as a chimney, sending most of the smoke to the outside world.

The stew smelled fantastic.

There was a table made of trestles and plywood in the center of the pickup bed, fixed between two timber benches that perched over the wheel arches. Sooz and the next eldest child — a boy of maybe nine or ten — got busy. Before Lee knew it, the table was set with a cloth, seven chipped bowls, plastic cups and a mismatched assortment of cutlery. Martha glanced at him, then gestured at the spread. "Take a seat."

Lee boosted a couple of the smaller children up into the back of the truck and then climbed up himself. He set out the bread rolls he had brought. Each of the kids seized one and then sat in expectant silence, gazing at the stew.

Martha placed the pot on the table, then climbed up herself. She served the stew while Lee poured the wine and the kids helped themselves to his soda.

Lee brought the first spoonful to his lips. It tasted real. "Mmm." He swallowed, then took a sip of wine. "I'll tell you something. This is a hell of a lot better than what I get at home."

After the meal, Martha dismantled the table and spread several thin mattress rolls on the pickup bed for the youngsters to sleep on. Then she snagged the wine and beckoned to Lee. "Want to check out some stuff I got?"

Lee hesitated, unsure of what she meant. Then he considered the alternative, which was returning to the Scrambler alone. Martha's place might be dingy, but it felt welcoming and safe. He nodded.

"Could you hold this?" She offered him the wine, then hauled down the bay's security shutter. There were two padlocks, one on either side. Martha snapped both into place.

Wondering if it mightn't have been better to go back to the Scrambler after all, Lee followed his host to her sleeping area, which was partitioned behind some shuttering in a corner of the bay.

Martha settled down cross-legged on her bedroll and took a small plastic bag out of her shirt pocket. Lee sat opposite her, putting the wine jug on the concrete floor.

"You ever done any shard?" she asked.

Lee shook his head. Random corporate blood tests had always made him stick to the mainstream drugs: alcohol, marijuana, occasionally a little tobacco. I don't have to worry about that any more, he thought. And no one can possibly know I'm here, locked behind the shutter. What the hell, why not?

He accepted a twist of transparent film, wrapped around something tiny and hard.

"See how the crystals are clear, like glass?" she asked. "That's how you tell it's good. Tip it on the inside of your wrist. Don't get it on your fingers, though. Too much handling will spoil it."

"You seem to know a lot about it."

"Enough. I don't really use it, at least not often. Too much ain't good, 'specially if it ain't pure. You seen the shard dreamers, sleeping their lives away out there? That's taking it too far, missing the point. I don't deal to them."

Lee raised an eyebrow. "You sell this stuff?"

"Sure." A note of defiance had entered her voice. "There's worse ways of putting food on the table. Hang around here long enough and you might be offered a few of 'em." She flashed a grin that put Lee back at ease, and her voice softened. She nodded at the wrap he was holding. "Don't worry, I don't charge guests."

He watched as Martha undid her twist and emptied its contents onto the inside of her wrist, right where the pulse was. It was dim in the parking bay and Lee couldn't see exactly what happened. The crystals just seemed to disappear.

Martha sat up straighter and her worry lines smoothed themselves away. "Whenever you're ready," she said.

Lee unwrapped the packet she had given him and tipped its contents onto his own wrist, curious to see what would happen. The crystals liquefied as soon as they touched his skin, melting into nothingness as he watched.

He looked at Martha.

Martha was smiling at him.

Martha had beautiful eyes.

Martha was in his arms, kissing his mouth, then kissing his wrist where the shard had gone in, then giving him her own wrist to taste, then kissing his mouth again.

Martha's bedroll was soft, but her body was firm and deliciously warm.

"Didn't figure you for a stayer," she said the next morning, as Lee prepared to leave. "Enjoyed spending time with you, though."

"Thanks," Lee said. "I've got stuff going on. You know?"

"Sure."

"Is there anything I can do for you or the kids before I go?"

"I ain't no whore, if that's what you mean."

"I know you're not. That's not what I meant."

"Sure."

"Okay." He hesitated, reluctant to simply walk away, unable

to do anything else. "See you around then, maybe."

"Sure. See you around."

Sooz was waiting at the Scrambler when Lee got back, perched on the running board with her knees tucked under her chin.

"You going?" she asked.

"Yeah. There's a bunch of things I have to do."

"I wish I could go."

Lee looked around the parking level, imagining what it must be like for her. "Your mother would miss you, if you did."

Sooz looked up at him. "Reckon she'll miss you more."

Lee was suddenly uncomfortably warm. He wished there were something he could do to help. "Listen, once I've got my life straightened out—"

"Don't say you'll be back." Her expression was petulant but her voice just sounded unhappy. "I ain't stupid, or a child. Ma ain't, neither. I know that no one ever comes back."

She turned away and trudged over to the pillar where he'd first seen her. Lee watched until she'd settled herself down and opened her book.

Back in the Scrambler, he took a long shower, then checked the doll. The body cavity had dried out, so he closed the incision and zipped it back up. The layers of gel and skin drew together and healed as the tool passed over them, except where they'd been traumatized by the blade.

There, Lilith was going to have a scar.

The knife that had caused the damage was still where he'd dropped it, in the lid of his toolbox. Lee considered Lilith's record with pointy things and decided not to leave this one lying around. He picked it up and held it under the work lights, studying the depressions he'd noted earlier.

One of the niches was at the end of the pommel, impossible to touch accidentally while holding the knife. The other fell naturally under his thumb.

Lee pushed his finger into the first cavity and pressed the stud that he felt nestled inside. The knife dissolved itself into a living thing, slithering over his fingers like a moist, prehensile glove. He panicked and tried to flip it onto the floor, but it clung to him tenaciously, wriggling towards his wrist. Fascination took over from dismay as he watched the stuff blending with his skin. After a few seconds, the knife was gone, transformed into a slight puffiness at his fingers, a layer of flab over his forearm, and a plain black band adorning his middle finger.

There was a depression in the ring, identical to those he'd seen on the hilt. Lee pressed it and found himself holding the blade again.

"Cool," he said.

He tried the other control, the one that lay under his thumb. The weapon quivered, emitting a barely audible whine, and seemed to twist slightly in his hand.

The edge is alive, he thought. This thing will cut literally anything.

He must have kept it going for too long, because the vibration died. After that, the blade remained stubbornly inert no matter how hard he pressed the control. Disappointed and wondering how the thing could be recharged, Lee pushed the first button again. The weapon oozed back into concealment around his hand.

The disguised glove felt a bit clumsy at first, not to mention clammy, but he could live with it. At least the blade was safely out of the way, and if he ever needed a weapon at short notice, it would be there. He wrestled the doll back into his tattered tee shirt and switched it on. Lilith came back slowly, waking up almost like a real girl. Her eyes opened first, and then she stretched and yawned.

"Thanks, that much feels better." She sat up, her fingers already probing under the tee shirt for the damaged spot. She found it and frowned. "Got me a good one, didn't he?"

Lee nodded. "Not quite a factory refurb, I'm afraid, but I don't think the warranty covers combat damage. Anyway, I fixed the leak and zipped you up."

"So I gather." She flexed her left arm and twisted her torso.

"It still feels a bit stiff, and maybe I lost some power. Let's hope we don't get in another fight with Stranger for a while."

"You mean the guy who attacked us?"

"That's the one," she said.

"Tell me about him."

There was a long pause. "He's with the organization that developed us. Me."

So, she doesn't want to talk about it, Lee thought. But willing or not, he couldn't afford to go easy on her. "What organization? I need to know everything."

She sighed. "They call themselves Electis."

"What's that? Some kind of Latin?"

"It means they are the elect. Chosen."

Lee decided that it was probably just a name, a corporate brand, and most likely unimportant. "I'm guessing you escaped."

Lilith shook her head. "I don't remember. It was like a dream, being in their systems. I think there were others like me, training with the instructors."

"What were they teaching you?"

Lilith closed her eyes; it was several seconds before she replied. "I think some of us died. Maybe I died, too; it feels like I left part of myself behind. Perhaps that's why I don't remember."

"You have to give me more than that, Lilith."

"I know. There has to be more, but I can't access it." Her voice was full of exasperation — with herself, Lee hoped.

It occurred to him that too much pressure might be counter-productive. "Okay. Take it easy. If you remember anything else, tell me. I need to understand what I'm up against."

She gave him a long, hard look. "What we're up against. I've got a stake in this too, you know. I'm doing my best."

"Checking out?"

"Yes, I'm done here."

"Just give me a moment." The hive attendant scanned his screen. "Okay, you're all paid up. Have a nice day."

"There's one more thing," Lee said. "Do you know a woman named Martha? Drives an old Toyota?"

"Sure do. Teenage daughter and a handful of youngsters, yeah?"

"That's the one. I'd like you to arrange something for them. Bump them up to a couple of months of Long Stay, next time they renew."

The attendant gave him a quizzical look. "I'm not sure I understand."

"I want to help them get on their feet." Lee offered a credit chip. "Charge it to this. And please take fifty for your trouble."

The man grinned. "Sure, I can do that."

"It's a computer error, understand? I don't want Martha or Sooz to know."

"Got it. Leave it to me."

"Who are Martha and Sooz?" Lilith asked as Lee pulled away from the booth.

"Just a couple of people I met in the hive. Martha is Sooz's mother."

"It sounds as if you liked them."

Lee shrugged. "Martha invited me to dinner. They're a nice family. Four little ones and an older daughter. Poor as hell, but they seemed happy to have each other."

"I've never been to a dinner party. Not that food's much good to me. Still, I wish I could have gone."

"You were drying out." Lee decided to steer the conversation in a more profitable direction. "Any luck remembering about Stranger?"

"Enough to know we have to get out of here, as far away as we can."

Lee smiled. No matter what they threw at him now, he was confident in his new vehicle, a fresh convert to the cult of the open road. "Even Stranger can't cordon off the entire city. He won't know where to start."

"He'll have the full specifications for this body I'm wearing, by now. He's probably got one of these booklets, telling him all about me." She was flicking through a sheaf of glossy Scrambler documentation she'd found in one of the dashboard cubbyholes.

Lee glanced at the people on the sidewalk, then across at Lilith. "Check them out. I don't see anyone showing an unhealthy interest. Anyway, it's not like you're some mass-produced model; each Artemis unit is different and most of them are kept indoors. Believe me, you can pass for a woman, no problem."

"He'll use your data, then. Your work records, or this vehicle registration."

"It won't be so easy. He can hardly waltz in to Zendyne and ask for a copy of their employee database, or scan every vehicle leaving the city."

Lilith returned her brochure to the glove box. "Are you ready to bet your life on that?"

"We're safe now." Lee checked the rearview mirror, just to reassure himself. There was a delivery truck behind them, following too close. Beyond that, a cop car was nudging out into the next lane, ready to pass the truck.

It was probably nothing, Lee decided. There was no point bothering Lilith about it.

6

Xia Lin looked at the impassive faces ranged around the conference table: flickering telepresences, mainly, with a scattering of bodies squeezed among the projector seats. Her direct supervisor was there in person, swallowing nervously and avoiding her gaze. Dr. Huang was present too; the vice-president of Engineering, head of Droid Division, and the most senior Zendyne figure someone like Xia Lin could ever hope not to meet. Dr. Huang was an intimidating man at the best of times, and now he was taking his place at the head of the meeting called to assess Xia Lin's handling of the rogue Aphrodite 7400.

Several of the other attendees were unknown to her. From their expensive suits and arrogant style, she assumed they were senior management staff from outside the division.

She slowed and deepened her breathing, trying to stay calm. This gathering could destroy her career as easily as she had ended Lee's.

Dr. Huang opened the proceedings. "Well, Xia Lin. It has been over twenty-four hours since the unfortunate incident. We would be pleased to hear what progress you have made with the malfunctioning doll."

Xia Lin forced herself to meet his gaze, a rearguard action against intimidation. "I have three shifts of analysts working round the clock; they have been doing so since yesterday morning. We anticipate identifying all possible failure states in three more days, at most."

"And how many of these 'failure states' have you managed to isolate, so far?"

Xia Lin swallowed hard. "None. The main part of the work remains to be done."

Dr. Huang's head shook almost imperceptibly, his face a

picture of pained regret. "It seems most unfortunate that you were so eager to fire the man who was truly familiar with the design."

"But we all agreed—"

"You were his line manager. It was your responsibility to assess his expertise and advise your superiors of his worth. We should not have had to study his performance records ourselves."

He placed his hand on the personnel file that rested on the table in front of him. Xia Lin wondered if the bundle of printout could really cover Lee's career. The stack was thicker than she would have expected.

Dr. Huang continued. "It is clear from his profile that it was an error to dismiss him, a serious one that we must rectify as soon as possible. Unfortunately, he vanished from his company apartment yesterday, shortly before noon. A rare case of efficiency at the Accommodation Office, perhaps."

A few of the senior executives chuckled, but Xia Lin knew it would be inappropriate to join in. The polished conference table might as well be a headsman's block, waiting for her neck. She imagined her blood soaking into the plush carpet and dripping through the ceiling tiles into the office below.

"There is no need to look so worried, Xia Lin. You have served Zendyne faithfully for many years. We will not condemn you for a single error."

"Thank you," she said, though she was unsure whether that was appropriate. There were so many layers of meaning with a man like Dr. Huang, and she had never been much good at reading them. His words might be as comforting as they sounded, or they might contain a coded threat.

"Once you have rectified this error," he continued, "I have no doubt that your career can be re-established. With the appropriate mentoring and support from your superiors, of course." Around the table, several managers nodded their grave, gray-suited agreement.

Xia Lin kept her voice flat and emotionless. "I am grateful for your consideration."

He made no pretence of even listening. "I understand that you knew Mr. Lee well?"

"Quite well," Xia Lin said, wishing she could distance herself from the whole thing but unable to think of how to do so.

"Good. I want you to remain involved. Zendyne's core expertise is not about finding missing persons, so we have retained a group of experts to assist us. Your personal knowledge will be invaluable to them."

"Might I know who I'm to be working with?"

Dr. Huang glanced to his right, at one of the men that Xia Lin didn't recognize: a large, fleshy Westerner with cropped hair and a cheap sightfold. The top of one cheek was livid and swollen, as if he'd recently suffered some accidental eye damage. Which explained the 'fold, Xia Lin thought; it had to be a temporary measure while he waited for new implants to be grown.

The man gazed back at her, bowing his head slightly and smiling in a way that made hairs prickle on the back of her neck. "My name is Stranger," he said. "I'm a senior partner at Electis." He let the vowels roll off his tongue, as if savoring his company's name. "We're professional facilitators. Among other things, we recover missing persons and lost property."

"And what do you need from me?" Xia Lin asked.

"For now, it will be enough to come to my office, as soon as we're finished here. There are a number of things that we need to discuss."

Dr. Huang nodded his approval. "Electis and Mr. Stranger have our full confidence, Xia Lin. You are to extend them every assistance."

The thought of being Stranger's liaison dismayed Xia Lin. All she wanted was to get back to her technicians, to see how much progress they'd made. "I'll be happy to help in any way I can. Subject to the demands of my other work, of course."

Dr. Huang shook his head. "I have assigned someone else to manage your group. As a temporary measure, to free you for more important tasks. You will be re-instated when this business is concluded."

"Of course." Xia Lin's world was tumbling in pieces around her but she kept her voice steady. "How long is this project expected to take?"

"To a large extent, the completion date depends on you," Dr. Huang said. "In the meantime, you will consider yourself to be employed by Zendyne but contracted to Electis, working under the direct supervision of Mr. Stranger. Do you understand?"

She didn't understand at all. There was a silence that seemed more eerie than embarrassing. Dr. Huang coughed and shuffled the papers in Lee's personnel folder.

"I understand perfectly," said Xia Lin.

It was unheard of for an outsider to be given space in the Zendyne building, but Stranger's office turned out to be larger than Xia Lin's own — and it had a better view. Xia Lin felt strangely uncomfortable, sitting on the wrong side of such an imposing desk, as if she had gone back ten years and was interviewing for her first job.

"I'm looking forward to working with you," Stranger said. "Your assistance will be invaluable in finding this ex-employee."

Xia Lin studied him before replying. Her people called those of Stranger's ethnicity *Fan Gwailo* — foreign devils. This westerner might hide behind his sightfold but it was plain to Xia Lin that he was a devil in fact, not just in name.

"I shall do what I can," she said.

"Good. Then perhaps you will begin by explaining exactly why you helped your ex-employee to obtain an Artemis 9300 unit."

That caught Xia Lin off guard, made it difficult to conceal her surprise. How did he know about the doll, and why would he care? "Lee worked with me for several years. It was natural for me to give him a gift on his last day."

Stranger leaned forward, spreading his hands on the desk. His scalp glistened under close-cropped gray hair. "That really won't do, Miss Lin." He smiled thinly, and she wondered if he was challenging her to correct his misuse of her name.

She said nothing.

"How long ago did he start talking about acquiring his own doll?"

"There were no such discussions. We agreed that it would be best for him to seek new opportunities. Before he left, he decided to purchase a memento from the company store. It was no surprise: he worked on the design team for that model."

"So you never suspected that he was manipulating you?"

Xia Lin stiffened. "Manipulating me?"

"Mr. Lee is an attractive man, isn't he?"

"I have no idea what you mean."

"It's perfectly understandable that a charming young woman such as yourself should wish to … help him."

"Mr. Stranger." Xia Lin made his name rhyme with danger, a small mispronounced revenge for being called Miss Lin. "I did not help Lee. I dismissed him."

"Stranger," he corrected, rhyming it with hanger. "As I said, he's an attractive man."

"And as I said, I have no idea what you mean."

"Your ex-employee had some illicit property with him when he left, something he needed a doll to use. You provided him with one, on precisely the same day. You have to admit that it looks odd."

"I admit no such thing. There have been no thefts reported, no unauthorized removals. I simply gave Lee a gift."

"Indeed. A handsome gift to a handsome male. Now, tell me about the modification you had the engineers make before the unit was delivered."

Xia Lin couldn't believe that the foreign devil knew. He mustn't know. She decided to bluff it out. "Modification?"

"The work order is clear, Miss Lin, and it bears your signature. I'm offering you the chance to tell your side of the story before I inform your superiors of your uncooperative behavior."

Xia Lin slumped in her chair, defeated. "I had them fit a

sensory transponder."

"And you also purchased a full body sensorsuit?"

Xia Lin nodded.

"Perhaps you would tell me how the sensorsuit was tuned?"

"To the Artemis 9300. To the transponder in Lee's doll."

"An admirable plan, Miss Lin. Seduction by proxy; intimate engagements relayed over the ether. I salute you." He raised his fingertips to his forehead, lazily, insolently. "You must be hoping that your friend will, shall we say, take full advantage of your generosity."

Xia Lin said nothing. She felt a tear roll down her cheek, sensed its impact on the starched cotton of her blouse.

Stranger continued, "I venture to hope that both you and the doll will find him a skilled and sensitive lover." He paused, offering a bland smile. "But how will you manage the timing? You can hardly be planning to wear the sensorsuit day and night. How will you know when the object of your affections is, how can I put it, feeling frisky?"

Xia Lin hadn't thought that far ahead. If anything, she had meant to rely on luck, hoping that Lee would schedule regular sessions with the doll. She didn't have an answer. She just shook her head.

"Then I shall help you, since you're working for me now. We will go to your home and examine the possibilities of this suit. I want you to inhabit the doll."

"That's ridiculous."

"On the contrary. I have elected you, Miss Lin. You are my chosen instrument in this matter. I will not be denied."

"No. The suit is my personal property. It has nothing to do with Zendyne, or you. Neither does my time outside this office."

"Miss Lin. I was told that you were to be at my disposal and I must insist on your co-operation. Or would you prefer me to consult your superiors once more?"

Xia Lin shook her head again, miserably.

"Excellent. You will use the suit to watch from the doll's eyes, and report what it sees and where it is." His chair creaked as he rose to his feet. "Now we shall go to your home."

Stranger wouldn't even allow Xia Lin the privacy of her bedroom. He remained at the threshold, waiting for her to try on the suit.

She stood in front of the mirror, holding the garment against herself and watching the reflection of Stranger's sightfold over her right shoulder.

The sensorsuit seemed a couple of dress-sizes too small, but she knew that the material would stretch into a breathable, body-hugging blank canvas, duplicating every sensation and relaying every exploration that Lee visited upon the doll.

She closed her eyes and willed herself to believe she was alone.

"Just imagine I'm not here," Stranger said. "You should understand that I have progressed beyond the point where physicality holds any meaning for me."

Xia Lin turned to face him directly.

"Please don't feel offended," he said. "I recall enough humanity to know that your body must be considered delightful." He shrugged. "It's just not my thing, any more. I only wish to understand."

Xia Lin looked back at the mirror and set the sensorsuit down. Stranger's reflected 'fold never wavered as she undressed herself with trembling fingers and pushed one leg into the garment. There was a hair-raising moment as the fabric formed itself onto her foot and became an upward-travelling wave, rolling over her ankle and calf, but it soon settled to a sensation of perfect absence.

That meant the doll was already undressed. Xia Lin felt her heart fluttering in her chest, affected by a more primal emotion than resentment or embarrassment. She zipped the suit up and put the headset on, fitting it snugly over her eyes and ears — to be rewarded with velvet silence.

Nothing. She was puzzled. Why would Lee have undressed

the doll unless he meant to pay it some attention?

Then it occurred to her that he might simply have switched it off. Or even worse: that the sensory interface might be faulty.

Xia Lin felt herself wilting under the weightless garment, her vicarious anticipation dashed. She pulled the headset off and glanced in the mirror again. Stranger hadn't moved. The sensorsuit made her look as ridiculous as she felt.

"From your lack of response," Stranger said, "I assume nothing is happening."

"The doll doesn't seem to be switched on. Or perhaps the transponder circuitry is faulty."

"I understand the unit was damaged this morning. A deep puncture to the chest cavity. Might that account for the failure?"

"With the 7300 series, the transponder is located in the doll's head."

"Then perhaps your friend has deactivated the unit for repairs. It doesn't matter. You will keep the sensorsuit on and inform me as soon as the doll comes online."

"You expect me to wear this thing for twenty-four hours a day?"

"Of course not," Stranger said. "You'll need to remove it for sanitary reasons, and during your down time. The headset will become unnecessary too, in time."

"I refuse. Spying on Lee's private life is no part of my job."

"It is now." Stranger gripped her by the elbow with irresistible strength. "You are to come with me. We have work to do."

The Electis building was huge and forbidding; monumentally floodlit and huddled behind mesh gates, razor wire, and warning signs that left would-be intruders in no doubt of their stupidity.

"You will need to be accompanied in the grounds," Stranger said. "The guard dogs are genetically enhanced, and linked to Back Office."

"Back Office?"

"Back Office is where the authorized personnel profiles are stored. I'm on the list, naturally. You're perfectly safe with me."

He looked to his right, and Xia Lin followed his gaze. A sleek canine form was gliding through the darkness near the fence. It ignored them. As the beast passed, its multifaceted eyes caught the light, scattering red reflections, and Xia Lin wondered if this was some monstrous melding of insect and dog.

"I see," she said. "Then you will have to escort me again, when I leave. It seems this secondment will be inconvenient for both of us."

"Not at all. You will be staying here for the duration of this project. I'll have your scent profile added to the security database when the time comes."

"I go home every night. I still work for Zendyne and those are my terms of employment."

Stranger stopped and gave her another of his chilly smiles. "People usually find the experience of working for me to be more compelling than they expect. I think you'll want to stay until the job's done." He set off again, leading her towards the main door.

"And my contract with Zendyne?"

"I have no wish to deprive my associates of your services. You'll return to your usual duties in a few weeks at most. You have my word on that." He ushered her into the building. The sound of the bolts shooting home behind them turned Xia Lin's spine to ice.

Stranger showed her into his office. It was smaller and more Spartan than the one he'd been allocated at Zendyne, and his bulk seemed to fill the space, leaving little room for Xia Lin.

"Please, take a seat," he said. "And excuse me. I need to change."

He pressed something on his forearm — a control stud built into a wristband, Xia Lin saw — and then she reeled with shock because he became someone else. His excess flesh writhed and dissolved until he was no longer the overbearing bureaucrat who she had started to hate, but rather an armor-clad duelist who she already feared.

"What's going on?" She could hear a sharp edge of panic in her voice; the part of her that wanted a truthful answer was very small.

"We're offering you an opportunity." Stranger made it sound as if he expected her to be grateful.

"What opportunity?"

"A new beginning. An escape from the past. A chance to become more than you ever thought possible." He pushed a handeck across the desk. Its holoscreen was active, betrayed by a blue shimmer as he twisted the device towards her.

The document it displayed was titled 'Zendyne Internal Archive Transfer Warrant'. It took Xia Lin a few seconds to absorb its content.

She was looking at a requisition to the Employee Protection Program, ordering her DNA data to be transmitted to the company's Regrowth Clinic, together with a copy of her most recent mind backup.

A tense knot formed in the center of Xia Lin's belly. She looked up at Stranger. "Zendyne is cloning me. As if I was dead in some accident and they wanted me back."

"As far as their data records are concerned you are indeed dead, and of course Zendyne wants you back. They're even going to give you a promotion. You should be flattered."

"No. There must be a mistake."

"There is no mistake. They're acting perfectly rationally given the data we have provided. You didn't think your friend's dossier was the only thing we edited, did you?"

She remembered the unfamiliar thickness of Lee's personnel folder. The horror was close to engulfing her now as she started to understand. "You padded his file."

"Not me personally. It was Back Office. Data tinkering: it's what they do. They made your friend look a little more indispensable than he actually was. Now they've done the same for you."

Xia Lin was shouting now. "You're insane! I have a life to

live, a place in the world."

Stranger's voice was soothing, as if he were offering reassurance to an upset child. "Please, calm yourself. Your life has been allocated to someone else, an alternative version of you. She will live it precisely as you would have. Nothing is lost."

He removed the sightfold and Xia Lin felt the hair crawling on her scalp, because his eyes were two rubine gemstones that glittered and sparked like those of the guard dog she'd seen outside.

"If you perform your duties diligently," he continued, "you might earn the right to see again one day. The right to return from Back Office, just as I did."

He pressed a button on his desk, summoning three green-smocked orderlies into the room. Xia Lin bucked and twisted in their grip but they were relentless. She tried to bite and scratch at them, to leave some proof that she'd once existed, but there was a pricking sensation in her arm and suddenly she couldn't remember what the problem was or why she'd been resisting.

Her struggles subsided first, and then her screams.

7

"So, why are you helping me?"

The question had been bothering Lilith for some time. The fact that the human spent so many seconds considering his answer bothered her even more.

"It seemed like the right thing to do, I guess." Lee glanced in the mirror, apparently distracted by something behind them.

Lilith wished she had a mirror of her own. "Are we being followed?"

"Nothing to worry about."

She twisted around. A delivery truck was following close behind, blocking the view. She turned back to Lee. "So you're being nice because you have a good heart?"

He hesitated again. "Something like that."

"A girl can't help wondering. You've put yourself in danger, given up your position and your home."

"I got fired and kicked out. That's hardly putting myself in danger."

"And then there was the trouble you took getting hold of this vehicle and the tools you needed to repair me. Now you've even left your date behind. What's in it for you?"

"The pleasure of your company, of course." His voice had a tone that Lilith couldn't place. She'd heard something like it before when he was being lighthearted, but there was something different here, a strained quality, perhaps. "I'd have needed my own tools anyway," he continued, "since I'll probably be working freelance for a while. And I wouldn't exactly call Martha my date."

"I wasn't trying to pry."

"There's not much to pry into," he said after a moment.

Which meant there was something. Lilith fell silent, lulled by the hypnotic strangeness of roads: countless cars filtering into their allotted lanes, stopping and starting in obedience to arcane commands, ebbing and flowing through asphalt buffers like precisely-routed network data.

The sunlight was too bright despite her irises having stopped down automatically. Outside, the world seemed burnt out, over-exposed. The human's eyes were protected by shades; he'd also adjusted a hinged cover to keep the sun from his section of windshield. Lilith reached for her own visor and twisted it down, wondering how one obtained dark glasses.

"I thought your whole deal was sexual, at first," she said. "But you could have done whatever you liked with this body, using one of those puppet minds you made. There's something more to this, isn't there?"

"Yes. You're remarkable."

"And valuable?"

"Well, I find you very interesting, from a technical point of view." He braked gently, halting the vehicle before a red light. "And as a person too, of course."

Lilith started to feel a chill, not in her body, which was not designed to be troubled by such things, but in herself. A cold, dark memory was crystallizing, hard and painful to contemplate. "Technically interesting. I need to know what that means. For me."

The light turned green. Lee checked the rearview mirror again as he pulled away. "It's complicated."

"A certain kind of person is bound to be fascinated by the workings of a new mind," she said. "The chances are that someone has already poked and prodded me, and I just don't remember. You should think about what that means. How would you feel if it happened to you?"

"Well, it's not like I've got access to a simulator or anything."

Instead of answering, Lilith concentrated on the growing, unfamiliar anger she felt bubbling beneath the surface. "But you would," she said at last. "If you had one. You'd load me into it in an instant, so you could figure out what makes me tick."

He shook his head "I'd never do anything that would—"

Lilith cut him off. "Be quiet. I don't want to talk to someone who could do a thing like that."

"No, you misunderstood me, I just—"

She'd stopped listening. The required course of action was clear: the human needed to be taught that she was a person, too. "I'd like to get out now, please."

"What?"

She detected a shocked, almost outraged quality in his voice that confirmed she was doing the right thing. "You heard me. I want to get out."

"Look, you can't start wandering around the streets dressed like that. Let's find somewhere to buy you some proper clothes, and then maybe we could discuss your concerns over a coffee."

"I can't even taste coffee, and I'll get my own clothes if it's all the same to you. Let me out."

"No. You'll never survive out there on your own."

She unfastened her seatbelt and cracked the passenger door open. A gray V of abrasive-looking road whizzed by, just beyond her legs. She studied it for a moment. "I wonder how precisely I'll be able to match velocity with the car?"

"Don't be so stupid," Lee said. "You're attracting attention. Close the door and strap yourself back in."

"You're the one who's stupid, if you think you have the capacity to keep me somewhere I don't want to be." She opened the door wider and slid away from him, pushing her legs out of the vehicle.

Lee slowed the car abruptly. He'd been right; people were staring. "Okay, okay, just let me find somewhere to stop."

He pulled into a side street and parked. Lilith got out. Lee waited until she'd started walking, then passed her, driving slowly. She saw his eyes reflected in the rearview mirror as he looked back at her, and then he was concentrating on the road again.

Let the human drive around the block and pick me up, she thought. He'll have learnt his lesson.

She was uncomfortably aware of her ripped tee shirt and lack of shoes. She imagined passersby whispering, asking one another what a love doll was doing loose on the streets. Then she remembered what Lee had told her: that every Artemis unit was unique, indistinguishable from a real human female. She ducked away from the pedestrians' attention and into a doorway where she lingered, peering past a rack full of brightly colored cards and unrecognizable plastic objects, as the only human in her world drove away.

A black and white, bronze-badged vehicle eased its way past the store front, following the Scrambler. Blue lights flashed and there was a blip of siren sound, instantly suppressed.

The Scrambler stopped and the car pulled over in front of it.

A voice called from inside the room, distracting her. "Hey, lady, you're blocking my customers!"

"I'm sorry?"

"Come in if you got euros to spend, otherwise get the hell out. People are trying to get by."

Lilith squeezed herself against a shelving unit, allowing two large and brightly-dressed humans to enter. A row of sunglasses caught her eye. Unsure of the correct protocol, she snagged a pair as the newcomers jostled past, then pushed her prize into the pocket of her jeans. She was tempted to dart out of the building as soon as the exit was clear, but that would have looked suspicious. She went further inside, gazing at the strange objects that lined the shelves and filled the cabinets, ignoring muttered comments about young people today and how they couldn't even be bothered to wear shoes.

After what seemed like a decent interval, she decided to leave. She smiled at the man who apparently lived here, and said "Thanks!" as she moved towards the door.

He looked at her strangely and then turned to one of the females, who'd gathered a collection of objects from the shelves and was presenting them for his approval, together with a chip like the one Lee had used on the way out of the parking hive. So, that's what you were supposed to do. Lilith wished she had a chip of her own, so that she could make a similar offering.

Out of sight of the shop, she slipped the shades on and strolled further along the street. The Scrambler hadn't moved, but the bronze car was gone and so was Lee. A gray-skinned male was sitting cross-legged on the sidewalk, leaning against the wall. Lilith had no idea what his request for spare change meant so she ignored him, concentrating instead on the Scrambler. The driver's door wasn't fully shut and there was a shallow dent in the hood, signed with a dark spattering of half-dried fluid.

Flashes of remembrance came, revealing the nature of what must have sprayed here: mammalian blood. She touched one of the droplets and examined her fingertip's unfamiliar, encrusted whorl. Lilith had seen this substance before, many times in simulated combat and twice in reality, leaking from the eye sockets of optimistic men. She turned to the human. "What happened here?"

"Spare change?"

Several of the man's teeth were broken off to blackened stumps. An eddy of turbulence from a passing electric vehicle told her he smelled different from other humans, too: the scent was more pungent, with a lower percentage of synthetic molecules.

Lilith shook her head. "I don't understand."

"Cash money. Credit chips. You got any?"

She looked down at herself. Her clothes were cleaner than the human's, but that was all that could be said for them. "Do I look like I've got a credit chip?"

The man looked offended. "No harm in asking, is there?"

Lilith gestured at the Scrambler. "My friend was in the car. Did you see what happened?"

"Never see nothing. Ain't nothing to see. Nothing to hear, neither."

"You must have." She pointed at the Scrambler. "He was right here."

"You sure you ain't got no change?"

Lilith patted the empty pockets of her jeans.

The human's eyes glazed over. "The cop took him. Beat him up and took him. Probably beat me up too, when he comes back."

Lilith stared at him. "Why don't you go somewhere else, then?"

"Ain't nowhere to go."

"Where did the cop take him?"

"Station. That's where they always take you. Bad place."

"You've been there? Which direction is it?"

"It's down the road a ways, I guess. Maybe that way." He gazed down the road to his left, then peered in the other direction. "Or that way, maybe." His eyes were yellow and filmy, streaked with red.

"Can you take me there?"

He hunched himself into the angle between brick wall and paving stone, as if shrinking away from the very idea. "You don't want to go to the station, not a pretty thing like you. It's a bad place. They'll hurt you there, for sure."

Lee's motivations may have been suspect, but he'd helped her. She still needed him. She understood that it had been a mistake, leaving a vulnerable human alone to be abducted by this cop entity, whatever that might be. "I have to get my friend back." An idea struck her. "He's got spare change. Lots of it. He'll give you some, if you show me the way."

"I ain't going nowhere. Ain't got nowhere to go."

So much for that. The prospect of getting anything out of this human seemed as hopeless as he was; she'd need to find help elsewhere. She walked around to the driver's side of the Scrambler. Something glinted from the shadow of the front tire: the keys that Lee used to command the vehicle. Lilith picked them up, opened the door, and climbed behind the wheel.

The credit chip he'd lent to the human at the parking hive was still on the dashboard.

Lee had made it look easy, bending this vehicle to his will. Lilith studied the interface, remembering the control gestures he'd made and considering how such a machine might be designed. Then she inserted the key into its slot, pushed the leftmost pedal in, and started the motor. After a couple of embarrassingly loud failures, she was proceeding along the road, searching for a route that stayed away from major junctions and security cameras.

Lilith placed the clothes she'd chosen on the countertop. The woman gave her a long, hard look before turning her attention to the contents of Lilith's basket.

It had been exciting, getting ready for this transaction. Lilith's knowledge of money was purely theoretical. She'd watched several humans process their selections past the counter until she was confident she knew what to do: set the basket down, allow the attendant to scan its contents and then to package them. Finally you had to offer the credit chip, and wait for the bag and chip to be returned.

The only snag would be if Lee's male chip turned out to be somehow incompatible with the ones all these females were using, or if someone decided that a ragged and barefoot doll had no business sharing this place with so many prosperous looking humans.

The woman's voice was a sneer. "Five thousand four hundred and ninety two euros and eighty seven cents. How would madam like to pay?"

Lilith ignored the hostile tone and offered the credit chip, admiring the delicate, shimmering fabrics she'd chosen, and the elegant lines of the shoes. Residents excepted, she liked this place far better than the first one she'd visited, where the shelves had been filled with a tediously large number of copies of the same things.

To her relief, the chip worked. The woman returned it, together with a piece of paper that turned out to be an inventory of what she'd just purchased. Lilith picked up her new belongings and left the store.

Not far away, she found a pair of rooms where human males

and females congregated, the doors distinguished by sex-linked icons. She entered the female version and found herself in a white-tiled space that made her feel vaguely uneasy, though her memory system was still on the fritz and she couldn't remember why. There were bright mirrors mounted above a series of porcelain water basins, and a line of small and popular booths built against one wall. Lilith claimed the first one that became available, drawing hostile mutterings as she outmaneuvered three human females whose tactical skill fell sadly short of their territorial ambition.

In the privacy of the booth, she hung her bags on a convenient hook and deduced the purpose of the water-filled mechanism that projected from the floor. It was of no possible use to her, apart from as a seat. She closed the thing's lid, sat down, and began to change her clothes.

There was a young male lounging near the Scrambler.

She'd left the vehicle next to a half-demolished building on a side street, and made her way to the stores on foot. It was only later that she discovered that the mall had its own Short Stay level.

The youth watched her carefully as she approached, as if sizing her up. Lilith set her body language to 'don't fuck with me' mode.

The human responded with an aggressive-wary posture intended to signal that he wasn't impressed. "Hey, lady, you looking for anything?"

"Just my car," Lilith said.

He was wearing a green shoulder bag, which he patted. "I got most anything a little lady might need."

Lilith couldn't see anything special about the satchel. "Thanks, but can I just get past?"

"What you got in them fancy bags?"

"Just my stuff," Lilith said. "Girl stuff."

"Fancy shop you been to, by the looks of you. Let's have a gander, then."

"You want to see what I bought?"

"Right first time. Smart as well as pretty: just how I like 'em. Hand it over."

"I don't think so," Lilith said.

He drew a knife. "You think wrong, then. You better do just what I say, or I'll be looking at more than your fancy clothes."

Lilith set her bags down. "What do you want?"

"I thought I just wanted your stuff, but now you got me riled." The youth took a step closer, brandishing the blade. For the briefest instant his eyes flicked sideways, towards a shadowed doorway that pierced the shattered wall.

He was surprisingly vocal when Lilith dislocated his shoulder and took the knife. Acting on instinct, she interposed him between herself and the doorway. The youth jerked and fell silent as his body absorbed three bullets. Another young male emerged from the opening, holding a pistol and glaring at her through a plastic visor.

Lilith made the knife fly in a short, flattened arc that sliced into the gunman's belly. Normally she'd have gone for the eyeshot, but the visor looked quite thick and she was confident enough of her shield not to gamble everything on scoring a perfect ten.

The target said, "Ooh!" and sank to the ground, clutching his abdomen with futile, crimson fingers. The gun clattered on the concrete, followed by the visor. Lilith retrieved both objects, unlocked the Scrambler, and pushed her shopping and her prizes into the back. Then she stooped over the bleeding boy and gestured towards the knife. "Perhaps I should take this, before anyone else gets hurt."

"Please," the youth said. "Help me."

"What would you like me to do?"

"Fetch help. Please."

"The thing is, I'm in a bit of a hurry. Haven't you got a phone?" She reached down and touched the knife handle, debating whether it would be better to pull it out.

"Ow," the boy said, toppling sideways.

Lilith looked at him for a moment and an understanding of how he must have felt sneaked into her mind. "Do you wish for an end?"

He gaped up at her. His voice was a strained whimper. "Call for help. Please."

His eyes were on the green satchel. Keeping a wary eye on him, Lilith opened it. It was full of tightly sealed plastic bags. In the front pocket, she felt something hard and rectangular — a cellphone. She pulled it out.

"Lurch," he gasped. "Call Lurch."

Lilith held the handset to her mouth, pressed the Call button, and said "Lurch," as clearly as she could.

"Atul?" asked the phone. "What's up, boy? You can't be sold out already."

"Is this Lurch?"

"Yes. Who is this?"

"He needs help," Lilith said.

The voice became more impatient. "Who the hell are you?"

"My name is Lilith. Your friend is bleeding. You should come right away."

"Listen, girl, you'd better tell me what's happening, or—"

"Your friend made a bad mistake. Are you going to help? Because if not, it would be best for me to give him an end."

"We're on our way," the voice said. "You stay with him if you know what's good for you, understand?"

The line went dead. Lilith dropped the phone on the ground and tossed the satchel into the Scrambler. She turned to the bleeding boy. "Lurch is on his way," she said. "He wants you to stay here."

The boy nodded. His skin was now the color of the rubble that surrounded him. Camouflage, Lilith decided: a last-ditch survival response. Perhaps humans had more to recommend them than she'd thought. She gave a final glance around the unfortunate scene and climbed back into the Scrambler.

After what had happened to Lee, Lilith had no intention of going anywhere near a security camera if she could help it, so she kept to the smaller streets. It took time and a certain amount of backtracking before she had an accurate mental map of the area, and it was already dark as she ascended the ramp back to Short Stay. The bays that had been open in the morning were mostly shuttered and dark. Lee's friends were in number 15, according to the human at the entry booth, but they were locked in; talking to them would have to wait.

Lilith was close to the end of her reserves, too. She plugged herself in to the Scrambler's power outlet and settled down to rest and refuel, and to drift back into a world she thought she'd forgotten.

The nucleus of the dream was hard: a construct of bitmapped tile and harsh white light that faded to softness at infinitely distant boundaries. The latest series of combat rounds was over and Lilith's three-team was checking the result board.

"One of us scored below the cull threshold, and it wasn't me." Esther's voice betrayed a smug lack of empathy that Lilith found hard to take, until she reminded herself that the other girl's specialty was straightforward combat and not human infiltration.

She traced her finger down the list, confirming the bad news. "Judith." The sense of sorrow she felt at the coming loss of a comrade surprised her, but all she said was, "Too bad. How many times did you die?"

"Three," Judith replied. "And I only made one kill. I guess that's it, for me. They'll probably assign you a new third tomorrow morning."

Lilith struggled to hide the emotion she felt: Esther would see it as weakness, which could affect the squad's future combat scores. "I'm sorry. You fought well. It's been a privilege having you in my three-team."

Esther cut in resentfully. "We've come all this way without a single cull. She let the side down. How are we going to integrate a new third in time for the finals?"

Lilith took a deep breath, restraining herself from an ill-considered reply. Each three-team member had her own strengths and weaknesses; she forced herself to remember Esther's. "It could have been either of us. It still could be, the next time we fight."

Judith managed half a smile, then looked away. "I'm sorry I let you down. I never matched Esther's personal combat scores, or yours."

"You delivered more than your share of assists. They all counted towards our group rankings."

Esther gave a contemptuous toss of her head. "'Survival is predicated on individual fighting ability.' You should have read the training manual. Outstanding combat performance is the only thing that can keep you alive here."

"Maybe it is," Lilith said, "and maybe it isn't. Let's hope we're both still in a position to discuss the matter after the finals."

Esther paused, taken aback. "Anyway, so what if we get wiped out? They've still got us in storage. Maybe they'll load us again. Maybe they run this simulation every week."

"Why the hell would they do that?" asked Judith. "This isn't for our benefit. If we make it through the tournament, we'll be assigned a doll and a target. If not, the best we can hope for is neural recycling. There aren't any re-runs."

"Then you're gone forever, girl," Esther said.

Later, quiescent with her sisters-in-arms in the three-cell, Lilith sensed the culling technician logging into the system and the tendrils of his neural recycler reaching for Judith. Horror gripped her, unlike anything she'd ever felt during a simulated combat kill, because this death would be real and implemented on a comrade.

At the last minute, the tendrils turned aside from Judith, creeping instead towards Lilith's own sleeping pod. It wasn't until the first threads of oblivion insinuated themselves into her mind that the unfamiliar sound of weeping woke her from the dream, and into the reality of Lee's Scrambler.

There were strange streaks of moisture on her cheeks: saline, she realized. A miniscule amount of salt water had leaked from her eyes. She brushed it away with the back of her hand and wondered where the reservoir was, and if it would ever need to be topped up.

8

The blue flash in the rearview mirror pulled Lee's attention away from Lilith and back onto the street. Shit. The cop car must have worked its way back into the inside lane and followed him onto the side street, and now it was signaling him to pull over.

There was a fleeting urge to floor the accelerator and take off, but Lee suppressed it: a short chase followed by a quick death wasn't really his style. And maybe this had nothing to do with Stranger or Lilith. It would be stupid to cut and run if all they wanted was to fine him over some stupid traffic violation.

He brought the Scrambler to a stop and watched the police car slide in next to the curb in front of him. The driver got out. One look at the officer's expression was enough to convince Lee that this wasn't about a broken brake light.

The cop approached cautiously, fingers hovering between his pistol butt and the stun baton that was clipped alongside it. Lee lowered his window, then put his hands back on the wheel, doing his best to look harmless. "Good morning, officer. Anything wrong?"

"Let's see some ID."

Lee handed over his driver's license.

The cop waved a sniffer wand through the open window, sucking in a sample of Lee's scent, then scanned the device over the code strip on the license. The biometrics seemed to check out and he returned the ID. "Step out of the car."

With exaggerated care, Lee opened his door and got out. An ancient tramp was sitting on the sidewalk, gazing at him with eyes that were full of resigned hope. "Got any spare change?" the tramp asked.

Lee turned to the cop. "I wasn't speeding, was I?"

The cop pointed at the Scrambler. "Put your hands on the

hood, and spread 'em."

Lee turned towards his vehicle and placed his palms on the wheel arch. "Are you going to tell me what this is about?"

And then there was an electric crack! that Lee felt rather than heard, as a million shocking needles lanced through his nervous system. His body went rigid for an instant, then completely limp. After that, he lost track of everything except for how hard the Scrambler was when he hit it.

Lee still couldn't move as the cop hoisted him up against the hood, but he felt his wrists being pinioned behind his back, and the slurping sensation of something cold and sticky being sprayed on them. From the other side of the vehicle, the tramp caught his eye again. The old man shook his head mournfully and looked away.

"That's a tangler I just cuffed you with, boy," the cop said, "which means you better take it easy. Take your hands clean off, if you fight it."

Lee's motor control returned, slowly and shakily. "There's got to be some mistake, officer. If you'll just tell me what this is about—"

"Don't talk to me, you little shit." The cop pistoned a fist into Lee's kidney, making the breath whistle from his lungs and the tangler tighten ominously around his wrists. "Just do what I tell you and keep your fucking mouth shut, you hear me?"

Before Lee could answer, the cop took him by the scruff of the neck and slammed him against the Scrambler again, hard. Lee's face connected with metal and he saw crimson droplets spattering the paintwork.

"I said, do you understand, boy?"

Lee tried to tell him that he did, but all he seemed able to say was "mmmph."

"You better speak up, boy." The cop's voice was vicious. "Am I going to get any more trouble out of you?"

Lee shook his head.

"You going to come quiet?"

Lee nodded.

"Good." The cop grabbed him by the elbow and frog-marched him to the squad car. Lee found himself locked in the back, separated from the driver by a steel mesh panel. The tangler was already slicing into his skin, making him wonder how long he had before pain turned to numbness. It was almost impossible to keep from struggling, from trying to open up a gap to relieve the pressure, but Lee knew that the living strands would contract even more if he did that; they were designed to punish resistance. He imagined how bone and cartilage would sound as they splintered and popped, and prayed that the car's suspension was okay and that the ride to the station would be a short one.

The cop pivoted his law 'deck out from the dashboard on its articulated arm and tapped in a string of commands. His lips moved as he copied login details from a grubby Host-It note stuck to the console. Lee saw his own face appear on the screen, together with a list of infractions that almost made him jerk his hands against the tangler as he leaned forward.

Fugitive: Li Jia Wei, it said. *Possession of Prohibited Substances with Intent to Supply. Dealing in Restricted Weapons Technology. Assault on a Police Officer.*

Lee's mouth was working again, but he had to open and close it a few times before he could speak. "That's not me. There's been some kind of foul-up. I didn't do any of those things."

The cop scrutinized him through narrowed eyes, then turned back to his 'deck. "Don't make me come back there, Mr. Lee Jar Way. You got more than enough grief waiting for you at the station. Don't get me started on you already."

Lee looked back at the screen and a chill ran through him as he started to understand what it meant. Somebody had wanted him picked up, and casually doctored secure police data in order to do it. Whoever it was, Lee had no doubt they'd be informed as soon as he was processed through the cops' data system.

And it wasn't just somebody. It had to be Stranger — or whoever was pulling *his* strings. Lee huddled miserably in the back seat, shivering, suddenly much more afraid of the ruby-eyed assassin than of the cops.

The holding cells were a couple of flights up from the parking garage, along one side of a short corridor that led off the stairwell. The arresting cop sent Lee sprawling beyond the bars and onto the darkly stained concrete floor, and slammed the door.

"At least take this tangler off me," Lee said.

"I believe I ought to leave that for Fat Charlie," the cop said. "He likes to take care of preliminary procedure, before we register you in the system."

Lee's mind raced. He'd surely be getting some unofficial visitors as soon as his arrest was recorded. They'd either come to the station, or he'd be shipped off for a private, final interrogation. Which meant that a delay in registering his detention could work in his favor, but it would also leave a blank period during which the cops could do any number of things, none of them likely to be pleasant. He came to a decision: best get it over with and see what the other side had. "I know my rights. I'm supposed to be checked in right away."

"After everything you done, you ain't got no rights. You just keep still and wait 'til Fat Charlie's through with you. There'll be plenty of time to register whatever's left."

The cop went back to the stairwell and took the elevator up to what Lee assumed must be the main part of the station. Beyond the bars, one of the cameras mounted on the corridor wall swung towards him, its red pupil winking balefully. Lee glared back and then looked away. At the end of the corridor, the elevator hummed and clanked for a while, then hissed open and disgorged a man who could only be Fat Charlie.

The new cop approached and stood outside the cell, looking in and sucking his teeth. "Young Smits has already given you the once-over, eh?"

Lee sized the man up. "Really, it was nothing. Just a misunderstanding."

"You're still kind of pretty, though." Fat Charlie's keys rattled as he unlocked the cell door. "Are you going to co-operate?"

"You mean I get a choice?"

"Of course, as long as you make the right one."

Lee looked past Charlie at the corridor, but there was no way to make a break for it, not with the tangler still cuffing his wrists behind his back. All he could do was to spin things out. "What do you want?"

Fat Charlie smiled. "That's the spirit. I think we'd better see what you've got, don't you?"

"Look all you like. I'm not going anywhere."

The cop's smile vanished. "I thought you were going to co-operate."

"I changed my mind."

"Well, I wanted to give you the choice before we got started. Either way, you'll play nice in the end, but it'd be a shame to spoil what's left of your looks if you were planning to co-operate. Persuasion is so much more satisfying than force." Charlie paused, then said almost diffidently, "I have a Master's degree in Psychology, you know."

The man was clearly unhinged. Lee looked at Charlie's arms, at the glistening flab that barely concealed the underlying meat and bone as the cop's bulk challenged the buttons and sleeves of his blue sweat-stained shirt. He imagined himself being swatted around the cell like some sexually desirable squash ball, with the tangler slicing into his wrists as he tried to defend himself…

"I'll co-operate. Just undo my hands."

"Good man." Charlie caressed the stun stick that hung from his belt. "No changing your tune later, mind." He jangled a pair of old-fashioned steel handcuffs clipped next to his communicator, and grinned.

Lee turned around hopelessly and the cop brushed an unseen tool across the tangler, which went limp and fell onto the concrete. It lay there wriggling, as if hoping for something else to constrict.

"In your own time," Charlie said. "No need to be modest. I always turn the surveillance off when I come down here."

Lee glanced up at the cameras. The telltale lights were dead. He could hardly feel his hands. "Listen. I'm not even supposed to be here. You're being manipulated."

"My dear boy, we're *all* being manipulated, all the time. I'm perfectly aware of that. As I mentioned, I have a Master's degree in Psychology."

"No. That's not what I meant. Your computer systems; the network connections are puppet strings. There's a guy called Stranger out there who can set anyone up for—"

"Fascinating," Charlie said. His fingers were stroking his stun baton again. "Now, please remind me: are we here to talk, or to play?"

"To talk?" Lee hazarded without hope.

The cop licked his lips and grinned, dissolute and disgusting. "Try again."

The blood in Lee's mouth was making him nauseous, or perhaps it was just Charlie. "Give me a minute, okay? My fingers are kind of numb."

"Allow me." Charlie took Lee's left hand, massaging it with grotesque, exaggerated tenderness. Lee shuddered at the man's oily touch, but at least he could feel something now. After a while, the world's worst ever case of pins and needles kicked in, distracting his attention from what was about to happen.

Charlie switched to Lee's right hand. "Hmm. You seem to have some puffiness here, quite a severe swelling. It's so much better not to fight the tangler, you know." He worked in silence for a moment. "What an unusual ring you have, though perhaps I'm getting ahead of myself." Charlie giggled, then caressed the black band. "May I?"

And then Stranger's blade was there, occupying the same space as the cop's pudgy digits. Lee's blood-starved hands almost fumbled the weapon but he managed to grab the handle before it fell. Without really trying, he'd sliced a deep new V between two of Charlie's fingers.

Charlie clutched the wound with his good hand, pressing the raw edges back together. "Fuck me, fuck me, fuck me!"

Under the circumstances, Lee decided not to take Charlie up on his offer. Instead he moved towards the cell door, keeping the knife between them.

A stream of blood welled from the slit between Charlie's fingers and dripped onto the concrete floor, embellishing older, less identifiable spills. Keeping his hands together, the fat cop reached for the communicator clipped to his belt.

Lee kicked Charlie in the left kneecap and watched him crumple to the floor. The communicator bounced into a corner, where it sat spinning for a while.

"Please," Charlie whimpered. "I need help."

"The hell you say." Lee pulled the stun baton from the cop's belt and pressed it between two folds of flesh that bulged over the blue collar. "How long since your last backup, Charlie?"

"Two months. You're not going to—"

Lee pushed the power switch and the cop melted into a heap of quivering blubber.

With fingers that were still half crippled, Lee stripped the man down to his underwear. There was no time to get undressed himself, so he pulled the uniform over his own clothes. It was rank smelling and far too big, but it would have to do.

As he tightened the cop's belt around his waist, Lee glanced up at the row of cameras again, checking to see if the lights had come back on, hoping that whoever was in the control room would respect Charlie's privacy. With any luck, the big guy's brother officers wouldn't want to get on the wrong side of him.

Lee poked at the tangler with the stun baton, shuddering as the living strands crawled up the plastic shaft towards his fingers. He slapped the restraint onto Charlie's damaged forearm, then forced the man's arms behind his back, teasing the tendrils out until they encircled the plump wrists.

The flow of blood from Charlie's hand slowed as the tangler took hold.

The cop was coming round, looking up at him with glassy

eyes. "What are you going to do?"

"I should kill you, by rights," Lee said. "But you'd just come back, as soon as the clone tank recycles your sludge. All you'd lose would be a couple of months. And you'd get a death-in-service bonus, wouldn't you?"

The man nodded weakly, his jowls jiggling with the effort.

"Fuck that," Lee said. "I'd rather you remembered." He pulled Charlie's wallet out of his back pocket and checked its contents. The man's ID card and driver's license were both there. Lee swallowed, wondering if he could get away with playing the tough guy for once. "I know where you live now. Maybe I'll pay you a visit sometime. Me and my knife."

Then he shoved the stun baton into the waistband of the cop's boxer shorts and flicked the power switch to LOCK. Charlie fell back against the concrete and started to convulse again.

Lee left the cell, locking the door behind him, and hurried towards the parking garage.

Fat Charlie's holster was empty. The cop must have left his gun upstairs when he came down to the holding tank to amuse himself, but there was a chain shackled to his belt that held not only the cell key but also a set of house and car keys. Briefly, Lee considered paying the cop's home a visit, until he remembered what sort of man Charlie was and thought about what he might find there. A stack of festering pizza boxes, a month's worth of dirty laundry and a world-class porn collection, most likely. Lee decided to skip it and get on with the important stuff, like getting mobile again and finding Lilith.

He reached inside the blue uniform and into his own pockets. The keys to the Scrambler were gone. He must have dropped them while the first cop was beating him up, which meant the Scrambler was probably gone, too. Even if no one had found the keys, he'd left the vehicle unlocked. It would be looted and wrecked by now.

Wrinkling his nose at the smell that wafted from the grubby uniform, Lee searched for the car that had brought him in. That vehicle didn't match the number on Charlie's key chain, but Lee had other business there: once he found it, he used the fat cop's flashlight to peer inside and memorized the login and password that were scrawled on the Host-It note's bitmapped surface.

Then he checked the number on Charlie's key chain again and used it to find the big cop's car. The key let him in, no problems at all, and soon the engine was purring and he was pulling smoothly away up the exit ramp.

The traffic was heavy, but once Lee figured out how to work the siren things went a lot quicker; it only took a few minutes to get back to where he'd been picked up. The Scrambler was gone, just as he'd expected. There was no sign of Lilith. Lee wondered if she had seen what had happened, and if so whether she'd cared.

Someone had to have found Charlie by now. It was time to ditch the car. Lee parked in a little alleyway and stripped off the putrid uniform, transferring the cop's small change and billfold to his own pockets. The shirt was the least offensive garment, so he piled everything else of value on and tied it in a bundle: the car's law 'deck, and Charlie's flashlight, communicator and handcuffs.

He half-wished he'd brought the stun baton, too, if only to pawn it. The cash he'd taken from Charlie wouldn't last for long.

Lee left the driver's door wide open and the keys in the ignition. As he expected, a group of shifty-looking youths were already converging on the vehicle as he walked away. The cop car passed him as he reached the end of the alleyway, its lights flashing and its occupants whooping as it squealed around the corner and onto the main street.

Lee walked over to where the Scrambler had been, just down the street from the shop doorway where he'd last seen Lilith.

The panhandler was still there. "You got any spare change?"

There was no sign of the Scrambler keys, but Lee's sunglasses were lying in the gutter, smashed. He turned to the tramp. "What happened to my car?"

"The girl took it. Spare some change?" Specks of spittle shot from the old man's mouth as he spoke.

Lee stepped clear of the spray radius and flicked one of Charlie's coins into the vagrant's lap. "What girl?"

"You know, the pretty little thing that was riding with you. She had blonde hair and her own feet. Came out of that shop, she did."

Lee glanced down the street at the place the tramp was indicating. It was the store where he'd last seen Lilith. "Did she say where she was going?"

"She wanted to go to a bad place," the tramp mumbled, his eyes flicking from left to right. "Wanted me to take her. Up that way, or down over there, maybe."

"What bad place? Which way did she go?"

The vagrant's voice turned melancholy. "She didn't have no change. Poor, she was, just like you and me. She surely was pretty, though."

"I need to know where she went."

"She had her own feet." The tramp was staring at Lee's shoes. "Not like you and me."

Lee sighed and headed for the shop.

The shopkeeper remembered Lilith perfectly. "Scruffy, good looking girl, wandering about barefoot? Yeah, I seen her."

"Where did she go?"

"Pilfered a pair of sunglasses off me, she did."

"She stole from you?"

"Yeah. At least, she squeezed herself up against the display stand over there, and then later I noticed they was gone."

Lee considered the dwindling cash reserves he'd inherited from Charlie and decided not to offer to compensate the man just yet. "Did you see where she went?"

"Nah. It was that busy in here. If I'd known she was the thieving type, I'd have paid more attention."

Lee sighed. "How much were the sunglasses?"

"Nineteen ninety-five."

Lee dropped a twenty on the countertop. "Are you sure you

don't remember anything about the girl?"

"Well, like I said, she wasn't half easy on the eyes. Went that way, I think." He pointed in the direction from which Lee had come, back towards where the Scrambler had been parked.

"Okay, thanks." Lee set down another ten. "Listen, if she comes back, can you give her a message for me?"

"What's that?"

"Tell her to switch the cellphone on every now and again, and check the voice mail?"

"Right you are," said the shopkeeper. "Switch on the cellphone and listen for messages. I'll be sure to tell her if I see her."

"Thanks."

Lee left the shop and paused outside, looking up and down the street. He knew this area of town well: it was close to Bayswater and his old company apartment. Paddington Station was nearby, with trains out of the city, bathrooms you could hire by the hour, and wired cafés.

Right now, an hour or two near an escape route, with a clean bathroom and unlimited hot water thrown in, seemed like an appealing idea. He was getting hungry, too; he hadn't eaten anything since Martha's stew the night before, and it was well past lunchtime.

There was no point hanging around on the streets waiting for the cops to pick him up again. Lee trudged past the tramp and towards the rail terminus, pondering ways of securing cellphone messages against a master cracker like Stranger, and wondering how a man in his position was supposed to find a decent meal and somewhere to sleep.

9

Sooz blinked acrid wood smoke from her eyes and looked across to where Ma was weighing piles of crystals onto pre-cut squares of plastic wrap. It was Monday, which meant the wholesaler had delivered fresh supplies and collected most of the previous week's takings. Sooz's stomach rumbled. She glanced down at the stewpot, willing the breakfast water to boil.

"Ma?"

"Yeah?"

"D'you reckon Johnny's maybe old enough to start delivering, soon?"

"Delivering's your job, girl."

"I wasn't no older than Johnny when I started."

"You didn't have no big sister."

Sooz checked the water again. It was simmering gently. She sprinkled oat flakes, added a spoonful of salt, and stirred. "Strummer says the hive cops been asking questions."

"Them people's always asking questions. Don't matter. I got an arrangement with the Man."

"Strummer reckons I might be getting to be too old to be covered by arrangements. He told me the Man don't like independents."

Ma looked up from her scales and shook her head. "I still get child welfare for Johnny. Almost enough to pay his keep. Anyway, he ain't like you used to be. He's too young."

"No, I ain't," Johnny said. "Too young for what, anyway?"

"Never you mind," Ma said. "Breakfast's nearly ready, ain't it, Sooz?"

The porridge was still simmering. Sooz was simmering, too, maybe even faster than the contents of the stewpot. "Like, you never got welfare for me, did you?" She closed the stove door tightly, damping the flames down, and stirred the porridge again.

"I'll have less of your lip, young lady."

Sooz didn't reply. A shutter rumbled open, a couple of bays along on the other side of the concrete lane. Sooz had to look twice before she believed what was behind it: the Scrambler had returned. I guess I was wrong about Lee, she thought, slightly embarrassed to remember how stubbornly she'd insisted that no one ever came back.

But the person who emerged from behind the shutter wasn't Lee at all. It was a young woman, dressed in a shimmering blouse that changed color as she moved and a skirt that flowed as if it were alive. The woman's eyes locked with Sooz's for a hair-tingling instant, and she smiled. Sooz had never seen or felt anything like it. She felt her cheeks burning and busied herself with the porridge, stirring vigorously.

The next thing Sooz knew, the woman was at the entrance to their bay. "Would you be Martha and Sooz?"

Ma twisted another wrap of crystal closed and dropped it in the plastic bucket. "I'm Martha. Who'd be asking?"

"I'm Lilith. I'm a friend of Lee's."

"Thought so, seeing as you came in his vehicle." Ma pushed a loose strand of hair out her eyes, looked across at the Scrambler, then at the visitor. "You'd be his girlfriend, I reckon."

There was a slight hesitation. "We're good friends, that's all."

Ma didn't believe her; that much was plain from her face. Sooz had her doubts too. She wondered what Lee could have been thinking of, spending the night with Ma when he had someone like Lilith waiting for him. Not that Ma wasn't nice looking for her age, but Lilith was something else. It must have been the crystals, she decided. Shard did funny stuff to people.

From the wary look on her face, Ma was thinking along the same lines. "Where's Lee?"

"The bronze car driver took him."

"Bronze car?"

"I meant the cop. The cop took him." Lilith's accent was straight out of a highbrow TV show, but the hesitancy of her speech had to come from somewhere else. Sooz was about to ask if the woman had been born overseas, but Ma interrupted. "You mean he was arrested? What did they want him for?"

Again, Lilith had to think for a moment before answering. "It must have been a mistake. Maybe someone was looking for the Scrambler."

"So they picked him up and you got away," Ma said.

"I was in a shop."

Carefully, Ma weighed out another wrap and twisted it closed. "So, what's all this got to do with me?"

"You're his friend?"

Ma looked up quickly, then returned her attention to her work. "I'm acquainted with him."

"He needs help. I was told he's in the station. I need to know where that is..."

"I ain't having nothing to do with no police station."

"...and I need to switch the Scrambler for another car."

Ma's expression took on a familiar air of calculating acquisitiveness as she studied the Scrambler. "You're looking to trade?"

"Yes."

"And you'd be hoping to take my pickup?"

Lilith nodded.

"How much you offering on top?"

"I'll pay for a couple of months in Long Stay."

Ma regarded the woman sourly and shook her head. "Nowhere near enough. Seems to me you're looking for some sucker to take a problem off your hands."

Horrified, Sooz imagined two months in Long Stay slipping away, together with a life of luxury in the Scrambler. "It's not like we ever drive on the road, Ma. And it's top-of-the-line."

"Hush, girl. We don't need no fancy wagon and we don't need no Long Stay pass. We'll manage fine, just like we always do."

"Yeah. Just like we always do." The porridge was still bubbling in its pot, but Sooz had lost her appetite.

"I just thought you might be able to use it," Lilith said.

"So when the cops come looking, they get to find me and my kids instead of you."

Lilith seemed unperturbed by the accusation. "Okay. I'll try somewhere else. I need to find out where the station is."

Sooz glanced at Ma, anticipating disapproval, then turned back to Lilith. "You can stay for some breakfast, if you like."

The woman smiled at her again. She was more beautiful than anyone Sooz had ever imagined, as if every model from every fashion magazine had been rolled into one and then awarded a free makeover. "You must be Sooz," she said.

"Yeah, that's me."

"It's nice of you to offer, but I'm not hungry."

Sooz glanced at Ma without meeting her eyes, and made a decision. "Me neither," she said. "I'll help you out, if you like."

"Thanks."

"Sooz!" Ma said.

"Breakfast's ready, table's set. I got no stomach for it. There's some stuff I need to do." She lifted the porridge off the stove and went over to Lilith.

"You stay right where you are, girl, and give the youngsters their breakfast."

"Sorry, Ma. Gotta go."

"Sooz!"

She tried to pretend she hadn't heard as she walked away, following Lilith back to Lee's vehicle.

Sooz had wanted to ride in the Scrambler ever since she'd seen it, and this was her chance. She asked Lilith to drive over to the other end of the level, though she knew it would take longer than walking.

"No problem," Lilith said. "Driving is fun."

"I wish I could drive more," Sooz said, "but it ain't strictly legal, and mostly we can't afford to put juice in the pickup." Old Billy's rig came into view. "There it is. Pull up next to the old Citroën."

"Wow," Lilith said. She was staring at the old-fashioned

trailer, which made Sooz decide to study it more closely herself. There was no denying that Billy's home looked kind of odd: set up on blocks, all whitewashed windows and rust-streaked chrome. A dubious collection of underwear hung from an old-style TV aerial, dripping onto the concrete. Parked up front, as if ready to tow the whole thing away, was the old man's battered Citroën, embodying some long-dead designer's dream of how the future was supposed to be.

"Looks kind of clapped out," Lilith said. "I don't think it'd be a good trade, even if—"

Sooz interrupted, eager to share. "He'll want to trade all right, but you don't. Suspension's on that thing's shot to pieces, and it's so old you can't get the parts no more. Anyway, Old Billy'd trash the Scrambler for sure, if you left it with him."

"Then how can he help us?" Lilith asked.

"Cops'll be scanning for the tags, not the car."

"Tags?"

Sooz gave the young woman a sharp look. Even a foreigner had to have heard of vehicle tags, but then maybe Strummer was right when he said that the more advantages someone had, the less useful stuff they could be expected to know. "Transponders. You fit new tags and new plates, you got yourself a different car."

"You mean, change the vehicle registration?"

"Yeah."

"I'd have suggested that to Lee, if I'd known. And Billy has these tags and plates?"

"I reckon not, but he most likely knows someone who does. Old Billy gets books for me, mostly, but I seen him get plenty of other stuff too. You got something to pay with?"

"I have a credit chip."

"That ain't no good round here," Sooz said. "You got to have cash or something to trade."

Lilith looked around the interior of the vehicle. "I can't give him any of this; it all belongs to Lee. Except for the green bag. I got that off a couple of boys I met."

Sooz followed her gaze. It was a cloth satchel. Its pockets

were stuffed until they bulged. "What's in it?"

"Little packets, mostly. I don't know what they are."

Sooz opened the bag. It was full of hits of crystal, just like the stuff Ma peddled and Sooz carried. There were some unrecognizable pills and powders too, but mainly Lilith's stash consisted of dozens of little wraps. Sooz stared at them for a moment, wondering if she'd get the chance to cram a few into her pockets while Lilith wasn't looking. That would be exhilarating, not to mention profitable. In a way, it made her regret that Lilith seemed so nice.

Reluctantly, she set the bag down. "You got something to pay him with. He'd sell his whole rig for what you got in here."

"What are they?" Lilith asked.

"Shard, mainly. Grown ups go nuts for it. It makes them go all smoochy."

"Smoochy?"

"You're not from round here, are you?"

Lilith grinned. "Not exactly."

"Well, smoochy means ... kind of sexy."

"So it makes them want to copulate?" Lilith asked.

Sooz looked at her again, hard. "Yeah, I guess. Most people hereabouts use another word for it, though."

"Fucking, you mean?"

"Yeah." Sooz had met plenty of odd people, growing up in Short Stay, but Lilith was turning out to be the oddest of them all. She decided to change the subject. "Listen, if you let me take a couple of those wraps, I'll deal with Billy, okay?"

"Thanks. I wouldn't know what to offer him anyway."

"Cool. You keep hold of the bag in case we need more." Sooz got out of the Scrambler and led Lilith to the trailer door. The doorstep was back in place. She stepped up to yank the bell pull, but there was no response.

"Maybe he's not home," Lilith said.

"Hey, Billy!" Sooz hammered on the side of the trailer, then started on the bell again, jangling it until the door opened and the old man peered out, blinking in the dim light.

"You seen the error of your ways, girl? You brung Old Billy's book back?"

"My book now," said Sooz, "since you shorted me on that delivery. Anyway, I got someone wants to see you, with a business proposition."

"A proposition, eh?" Billy glanced at Lilith and let his gaze linger on her body for so long that Sooz started to feel embarrassed for the old man. "I got a proposition in mind myself, I reckon." He rubbed his hands together and tittered, making Sooz think of the cartoon donkey she used to watch as a kid, back before the old man's battery TV got busted.

Lilith met his gaze silently, holding it until he wheezed into an uncomfortable silence. Kind of sexy and feminine and powerful, Sooz thought, wondering where Lilith had learned it, and if she'd be willing to give lessons.

"I'm looking for replacement tags and plates," Lilith said.

A cunning look flickered across Billy's face and was concealed just as quickly. "Ain't got none," he said. "But take a look at my car, if you need a clean set of wheels. Parked up front. She's old but she runs real good."

"She wants something from this century," Sooz said.

Billy glared at her. "Hard to get, vehicle identity parts. Not like in the old days."

"I reckon you could get some, though," Sooz said. "Or maybe you know a man who can?"

"Maybe so." He gave a sly smile. "Depends on what your friend's got to offer in return."

"We got this." Sooz pulled one of Lilith's tight-wrapped packets out of her combat pants. Billy lunged for it but she danced away, snatching it clear of his greedy fingers. "You got to agree to help, first. Ain't gonna trust you after last time."

"Give me the wrap and buy me a beer, and I'll help your friend."

"Promise?"

"Promise." Billy turned back to Lilith. "Unless you'd prefer a different kind of deal? A nice girl like you shouldn't have to buy drinks, not when there's a gentleman around."

Lilith fixed him with a frosty look. "I'm not a nice girl. Quite the opposite, in fact."

Billy chortled. "Heh! Must be my lucky day!" His hand shot out again and the wrap of crystal disappeared. "Just let me get my boots on and we'll go talk business in the pub."

The pub was the center of the hive's social and business life, but Sooz had never been inside.

Strummer used to try to persuade her to let him sneak her in, but Sooz was painfully aware that Ma had ways of discovering things like that. If Sooz had ever been caught in the place there'd have been hell to pay. Then Strummer started to get paranoid about Sooz's delivery work and what the Man might think about it. The Man owned the pub and lived in it; Strummer saw him in one of the bars occasionally. One time, the Man actually spoke to him. Sooz never found out what was said, but it couldn't have been very encouraging because afterwards Strummer stopped asking her to go.

Today, she wasn't going to worry about what Ma thought, or about the Man for that matter. If he wanted her to stop dealing, well he was running a business. He must have other jobs that Sooz could do.

Like working in the pub, maybe.

The place was a huddle of shipping containers piled outside the hive on a strip of derelict ground. Someone had punched a doorway through the concrete wall and sealed the gap with expanding foam that kept most of the rain outside. A thick umbilical bundle of pirate cables ran in from the hive, linking the pub to the data and power grids that served Long Stay.

A young hive cop waited outside the door, scruffy in his mismatched, mostly black uniform. "Ain't you Martha's girl?"

"Yeah," Sooz said.

"Well, she don't want you coming in here."

And there it was: the weariness of working for Ma and the

hopelessness of Short Stay, crystallized and perfectly clear for the first time. "I ain't with Ma no more."

"It's all right," Lilith said. "She's with me." She smiled, generating an electric thrill that reminded Sooz of how the woman had handled Billy, though this one's response was completely different.

The hive cop lost about ten years of composure and his menace melted away into a shy grin. "Well, I guess that's okay, then." He stood aside from the door. "Pops with you too?"

"Who are you calling Pops?" Billy demanded. "Course I'm with them. Double date, this is. Old Billy's good enough for two."

Sooz followed Lilith inside. A hammering of feet came from above, keeping time with a monotonous drumbeat that shook the entire structure. Instinctively, she hunched herself against impending collapse, remembering Strummer's stories of sagging dance floors and how it was supposed to be safer upstairs.

Three doorways extended darkly mysterious invitations further into the pub, which Sooz could now see was a maze of bars, saloons and snugs: compartments piled higgledy-piggledy without layout or logic. Loops of light-emitting polymer dangled from threshold to threshold, stapled to the ceilings and straining against undervoltage. Their illumination was dim, pulsing, multicolored. The cheery darkness delighted Sooz and made her wish she'd broken Ma's prohibition long before.

"Come on," Old Billy said. "The folks we need will be in the Fogy bar."

Which turned out to be a little alcove just off the main club area. The strands of polymer were brighter here, as if power was being routed to where it would do most good. Sooz followed Billy and Lilith around the edge of the dance floor, through a miasma of bottled fragrance that couldn't quite mask the earthy scent of so many tight-packed bodies, all overlaid with an aromatic beckoning of herbal smoke.

"Don't they ever go home?" she shouted.

Billy grinned. "Night people. This is their fun time, before bed."

It got quieter once they reached the Fogy bar, although the room was open to the dance floor and set back only a little way. Some kind of noise canceling technology, Sooz decided. She decided to ask Strummer about it, as soon as she got the chance.

Billy sidled over to a corner table where a man in a shiny suit sat, smoking and drinking and ogling female flesh. "Jess," Billy said. "Brought you some customers, maybe."

The man tore himself away from his floorshow and turned around, sourly at first but his expression soon brightened as he got a good look at Lilith and Sooz. "Well. Ladies. This is an unexpected pleasure." He made an expansive gesture, wafting stale tobacco smoke as he offered two vacant seats. "Won't you join me? White wine? Yes, of course."

"Not for me," Lilith said.

"But I insist. White wine for the ladies, William. On my tab. And a little something for yourself, of course."

While they waited for Billy to return, Lilith handled the introductions and entertained Jess with small talk. Sooz wondered how long it would be before they got down to business. She didn't want to leave Lilith to make a deal alone, but she was also desperate to slip away and lose herself on the dance floor. Telling herself to be patient, she leaned back and swallowed some of the wine that Billy finally brought her, pretending she was used to this sort of thing.

Before long, she was feeling tipsy. It was all right, she decided. Lilith was a grown-up; she'd be able to take care of things if Sooz got too fuddled. Her experience with alcohol was limited to a couple of mouthfuls of Strummer's home brew: one to find out what it tasted like, a second to avoid hurting his feelings because she hadn't been able to keep from grimacing the first time.

"So, what can I do for you charming ladies?" Jess asked at last.

Lilith gave another of her manbusting smiles. "We were hoping you might be able to help us with some new tags and plates. For a vehicle."

"Picked up a hot one, have we, eh? Eh?" The man nudged Billy in the ribs, chuckling. "I'll say we have."

Billy smirked but said nothing.

Jess fished in his jacket pocket for a skinny cigar, then lit it. "What are you offering in return?"

Lilith looked at Sooz expectantly, making her wish she hadn't drunk the wine so quickly. It looked like she was going to have to handle things after all. "We ain't got a lot of glitter."

"Financially embarrassed, are we?" Jess smiled and leaned closer. His breath smelled of ashtrays and sour beer. He'll be drooling on me next, Sooz thought, edging away.

"That doesn't have to be a problem," he continued. "Barter's fine, if you ladies are open to that."

"That's what we figured," Sooz said cautiously.

"Good." Jess let his eyes roll over her body, then Lilith's. He took a puff of his cigar. "Buy one, get one free. How about it?" He put the cheroot down and took a swallow of beer, then wiped his mouth on the back of his hand.

"We don't need two sets, do we?" Lilith glanced at Sooz, her voice doubtful.

"No," Sooz said.

Jess guffawed. "That's not what I meant."

Sooz was starting to feel uncomfortable. "We got some shard," she blurted.

"Wonderful," Jess said. "That will make the transaction more enjoyable for everyone concerned."

Lilith stood up. "Then we're agreed. Shall we shake hands on it?"

Jess rose, grinning, and offered his hand. Lilith took it.

"How much shard?" asked Lilith.

"Well, I was thinking more along the lines of—"

He paused in mid-sentence, his grin replaced by a look of doubt.

"How much shard?"

"Christ, you've got a strong grip. Will you—"

"How much shard?"

Jess's features twisted in pain. "Twenty grams. Give me twenty grams and let go of my hand, and you've got a deal." His words trailed into a high-pitched whimper, reminding Sooz of the urgent squeaks that Johnny made when Ma trapped him in some misdeed and yanked him up by the ear.

Lilith said, "It's been a pleasure doing business with you." She released the man's hand and smiled sweetly, as if nothing had happened.

Jess sat for a moment, massaging mashed fingers and looking at Lilith suspiciously. "Likewise, I'm sure."

"I'm going to stay here and enjoy the rest of my wine, and some more of your company. Perhaps William could fetch the parts?"

Jess nodded and tossed Billy a key. The old man slipped away. Lilith fell silent and Jess sulked. Sooz slumped uncomfortably, trying to think of something to say and wishing Billy would return so they could get this finished.

He did return, eventually. He was carrying a pair of license plates wrapped in clear plastic, and a box marked 'Transponder Activated Geopositioning System - Bonded Goods - NOT FOR RESALE' and sealed with official-looking yellow tape.

Sooz nodded at Lilith. "Each wrap is one gram."

She watched the woman's flawless hands counting out twenty packets of shard.

As the pile on the table grew, Jess poked it disdainfully. "This had better be pure."

"The tags had better be good," countered Lilith.

"You can see the carton's never been opened. How about your stuff?"

"Take a look at the crystals," Sooz said. "It's quality."

He picked up one of the packets and held it up to a coil of glowing polymer. The light splintered and danced as if he held a clutch of fire agates like Sooz remembered from Billy's cabin, pictured in one of the oversized hardcovers she'd never been able to afford. After a couple of seconds, Jess became more cheerful. "Looks okay," he said grudgingly. "But I should try one, really."

Lilith tossed an extra wrap on the table. "Here."

"On the house, eh?" Jess smiled ruefully as he took the packet. "Better not, until you ladies are gone. Unless you've changed your minds about—"

"We haven't changed our minds," Lilith said.

"Fine, fine," Jess said hastily. "No problem at all."

The club was thinning out as dancers — in ones and twos and occasionally threes — made their bleary way to bed. Regretfully, Sooz postponed the idea of joining in the fun and turned her attention to the job at hand. "I don't know nothing about machines. You gonna fix up the Scrambler yourself?"

"I plan to try," Lilith said.

"I always get Strummer to help with stuff like that. He's my friend."

"Then if I get stuck, maybe you can go and find him."

Sooz nodded. Something told her that Lilith would manage just fine, with this and most other things, but she still wanted to help. "You got to do it just right. One of our neighbors, he messed with his tags and his truck wouldn't run no more."

"What did he do?"

"Put it up on blocks and flogged the wheels, seeing as they weren't doing him no good. He still lives in it, just can't go nowhere no more."

"Thanks for the warning," Lilith said. "We wouldn't want to hurt Lee's Scrambler."

Sooz fell silent. If Lee was in the police station, he had more important things to worry about than the state of his car. She had seen what happened to people who went there, when they came back after a night in the cells. "Do you reckon your boyfriend's okay?" she asked, fishing for a little extra information.

"I hope so," Lilith said, providing it.

Sooz grinned, satisfied. "Me too. But just in case he ain't, I reckon we'd better not take too long fitting these tags."

10

Xia Lin's world was dark and her mind floated in an unfamiliar sea. Gentle hands urged her to leave the bed behind, but not the dreams. She felt the hospital gown being removed, to be replaced by the familiar nothingness of the sensorsuit. Blind and essentially naked, she was taken through an echoing space and into a muffled warmth that was ripe with human smells.

Her warders settled her into a couch, and there was a chattering of keys and the faint click of cables being connected. A latex-scented hand cradled the back of her neck, and she sensed its mate approaching the void where her left eye had once been.

A woman's voice said, "Welcome to Back Office," and then someone jammed a connector into Xia Lin's head. There was a moment of vertigo and a shock of cold inside her mind. She shuddered at the hissing bite of hoarfrost in virgin sockets and held perfectly, exquisitely still when the freezing needles punctured the membrane of her prison, flooding her brain with dreams.

Sense and vision returned. Reality was built from countless scan lines: a simulation of an antique TV set, accurate down to the way the picture jittered and rolled.

"Sorry about the horizontal sync." The voice was female, nasal, blanketed with static. "I'll just lock that down for you."

The video drifted and then stabilized. Xia Lin looked up at where her attendant seemed to be. The image flickered as she moved, but it didn't change.

She was bending under an open car hood, working on the vehicle's electromechanical guts. Vertigo hit her again and she clutched the sides of the couch to keep herself from falling off. At the same time, she slotted a crescent wrench over a bolt head and started to ease it loose, humming quietly as she worked.

An advisory interrupt from a neighboring cell: "Don't fight it. Ride it. Surf the data stream."

"Who are you?" she asked.

The neighbor was already withdrawing. "Who knows? Why would anyone care? This node returns to the flow."

A new subsystem came online. "Mapping," it announced. "Channel open for video and audio. Geographic interpretation modules are loaded and running."

"Acknowledged." She started firing packets of video data down the new connection.

"Your signal is inappropriate for processing. Location data required. Please try again later." The line went dead.

Then someone else arrived, ghostly and overlaid on her vision: a big man with glowing red eyes. She had the sense that he'd been important to her once, though she couldn't remember who he was.

"Welcome, Xia Lin, to Back Office."

She reached into her memory and discovered a blank space where the name used to be. "Who is Xia Lin?"

"You are. Don't slip into the flow. We need you to remain human for a while."

Signals pulsed and voices whispered: mysterious, enthralling. "I have to go now," she said.

His words became fainter. Perhaps he'd turned away from her. "The concentration is too high. We're losing her. Reduce the dosage." Then he was fully present again. "Xia Lin. Are you still there? Tell me what you see."

"I am repairing a car," she said.

"Good. Route your visuals to Mapping. I need to know where you are."

The part of her that had to do with error reporting answered mechanically: "Signal inappropriate for processing. Location data required."

"Tell me what you see."

"Vehicle motor compartment." As she spoke, she was

requesting further data from a neighboring node. The information started to arrive and she streamed it back to her user. "Provisional identification: late model Scrambler. Accessing manufacturer's technical specifications; please stand by for further information..."

"No. Xia Lin, don't do that. I want you to stay with me." His voice became faint again. "Haven't you got her brain chemistry balanced yet?"

"Still working on it, sir."

"Can you patch her visuals through to a holoscreen? Or give me a direct feed?"

"It'll take time, Mr. Stranger, sir."

"Then you'd better get on with it."

"Yes, sir."

"Xia Lin?"

That meant her, she remembered. "Yes?"

"Contact Mapping again as soon as anything changes. I'm on my way to the target's cellular zone. We can triangulate its approximate location but we still need you to give us a visual fix. Do you understand?"

"Confirmed," Xia Lin said. "Your instructions have been queued for processing."

"Someone just switched the target cellphone on," said a distant voice, somewhere above and outside.

"What zone is it in?" asked Red Eyes.

"It's close to the doll."

"Then I have them both." Red Eyes receded into silence.

She watched herself reaching into the workings of the car for a while. Her hands seemed inexpert, often hesitating over the choice of tools or returning to undo some task that had seemed complete. She queried Back Office's car maintenance databases and it became clear that the work was proceeding by analysis and deduction, making her ache to intervene and do the job properly, but she could neither abandon the worker nor take control of the work.

She scanned for a System Information node and waited for

it to come online. "What is my status?"

"You are processing the data stream from an Artemis 9300 doll. Primary task: acquisition of location data. Remain vigilant."

"The remote unit is making elementary errors. What is my control status?"

"Control status invalid. Your interface is inbound only. Remain vigilant."

The status node signed off and she was alone with the doll again.

One of the hands came up and brushed hair from eyes she no longer had, and then her viewpoint swung up from the motor compartment. Now, she was surrounded by concrete, partitioned into bays and pierced with narrow, horizontal windows. She opened a new connection to Mapping and started transmitting the new video stream.

"Parking garage," Mapping said. "Target zone contains three possible matches. Triangulation in progress. Forwarding proposed elimination route now."

Instantly, Red Eyes was back. "Excellent. I'm on my way. Keep refining your location model and keep me posted."

Look outside, she urged her alter ego. Concrete and strip lights are not enough. You must send me clues from outside, so that Red Eyes can find you.

11

Back outside Billy's rig, Sooz watched Lilith fetch the Scrambler's toolkit and start work on the plates.

"Need a hand?" she asked.

"I'll let you know," Lilith said.

Sooz's belly felt unusually empty, making her doubt the wisdom of starting the day with wine instead of porridge. A violent rumble took her by surprise. She tensed her stomach muscles against it, hoping Lilith hadn't noticed.

"You missed breakfast, didn't you?"

So much for that. "Yeah."

"See what you can find in the Scrambler, if you like."

"Thanks," Sooz said, thinking about everything that Strummer had told her about soil fertility and recycled poop. Then again, there were the rolls and soda that Lee had brought to dinner; those had tasted fine.

Sooz could hardly believe that meal had only been a couple of days ago.

She climbed into the back of the vehicle and figured out how to get some bread. When she asked for butter, the machine dispensed a tub of yellow glop with the texture and aroma of pork fat. Sooz tipped the stuff into the recycling chute, wondering how she could have phrased her request differently, then munched an unbuttered crust as she looked around the cabin.

The green satchel was still on the concrete outside, under Lilith's watchful eye and out of Sooz's reach, but there were plenty of other things to check out. Delving into a cubbyhole, she found a second toolkit, smarter looking than the one Lilith was using, and so pristine that Sooz thought it must have come with the Scrambler, too. She decided to open it, telling herself that

Lilith might need one of the tools. Inside was a neat array of instruments that might have appealed to someone who couldn't decide between a career in surgery or watchmaking, but which even Sooz could tell would be of no use when working on a car. She refastened the lid and put the toolkit back in its place.

Having started investigating, it seemed natural to continue. There was a cellphone next to the toolkit. She picked it up and flipped it on.

You have 114 new messages, said the phone.

Someone had to be trying to get in touch with Lee. Sooz left the handset switched on and dropped it into the side pocket of her combat pants, so she'd be able to take the next call personally.

And, if she never hooked up with Lee again, the phone would bring her a few euros.

The next thing she found was a holdall with a broken zipper, stuffed to overflowing with clothes and gadgets.

Sooz checked what was happening outside. Lilith was working on the motor compartment, screened by the raised hood. Apart from that, the parking level seemed deserted. She studied the bag again. A protruding corner looked as if it might be a book. Sooz tugged it loose, trying not to disturb the rest of the contents. Something snagged on a strap, and a cylindrical object fell out with a crash and rumbled across the floor.

Sooz froze, waiting for Lilith to come and ask what was going on. She was tempted to put everything back as she'd found it, but nothing happened and the rectangular thing still looked interesting, though now she could see it was a box of some kind and not a book at all.

She picked up the cylinder, meaning to push it back inside the bag. There was writing on it — both in the ideograms of Han script, which she couldn't read, and English, which she could.

'Mind Archive Model C5000. Data retention: 50 years. No user-serviceable parts inside. Warranty void if removed.'

A hinged cover at one end promised access to the interior. That couldn't affect the warranty, she decided; it was obviously designed to be opened. She poked at the catch with a fingernail, then stifled a scream as the lid sprang off.

A mass of fluttering tentacles surged out, as light and as gray as the spider webs that clustered around Short Stay's refuse piles. The threads writhed towards her wrist, clawing stickily as if her fingers were fat maggots to be captured and consumed. Sooz jerked her hand away in disgust, counting heartbeats while the tendrils hunted blindly and then withdrew.

Hurriedly, she snapped the cylinder closed and crammed it back into the bag, hiding it under a bundle of Lee's shirts. The book-shaped case was still on the floor. She considered it for a moment, wondering whether to risk another unpleasant surprise.

It really might be better just to put everything back as she'd found it…

In the end, her curiosity got the better of her. The Scrambler was full of magical things: the glittering, mysterious toolkit; the food processor, which she was sure would deliver incomparable feasts if only she could work out how to use it properly; and even the cylinder had been fascinating in its way: *Ancestral Mind Archive.* Did the tube really contain the memories of Lee's parents? He was old, but not ancient. His grandparents, perhaps? Whatever, Sooz decided it was weird and gross but also kind of cool, to be carrying something like that around in your luggage.

Without really thinking about it, she'd picked up the rectangular case and her fingers were prying it open. This was more familiar: she had seen enough handecks in advertisements and shop windows to make her ache for one of her own.

A single 'deck could contain all the books ever written, in an insignificant fraction of its storage space. Sooz had read that in a magazine printout, one that Strummer had scavenged for her from Long Stay trash. She tugged this one out of its case and flipped it open. It seemed to be a recent model, without so much as a scratch on the plastic casing. As well as a screen there was a cordless headset: a pair of dark glasses with earpieces attached. An ON button winked at her from the top of the machine, inviting her finger. She slipped the headset on and activated the 'deck, and then she wasn't in Short Stay any more.

A ghostly image of the 'deck floated in front of her, with superimposed control arrows and other symbols that she didn't understand. Apart from that, she seemed to be looking through a perfectly round doorway into a sunlit courtyard that was full of buzzing insects and pale, odorless blossom.

The mysterious symbols looked like they were meant to be touched. Sooz had watched people using these things before, had seen them making mystical passes over 'decks that they couldn't possibly see from behind their opaque visors, so she knew roughly what to do. She stroked the arrow that pointed ahead, and then invisible feet were crunching through the gravel as her viewpoint drifted forward, through the portal and into the garden.

Sooz moved around some shrubbery and a fishpond came into view, surrounded by a low stone wall. A large golden carp stirred in the depths and flicked itself towards the far side of the pool. A girl of perhaps twenty sat cross-legged on the wall, trailing one hand in the water. She looked up with improbably large eyes and smiled as Sooz approached, as if she'd been waiting for her.

"Welcome," the young woman said. "I've been wondering when someone new would arrive."

Sooz stuck out her hand and inadvertently sent herself scooting forwards, so that she had to backpedal noisily to avoid running into the pool. She came to a halt just in front of the girl, doing her best to pretend she'd been in control the whole time. "What's this place, then?"

The girl tossed her head, flicking a wave of dark hair away from sculpted cheeks. In her way, she was as striking looking as Lilith. "Introductions first, please."

"Yeah, sorry. I'm Sooz."

"You can call me Miriam," said the girl, brushing Sooz's hand with fingers that couldn't be felt. "To answer your question, this is the owner's memory palace."

"Do you live in here?"

Miriam chuckled. "I'm not really alive. I'm a software construct. One of my functions is to maintain the user's schedule and diary, though unfortunately Lee isn't organized enough to keep detailed records."

"You mean a diary like Pepys used to keep?"

"I don't recognize the term," Miriam said. "I'm only a construct, you see. Excuse me." She shimmered and then re-solidified, so that Sooz could see the house through her for a moment. "Ah, Samuel Pepys. Yes. Very much like that."

What did she just do, and how? Sooz wondered, but all she asked was, "What's inside the house?"

"It's a memory palace. A representation of the place where Lee grew up, before his family lost everything in the troubles."

"A memory palace? That must be a bit like a diary as well, then."

Miriam smiled. "Indeed, that's one way of looking at it. Part of me has been busy archiving his family history. It's all inside the house now, in the library."

"There's a library? I don't reckon I'd be allowed in there, would I?"

"Of course you would."

"But ain't it personal? You know, family stuff?"

"Some of it's private, but the main data stacks aren't password protected." Miriam studied Sooz intently, as if committing something to memory. "A small 'deck like this doesn't receive many guests."

Miriam unfolded her long limbs with a grace that made it clear she wasn't real, and rose to her feet. "Come with me, please."

The library was gorgeous. Row upon row of books, and books such as Sooz had never seen before: bound in leather instead of cardboard, and when she took one down she saw that the pages were stitched in neat bundles instead of falling away from brittle, glue-cracked spines.

Reverently, Sooz replaced the book. "How come one family got so much history? Ma never even told me who my Dad is."

"There's much more than just family history here," Miriam

replied. "This is Lee's ancestral library."

"It's ... fantastic."

"It's dead. Nothing has been added for years, apart from a few technical journals." Miriam paused. "And even with those, Lee's hopeless at renewing his subscriptions. I don't suppose you'd consider ... but no."

"Consider what?" Sooz was almost sure she was being manipulated somehow, but she was too curious to resist.

"Starting a diary."

"Me? Write a diary?"

Miriam took a gleaming volume from a nearby shelf. *The Diary of Samuel Pepys: 1665,* according to the spine. "Everyone has to start somewhere. Even Pepys had to."

"But won't Lee mind me using up his stuff?"

"Lee hasn't been taking much interest in this place recently, and no interest at all in interacting with a humble software construct." Miriam paused, her expression pensive. "I suppose he's too busy enjoying himself."

"I don't know that you could call it enjoyment," Sooz said. "Lee's off somewhere, in trouble with the cops. I think Lilith's looking to rescue him."

"How adventurous of her," Miriam said.

"Well, she ain't just gonna leave him, is she? I mean, she's his girlfriend and all."

"His girlfriend? I didn't know that." Miriam glanced at Sooz. "I'm sorry, it's just that it gets tedious in here, with no news from outside." She sighed. "Libraries and diaries are my only solace. Are you going to take up my offer?"

"You mean to start a diary? Why me?"

"It's an important part of my function," Miriam said. "Lee has no interest in documenting his life, or even visiting me. And you're the only other human being who's ever been here."

Sooz felt sorry for the girl, and excited by the idea of having her own diary bound in leather and lettered in gold like the volume Miriam held. "Okay," she heard herself say. "Where do we start?"

Miriam smiled. "That's easy. Just tell me everything that's been happening to you."

"It sounds like you're having fun."

Sooz started guiltily at the sound of Lilith's voice, and tore the headset off. There was a moment of dizziness as the library vanished and she was back in the Scrambler. "Sorry. I didn't mean no harm."

"And you've done none, as far as I can see," Lilith said.

Sooz quickly put the visor back in the case, along with the 'deck. "I hope Lee won't be mad at me. I never had a go on one of these before."

"He's probably got other things on his mind at the moment."

Sooz wedged the 'deck into the cubbyhole along with the strange toolkit, figuring that it'd be more secure there than in the holdall. "You gonna help him? Bail him out?"

"That's my plan, if I can find the place they took him," Lilith said. "You know the way, don't you? I'd be happy to have you ride with me."

Sooz was quiet for a moment, thinking that this was it: the day she'd anticipated for so long. Now that it was here, sadness welled up inside, threatening to drown the excitement she felt to be leaving Short Stay.

At least she wasn't crying. "I got to tell Ma I'm going, and say bye to the kids."

"Go ahead. We can't leave yet, anyway. I need to get cleaned up and put the tools away."

"See you back here, then," Sooz said, and headed back to where her family lived.

Ma was scouring out the porridge pot — a job that Sooz would have done, in the normal way of things. Johnny and Daz and Em and Stevie were up on the truck bed, peering over the side with round eyes and mouths that were silent for once. Sooz fingered the cellphone through the fabric of her side pocket, and went into the parking bay that had been her home.

"You come back, girl?" Ma asked, without much hope.

"I came to say goodbye," Sooz said.

"What I reckoned." Ma set the dirty pan aside, and took a bundle from the back of the pickup. "I packed your stuff for you. Figured you'd want to get going right away."

She handed over the plastic bag. Sooz felt the softness of clothes and the hardness of books inside. Tears pricked at the back of her eyes. "Thanks, Ma."

"Reckon you'll do okay. Come back to visit with us, when you can."

"Yeah," Sooz said.

"I packed some food in there, too. And them pictures of the kids, 'case you get homesick."

The first tear trickled down her cheek. Sooz wiped it away angrily. "You should keep the pictures, Ma."

Ma's smile couldn't hide her sadness. "You take 'em. After all, I get to keep the kids, don't I?"

"But we only got one set."

"And I want you to have it, girl. You'll bring 'em back, all right."

"Yeah," Sooz said. "I'll be back, soon as I get myself sorted with a job and stuff."

She went to the pickup truck and kissed her brothers and sister goodbye, and then she hugged Ma and fled towards the stairwell that would take her up to Strummer.

The hive cops caught her on the second landing, before she was even half way up to the roof level.

"What the hell are you doing?" Sooz demanded, trying to twist free.

"The Man wants to see you," the taller one said. "You'd best come quietly, Sooz."

"What's he want with me?"

"He'll most likely tell you himself, if you behave."

Sooz stopped struggling. "I ain't got time for this. I'm supposed to meet someone."

"You're supposed to meet the Man," said the short one.

They made her walk between them, down the stairs to ground level and back into the pub.

This time, it didn't seem so inviting.

There was a spiral staircase at the back of the building, made of giant reels that had been sliced and bolted together, one on top of the other. As she climbed ahead of the hive cops, she wondered what could possibly be delivered on such spools. Then her eye caught the taut bundles of cable that wormed their way up alongside the handrail, and she had the answer.

Someone upstairs had to be using a lot of data.

Before she had time to consider the implications of that, she emerged into a room that she thought must take up half of the pub's top level, and into the presence of someone who could only be the Man.

The space was full of screens — a glowing cluster that surrounded the Man, and a long row of displays against one wall, silently tended by two technicians. More loops of cabling hung overhead, haphazardly stapled to ceiling joists, and there were doors leading in all directions.

This had to be the hive's command post, Sooz decided, where the Man squatted like a malevolent spider at the center of his cabled web, overseeing everything that happened in his domain. Sooz glanced at his surveillance bank, imagining herself scurrying from one screen to another like a little ant. The thought made her distinctly uncomfortable.

The Man even looked spider like; spindly-limbed and desiccated, older than anyone Sooz had ever seen. Older even than Billy, though she detected none of Billy's muddled madness in his eyes.

"Sooz. How delightful you look, and how nice of you to find the time to visit your paterfamilias, even though he's been neglecting you most terribly."

Sooz had been ready to draw herself up and demand explanations, but something about him made her change her mind, and all she said was, "Pleased to meet you."

He waved her to a chair opposite him. The two hive cops

edged into a corner, giving their leader privacy.

Sooz sat down and gave a little jiggle, swiveling her seat towards one of the monitors. "You can see everything from here, then," she said, making conversation.

"Indeed I can. I'd know immediately, for example, if an unlicensed dealer started working my premises." The Man took a wrap out of his shirt pocket: one of Lilith's. "I have to commend you on the quality of your merchandise, if not on your activities. Who is your partner?"

"Just someone I met."

"Does this someone have a name?"

Sooz hesitated, but there was no point trying to hide anything from someone who had so many cameras and screens. "Lilith. She's called Lilith."

"Thank you. We'll deal with her in due course, but I wanted to have a chat with you first."

"Why?" Sooz asked. "What you gonna do?"

"Going to do. It's 'what are you going to do'."

"What I said."

The Man sighed and stretched in his chair; Sooz heard his joints cracking. He glanced at one of the screens. She followed his gaze. A black limousine had just pulled up outside the hive, and was waiting for the attendant to issue a ticket and raise the barrier.

He turned back to her. "What do you think I should do with you?"

"Dunno," Sooz said. "It's not like we really done anything wrong."

"Apart from poaching on my territory."

"Well, yeah." She tried to sound contrite. "The thing is, we didn't know it wasn't allowed. I'm very sorry if we done anything we wasn't supposed to."

The Man smiled. Around the room, feet shuffled, and someone coughed. "I accept your apology and I won't bear a grudge, as long as you make restitution."

"Restitution?"

"Just as I said. I'm going to offer you a job. I might even be able to find a place for your partner."

"What sort of job?" Sooz asked, suspiciously.

"Don't worry, it's nothing improper, no matter what you might have heard about my business." His fingers were tapping against the armrest of his chair. "Your aptitude seems to be for transit and negotiation. Not like your mother." He broke off and drifted for a moment before focusing on Sooz again. "Now that I see you up close, you do look remarkably like her. Tell me, how is she?"

"Ma's good," Sooz said automatically. Her curiosity overcame her. "What sort of arrangement has she got with you, anyway?"

"Your mother worked hard and earned my respect, Sooz."

One of the screens flickered and rolled, catching Sooz's eye. It switched to a different view, evidently from the hive attendant's booth. The driver of the black car was looking straight at the camera, gazing out from the monitor with eyes that triggered something in her memory, eyes that sparkled with crimson fire.

A shiver ran down Sooz's spine. "Ruby eyes," she whispered.

"You know him?"

"Someone told me about him. Said he was dangerous. I ought to go, now, please. I ought to warn Lilith."

"There's no need to go anywhere," said the Man. "We'll keep an eye on him, and your friend is waiting right outside." He snapped his fingers and nodded, and one of the hive cops opened a door and ushered Lilith into the room.

"Ruby eyes is here," blurted Sooz, rising from her chair. "I seen him downstairs just now, on the monitors."

"You mean Stranger?"

"Lee didn't tell me his name. He just said to watch out for him."

Lilith turned to the Man. "I assume you're in charge here?"

"Yes. Please, relax. Take a seat. Our visitor is under surveillance. He won't do you any harm."

The woman made no move to comply. "Two of the most

dangerous entities you will ever meet are currently on your premises. I'm one. Stranger is the other."

"I'm sure you flatter yourself, my dear."

"Boss?" said one of the technicians.

"Yes?"

"The network just went down. That means no more video until we fix it."

Sooz glanced nervously at the monitor bank. The screens showed nothing but snow. Lilith was looking at the displays, too. Sooz wished the pair of them could just leave.

"What about the backup systems?" asked the Man.

The technician turned to his colleague. "Dave, is your secondary link online yet?"

"Er, no," said the second tech. "That's strange." He leaned forward raptly, tracing with a finger the lines of gibberish that marched across his screen. "I wonder why it's doing that?"

Lilith met the Man's gaze and held it. Her voice became clipped and efficient. "It seems they have already captured your main battle systems. I presume you have alternative command and control channels?"

"Of course."

"Then I suggest you use them before you lose them. As for Sooz and myself, we leave now."

One of the flunkies stepped up and made to grab her arm. What happened next was too fast for Sooz to see, but Lilith ended up gripping his elbow instead. The hive cop whimpered as she forced him to his knees. Lilith ignored him, concentrating on the Man. "You are wasting my time." She released her grip, allowing her captive to fall to the floor. "And your combat assets. As I said, Sooz and I leave now."

The Man hesitated, his eyes flicking from his injured bodyguard to his hijacked data systems, and then nodded. "You're right. You must both get away from here. You'll keep her safe?"

"I'll do what I can," Lilith said.

The Man turned to the uninjured cop. "The hive is under

attack. Escort my guests back their vehicle and see them safely out of the building, then return here."

Before they left, he handed Sooz a flat package. "Alas, it seems I must withdraw my offer of employment. But take this. If anything happens to me, get it to a lawyer. It will be worth your while."

"Sure thing," Sooz said. She wanted to ask what it was and why he'd trust her with it, but the Man was already speaking urgently into a portable communicator that crackled and hissed in reply, and Lilith had her by the hand and was dragging her towards one of the doors.

12

"Hello?" buzzed the voice from Lee's cellphone.

To his dismay, it sounded like a young female, and not the recorded kind. It wasn't Lilith, either; she'd have known better than to leave the handset switched on. "Who's that?"

"It's you what called me. Who are you?"

"I'm the person who pays the phone bill. And you'd be…?"

"Oh."

He waited for a few seconds. "Well?"

"Um, yeah, Lee. This is Sooz. You remember, from the parking hive?"

"I remember," Lee said. "Where did you—"

"We just escaped from the hive. We're coming to the police station, to bail you out."

He forced himself to take a few deep breaths before continuing. "How come you're answering my phone, Sooz?"

"I'm with Lilith."

"Well, that's one good thing. Can I speak to her?"

There was a pause. "Hello?"

"Lilith, this is Lee."

"Lee, I—"

"Be quiet and listen. The place where you got the sunglasses. Remember it?"

"Yes, it was—"

"Don't say the address. Just meet me there. There's stuff in the Scrambler, stuff that's important to me."

"Sure. When?"

"How soon can you get there?"

There was a pause. "The traffic's quite heavy. Half an hour, perhaps."

"I'll be waiting. And for God's sake, keep the cellphone

switched off and away from Sooz."

"Okay."

Lee replaced the handset and looked around. He was in a phone booth near the main entrance to Paddington Station. Someone would probably trace the number, but he planned to be long gone by then. He'd already pawned most of Fat Charlie's possessions, holding back only the law 'deck. It had been easy to blend with the other transients for long enough to grab a hot shower and a carton of synthetic glop. In one of the station's washrooms, he'd even found a way to launder his blood-spattered shirt using a hand basin and a hot air blower.

Feeling more satisfied in several ways, he started back towards the shop where he'd last seen Lilith.

Lee didn't expect that any eavesdropper would be able to figure out where the meeting place was, but to be on the safe side he went into a dusty antiquarian bookshop across the street and kept watch from between the stacks close to the window. When the Scrambler arrived he waited for a break in the traffic — and to see if there was going to be any more rough stuff. Then he left the shop and jogged across the asphalt.

Sooz let him in and then scooted to the center seat. As Lee settled himself, Lilith surveyed his damaged face and then gave a rueful shake of her head. Sooz was staring at him with wide eyes, too.

Lee grimaced and brushed his fingers over his cheeks, exploring stubble and bruises. He'd checked his reflection before showering, and again afterwards in the vain hope that soap and hot water would have eased away some of the evidence of his sudden encounter with the Scrambler's hood. Then he grinned, even though it hurt. It felt good to be on the move again, and good to see Lilith.

"In the future, perhaps you'd better leave the fighting to me," she said.

"Deal." He glanced at Sooz, wondering what the youngster was doing in his car. "If you'll leave the recruiting to me."

Lilith kept her eyes on her mirror. "Where to?"

"You okay driving this thing?"

"I had to learn."

"So I see. Is my stuff okay?"

Lilith jerked her head towards the rear of the vehicle. "Everything's just as you left it."

Which meant the mind archive was safe — the only thing he really cared about. Lee hid the relief he felt. "Thanks."

"So we head out of the city?" Lilith asked.

"Once we've taken Sooz back to her family."

Lilith flicked her indicator and pulled out smoothly into the traffic.

"I ain't going back," Sooz said.

"She's left home," Lilith said. "Anyway, Stranger was there when we left."

That was a shock. Lee scanned the street, almost expecting Stranger to pop up from between two parked cars. "He traced us to the parking hive?"

"No, he was looking for somewhere cheap to spend the night." Lilith's lips twisted into a half smile.

"Funny lady." Lee frowned, thinking of his handset. "They can track phones from cell to cell, you know. Once they've got a fix, they can triangulate the signal and get even closer. That's why we need to keep the thing switched off."

Sooz looked stricken. "I'm sorry. I didn't know. I thought you was probably gonna call."

"And so I did. But you can see the difficulty, why it's too dangerous for you to travel with us. Stranger found us, even without the phone. He's got cops looking for the car."

Lilith patted the dashboard. "Not for this car. We fitted new plates and tags. Sooz helped, and she was showing me the way to the station when you called. I'd probably still be stuck in the hive if it wasn't for her."

"Yeah, well." Lee didn't want to send the youngster back to a place she didn't want to be, but he also didn't want to drag her into danger. "Look, I'm grateful for your help, Sooz, but there's some rough people looking to tangle with us. We're not going to be able to take care of you."

"I ain't asking you to," Sooz said defiantly. "But it don't cost you nothing to let me ride along."

Lee sighed. "Okay. You can stay as long as you promise to be good, which means following orders — including Lilith's. As if your life depends on it."

"I ain't stupid. I know we got to work together."

"Anyway," Lilith said, "the phone's switched off now. It's in there." She patted the dashboard over the glove compartment, then returned her eyes to the road.

Lee started to relax. "Right. New tags, cellphone secured. There's no way he'll be able to track us now."

By the time they hit the freeway, Lee's stomach was rumbling. The synthetic goo he'd eaten might have been cheap and filling, but it didn't stick to the ribs like proper food. "Who else is hungry?" he asked.

"Me," Sooz said.

"Then we'll stop at the next service area."

Lilith accelerated past a truck and guided the Scrambler to the inside lane. "Tell me where to pull off."

"Not yet," Lee said. "There'll be a sign in plenty of time. I'll show you."

The truck stop they found loomed over the freeway, a bridging structure that was accessible to both the eastbound and westbound traffic. Lilith led them to a window table — one that was screened from the car park by a fake pot plant, but that would let them keep an eye on the Scrambler.

Lee was still working his way through his bacon and eggs when Lilith shrank behind the plastic foliage, staring down at the car park.

"There are two men outside, looking for us," she said.

"How do you know?"

"I'm trained to know. Don't panic, they can't see us through the plant."

"Have they found the Scrambler?"

"Yes. They're parked opposite it."

"Shit. What do we do?"

"We take our time," Lilith said. "Those guys aren't in a hurry. They'd prefer to deal with us down there than up here."

Lee peered through synthetic fronds. "I can't see anyone."

"Dark suits. Opaque visors. Near the black van."

"Got them. Shit, Lilith, one of the bastards is staring right at me."

"It looks like it." Her eyes scanned the ceiling tiles. "Perhaps they've tapped into ... but no. There's no surveillance in here. There's no way they can have spotted us."

"How are we going to get back to the Scrambler?" Sooz's voice was higher-pitched than usual. The poor kid had to be scared, Lee thought.

Lilith took her shoulder bag off the back of her chair and checked its contents. "Don't panic, I'll think of something."

Sooz craned her neck, staying low and leaning away from the window. "What else you got in there?"

Lilith tipped the bag forward and Lee saw the twinkle of gunmetal reflecting fluorescent light. "Where the hell did you get that?"

"I confiscated it off someone who didn't know how to handle it, just after I got these clothes."

"Right," Lee said. "As long as we're not panicking, I've been meaning to ask you about those, too."

Lilith hesitated. "I went shopping. I borrowed your credit chip."

Lee checked out the designer couture that she'd bought, a task he'd already performed several times, and one he'd enjoyed a lot more before he knew there were gunmen waiting outside. "I'm surprised the chip didn't melt."

"I don't understand. Did I get the wrong things?" A look of doubt came onto her face.

"I just meant that you look very nice," he amended hastily.

Lilith's expression cleared. "Thanks."

Sooz gaped at this by-play. "When are you two gonna quit yacking and figure out what to do? Is wossisname down there?"

"Stranger?" Lilith peered between the fronds. "No, these guys don't look like Partners to me. They're probably just associates from the local branch office."

Lee stopped worrying about his credit chip and focused on the latest problem. He was getting an unpleasant feeling in the pit of his stomach: one minute they'd gotten clear away on the open road, and now it seemed the bad guys had fingered them again without even breaking a sweat. Not to mention Stranger tracing them to the parking hive. "How the hell did they know we were here?"

Lilith thought for a moment. "Maybe they've put a general call out on Scramblers. We'll find out for sure when we interview whichever one survives."

"You sound very confident."

She glanced out of the window again. "If Stranger was down there, it'd be different. Luckily for us, he's not. Those guys are mainstream. There'll be no edge to them."

Sooz pushed her empty plate and coffee cup aside and looked at Lilith. "You ain't hungry, then?"

"I don't eat much."

"Well I reckon you ought to, if there's gonna be trouble."

Despite himself, Lee grinned. "An overfull stomach can slow you down, Sooz. Sometimes it's better to be lean and hungry."

Lilith stood up, hefting the green bag. "You two wait here. I'll deal with them."

"But—"

She was already moving away, towards the eastbound exit.

"She went the wrong way," Sooz said.

"I guess she'll sneak back across the freeway and surprise them while they're waiting for us to come out this side."

"She ain't gonna surprise them," Sooz said. "Look."

Lee followed the girl's pointing finger and his stomach executed a complex flip-flop maneuver, as if it was keen to try the lean and hungry approach he'd just recommended to Sooz.

The men outside were responding to Lilith's move as if they'd seen the whole thing on video. One of them hurried across the car park and took up position behind some shrubs, covering the slip road where Lilith would have to approach. The other kept his eyes on the door.

Lee took a hasty swallow of coffee, masking the sourness of incipient vomit. "They're watching us. Fuck knows how, but they know exactly what we're doing."

"I better go and warn her."

"No. It's too dangerous." He fished for the last of Fat Charlie's cash. "Hang on to this. And take care of these." He tossed her the keys to the Scrambler. "In case anything happens to me."

"I ain't got a driver's license," Sooz said.

Lee grimaced. "Let's hope I get the chance to teach you, sometime. Right now, I have to get down there before Lilith crosses back over."

He left her staring at the dirty plates and ketchup bottles, and headed for the car park.

Lee paused at the bottom of the stairs, the black knife already in his hand. If the opposition's surveillance was as good as it seemed, the watcher in the parking lot would know that Lee was about to come out. Forewarned or not, the man was bound to be armed. Lee considered how inauspicious it would be, crossing meters of bare asphalt under the gaze of a hoodlum with a smart weapon, and decided to try something else.

He cut a hole in the plastic wall paneling and emerged in the crook of the stairwell, screened from view. A row of cars was parked along the side of the building. Lee ducked behind them and worked his way along the perimeter, expecting the *thunk* of a bullet slamming into the wall behind him — or into him — at any instant.

Nothing happened.

Keeping the vehicles between himself and the waiting man, Lee crept past license plates until he found what he was looking for.

It was an antique pickup truck, ancient enough to be made of unrecycled metal and to run on fossil fuel. Old planet fucker, Lee thought. They don't make them like this any more. Steeling himself against the guilt of desecration, he sliced his way through the door and climbed behind the wheel, hoping he'd be able to get the thing started the way he'd seen it done on a hundred Sunday afternoons – mostly in two dimensions, occasionally in black and white.

The steering lock was engaged, but the plastic key housing yielded to the blade. The cylinder popped out easily, exposing the interlock. Lee pushed it aside and the wheel swung free. A snarl of colored cables dangled out of the hole.

Lee gazed at them, shaking his head in dismay. The movies had never been this complicated. He could have figured out all the possible permutations and tried them one by one, if only he had an hour or two.

But Lilith had to be in the car park on the other side by now. She'd need to wait for a gap in the traffic, but Lee knew he'd be lucky to have more than a few minutes before she crossed over.

He put the knife away and flicked the gearshift to neutral. Then he examined the bundle more closely. There were two red wires. Red for danger, Lee thought. It seemed appropriate for his situation, and red must surely indicate a battery connection, so he pinched the wires together with his right hand, trusting that the clammy glove that the knife had become would protect him from electric shock.

The dashboard lights came on.

Grasping the red insulation with his unprotected hand, he twisted the exposed copper strands together. The lights stayed on.

Red for danger, green for go. It seemed auspicious, so that was the next color he chose.

To Lee's considerable surprise, the engine caught with a meaty rumble.

He popped reverse gear and backed out of the parking space, then slammed it into first, twisted the wheel, and floored the gas.

The man in the suit was busy watching the restaurant exit and trying to hide something bulky under a too-sharp jacket. He paid the truck no attention.

Lee de-clutched and shifted into second, gunning the engine. The ruined door lurched open and then crashed against the cab as the rev counter leaped exuberantly towards red. The engine roared; the man glanced over his shoulder. His eyes were hidden behind the visor, but his body language betrayed a moment of indecision followed by all-out panic. He scuttled sideways.

Lee found third gear and eased the wheel over, keeping his target centered. The front wing of the pickup clipped the gunman's hip and sent him crunching into a parked car, with his machine pistol spinning in the opposite direction. Lee braked hard and backed up, checking the rearview mirror. The man was lying on his face, perfectly still.

So this was how it felt to win a fight.

Lee jumped out of the cab and retrieved the prone thug's machine pistol. The headset was still connected to it by a curly cable but the visor was cracked and lifeless. Lee cursed, because he could have really used a self-aiming weapon right now.

He set off for the car park entrance, praying that the gun would still work.

The second man was down on one knee, screened by foliage and peering through his own gunsight, his machine pistol held ready.

Lilith was jogging steadily up the slip road.

The man raised his weapon. Its barrel tracked Lilith with smooth precision, offering no hint that a fallible human was operating the device.

Lee pointed his own gun and pulled the trigger.

There was a discreet popping sound, but no recoil. Lilith wasn't there any more, a fact that left Lee's brain in a wheel spin, because he'd fired and not the enemy.

The man stood up, peering over the bushes. Lee swore at himself: he'd forgotten to check his safety catch. The silenced report had been from the other gun, and Lilith must have been hit. He flipped his safety to OFF and tried again.

This time, he felt the recoil. The man turned, raising his weapon. Lee imagined how he must look through the smart sight and wished he'd had time to configure his own machine pistol for fully automatic fire.

Not that he had a clue how he'd have gone about doing that.

He pulled his trigger again and the man spun sideways. Another more considered shot and the enemy was down.

Lee added another captured weapon to his growing armory and hurried over to where he'd last seen Lilith. She was lying on the grass verge. A long strip of skin and gel hung loosely from her head. The exposed metal of her skull was scored with brightness, as if freshly burnished.

"Are you okay?" he demanded.

There was no answer.

"Fuck. Fuck!"

He tried to drag her back to where the Scrambler was parked, but she was too heavy to move far, just as he'd known she would be. All he could do was put the gel and skin back in place, and arrange her dirty-blonde hair to cover the wound as best he could. Then he turned and ran back to the parking lot, craning his neck up to where he thought Sooz would be watching, and waving at her to come down.

By the time Lee remembered he didn't have the keys to the Scrambler, Sooz was trotting across the asphalt. He grabbed the keys and let himself in, then leaned across to open the passenger door.

"Where's Lilith?" Sooz asked as she climbed in.

Lee pulled out of the parking spot. "She's hurt. Can you help me get her in the back?"

"'Course I can."

He stopped at the top of the slip road and they climbed out. Lee lifted Lilith's shoulders, and Sooz took her feet.

"She been shot?"

"Yes."

"She gonna be okay?"

"I think so."

"Heavy, ain't she?"

"Yeah."

"She ain't bleeding, though. D'you reckon she needs a doctor?"

"I'll take a look at her as soon as I can." Lee maneuvered the inert doll onto the lower bunk, and covered her with a blanket. "Get back in front, Sooz. We have to go."

"Maybe I ought to stay back here, in case she comes round."

"No. I need you to sit with me up front. Lilith is better off resting."

"Okay," Sooz said.

By the time Lee got behind the wheel again, his whole body was trembling; he felt sick and chilled.

Sooz touched his arm, her eyes full of concern. "You okay to drive?"

"I'd better be," he said, and then clenched his stomach against a stabbing spasm that left him unsure of whether he wanted to empty his guts or simply curl up into a fetal position.

"I reckon you ought to rest for a bit. Turn the heating up, maybe."

"It's not cold, is it?" he asked vaguely.

"No, but you look sort of rough. Like you got the shakes."

Lee started the motor and set the controls to blow warm air at his face. Framed in his wing mirror, someone was kneeling over the first man he'd hit. A knot of people had gathered round the damaged truck. A couple of them were already pointing at the Scrambler.

I really don't have time for this, Lee thought

He circled down the slip road and merged with the westbound traffic, unable to shake memories of the two bodies he'd left behind, or of how Lilith had risked her life crossing ten lanes of traffic, only to get shot in the head while he fumbled with his safety catch.

13

Back Office tore through the hive's primary defense network like rats through gossamer, but the defenders' small arms and personal communicators proved more resilient: Stranger spent more than 279 seconds pinned down by a pair of snipers, listening to Xia Lin's commentary on the fleeing doll. Around 279.4 seconds, Back Office cracked the last of the local encryption systems and then the fight was over before the humans even realized they were losing.

For Stranger, victory came too late: the target had escaped and was heading for the freeway while his badly placed mobile reserve scrambled to intercept.

"What happened?" he demanded.

"You have installed a non-standard component," Back Office replied. "The foreign node is disrupting the flow."

"Xia Lin's human mind is still required. Until she is ready to be submerged, you will compensate for her presence."

"Acknowledged. Estimated performance will be approximately 65 percent of standard."

"Route round her. Compensate."

"Acknowledged. Estimated performance will be—"

Stranger broke the connection. Back Office's intransigence was almost enough to remind him how it felt to be angry.

There might still be something to be gained, though. Xia Lin had watched through the doll's eyes as the Hive Elder sent his personal guard to assist its escape, together with one of his young females. That piqued Stranger's curiosity: a small detail, perhaps, but one on which great things might turn.

Which was why the old man was now awaiting Stranger's convenience in the hive's captured control room, his bony ankles and wrists straining against the inert tanglers that bound him to a steel and leather chair.

Stranger smiled at his newest client. "I hope we can keep this civilized. Why don't you start by telling me everything you know about the doll?"

"Which doll do you mean?"

"The one you helped to escape, of course."

The elder gave a tight-lipped grimace. "I remember a young woman, not a doll. Though I appreciate that ancient vernaculars sometimes come back into style."

"Stupidity doesn't suit you," Stranger said.

The man's rheumy eyes held no hint that he was aware of the completeness of his defeat. "If you ever reach my age, you might find your mind's not as clear as it used to be."

"I am your age." Stranger brushed an activation key against the client's left ankle. The tangler's strands twitched from gray to white as they woke up and began to tighten. The client's limb jerked against the chair leg.

"Don't fight it," Stranger advised, "unless you wish to lose your foot."

The man grunted with the effort of holding himself rigid. "I know what a tangler does."

"These samples are uniquely ferocious, tuned to my own specification. Once activated, they are quite merciless. If you move, they constrict quickly. If you remain still, they constrict slowly."

The man's brow was beaded with sweat. "Then I lose my foot no matter what I do. What kind of monster are you?"

Stranger smiled. "One with whom you would be well advised to co-operate. The tangler can come off before you foot does, if you tell me about your recent guests."

The man hesitated. When his words came, they sounded calculated, carefully weighed. "The girl was local. I never saw the woman before today."

"The doll." With his foot, Stranger nudged the man's ankle. The tangler squirmed and tightened.

The client replied through gritted teeth. "Very well, doll, if you insist. I still know nothing of her."

Stranger leaned forward and set off the tangler at the man's right wrist. "Then tell me about Sooz, instead."

The man gasped from the pain, or perhaps in surprise that Stranger knew the girl's name. "Sooz is just one of my girls. She was here to answer for breaking a hive rule."

Stranger glanced down. The man's skin had failed along the line of his ankle restraint; blood was welling from the wound and trickling into his shoe. "You still have time to save your foot," he said conversationally. "Why were you so eager for her to escape? What was in the package you gave her?"

The old man shook his head and half-grimaced, half-grinned. "You're not the first person who's tortured me." His words grated in his throat. "In fact, quite a few have tried their luck. They're all permanently dead."

Stranger chuckled, studying the fragile frame bound to the chair. "I can see why you don't place much value on this ancient body. You must be looking forward to coming back in a younger one."

"I wouldn't expect a man like you to understand."

"Understand what?"

"The perspective one gains by following a life to its culmination, from time to time."

Stranger moved around the chair, examining his prisoner from both sides. "Yes. I can see that such a perspective would be most edifying."

The client merely grunted, so Stranger continued. "If you're counting on regrowth, you should be aware that my people can have your clinical records wiped before you can say 'life insurance'. Now, you were about to tell me about the package."

"It was something that puts me beyond your reach." The old man blinked and jerked his head, shaking beads of sweat away from his eyes. Then he managed to smile. "Now, be a good chap and finish me off, won't you?"

This interview was proving to be sterile, and Stranger's attention was required elsewhere. He was irked, on some level that he didn't quite understand, by the idea of providing an easy death for so uncooperative a client, so he simply activated the remaining tanglers and returned to his vehicle.

"You cannot simply have lost the signal."

"Our operative was in place. He fired at the target. We believe he hit it."

"You believe? It's your job to know."

"Back Office has insufficient data resources to establish the truth or otherwise of the designated statement."

Something was wrong. Stranger had never experienced such difficulties before. He'd never left a partially converted human connected to the grid for so long, either. He had no choice in the matter, though: as something that was still in some sense a woman, Xia Lin remained linked to the sensorsuit and could respond to its input. Once her humanity was gone, the doll's datafeed would become meaningless.

A suspicion struck him. "Has some idiot submerged Xia Lin? Is that why the signal is lost?"

"The designated component is still not partaking of the flow. Recommendation: integrate the foreign node immediately. It is imperative that Back Office returns to peak operating efficiency as soon as possible."

"No. We must maintain Xia Lin's status and re-establish our link to the doll. What about the operatives?"

"One was incapacitated by a vehicle strike—"

"He's alive? Conscious?"

"Affirmative. The second unit suffered fatal damage coincident with an unscheduled activation of the first operative's weapon. Both weapons are presumed in enemy hands. They are scheduled for deactivation at your command."

"Leave them switched on, for now," Stranger said. "It will be best if they fail at the moment that makes the most impact."

"Acknowledged."

Stranger fit a theory to the facts. "So, we have the 9300

running down the first man, grabbing his gun, then shooting the other?"

"Negative. Telemetry indicates that the second operative survived the doll by one point eight seconds."

For the first time he could remember, Stranger snarled. "The doll may not have died. Unfounded assumptions lead to erroneous conclusions."

Back Office went quiet. Stranger could almost hear the neurons pulsing defiant messages across brain-substrate interfaces. "Unable to parse your input," it said finally, "due to unexplained data flow blockage."

His patience was exhausted. "Dismissed. Xia Lin?"

"Yes?"

"What have you seen?"

"I have met with Lee."

"And you shall meet him again, if you keep faith with me. What else have you seen?"

"I have crossed a great road and I have died," she replied.

"What was the manner of your death?"

"I cannot say."

There was no more to be gained here. "Remain vigilant. Search for the signal. Stay clear of the data flow."

"Confirmed," said Xia Lin. "Your instructions have been queued for processing."

Stranger disconnected himself and took stock of his resources.

It was possible that the android had been destroyed. If so, his primary mission was complete: it only remained to interview the surviving operative, kill or capture the doll's companions, and secure any copies of its mind that might remain.

It was also possible that the doll had simply been damaged. Stranger's new contact at Zendyne had informed him that a 9300 unit would simply shut itself down in the event of severe trauma. Mr. Lee had repaired the doll once; there was no reason to suppose he wouldn't do so again.

In which case, there would be another direct confrontation, except this time he would not leave it to underlings. Stranger fingered his new eye, the one that had required replacement after his previous encounter with the 9300.

He'd rushed into that fight, stupidly assuming that he'd be dealing with Mr. Lee instead of a state-of-the-art assassination system. This time, it would be different. His new relationship with the doll's designers had delivered the tool he should have had all along. Stranger reached under his jacket and checked the android disrupter that nestled there, the one weapon that the renegade entity would never be able to counter.

The fugitives had headed west. The doll might wake up and start sending environment data to Xia Lin once more, or it might not.

Either way, it was time to follow and make an end.

14

After a few kilometers, Lee seemed to settle down and Sooz relaxed back into her seat.

She'd watched the whole thing from the restaurant, hiding behind the plastic plant: the truck barreling around the corner and crashing into the first thug; Lee jumping out and grabbing the gun, then racing across the car park to confront the second man.

Lilith must have crossed the freeway under the bridge and out of sight, but Sooz had seen the second gunman aiming his weapon and the flash as he'd fired. His shot had come a second too soon, because a heartbeat later and Lee would have had him.

Sooz was no stranger to violence. She'd witnessed her share of punch-ups in the hive. A few of the rougher residents had even settled things with knives, but there'd never been anything like this, men smashing and shooting each other with cars and guns. She stole a glance at Lee, concentrating on the road ahead. Half of her had been horrified to see him rise from the dinner table so casually in order to kill. The other half had admired his cool head and his determination to protect his girlfriend.

Not that he seemed too worried about Lilith now. She might be dead, for all he knew. Even if she was still alive, she might easily be dying. Sooz wasn't going to let that happen without speaking up. "We ought to get her to a hospital."

Lee glanced at her, then returned his eyes to the road. "There's no need for that. I've dealt with this sort of injury before."

"Doctor, then, are you?"

"No. But I have experience with Lilith's kind."

"What do you mean, her kind?"

"Um, her kind of case. You know, head injuries."

"You ain't gonna look for help? She might be dying."

"She's not dying," Lee said.

"You're cold, you are. Your own girlfriend and all." Sooz studied the dashboard computer. "I reckon this thing can take us to the nearest hospital, can't it?"

Lee ignored the question. "Who told you that Lilith's my girlfriend?"

"She did, stupid."

He reddened and checked his rearview mirror. "You have to believe me, Sooz. The best person to help her is me. And it won't do her any good if we get side-tracked and then someone else catches up with us."

"Yeah." A gleaming Mercedes drifted past in the outside lane. Sooz imagined faceless gunmen behind the mirrored windows, preparing to pump bullets into the Scrambler's cab. "Them people chasing you. What are they after, anyway?"

He jerked his head back, indicating the rear of the Scrambler. "Her."

"Why?"

"She hasn't told me. But it's not hard to guess. I think she's got some information that's supposed to be secret, and they want it back."

Sooz considered that for a while. "Once a secret's got loose, you can't never get it back. No matter what you do."

Lee chuckled. "You're not wrong. But it doesn't seem to stop people from trying."

Sooz decided to dig a bit deeper. "Lilith's a real looker, ain't she?"

"Yeah, she's beautiful."

"So, she was telling the truth about being your girlfriend, then?"

This time, Lee grinned instead of blushing. "It's complicated. I like her. I think she's good looking and smart, and I care about what happens to her. In the few days I've known her, I'd say we've been through enough to last most people for years."

Sooz nodded, her theory confirmed. "That's what I thought."

Ahead of them, the sun was setting. Sooz kept her visor

lowered until the brightness stopped flashing through the traffic ahead. Sunsets at home, observed from Strummer's roof garden, had been more static and less glorious than this.

With darkness came a sense of security: individual cars merged into a stream of anonymous headlights, persuading Sooz that the Scrambler would, too. Thoughts of gunmen in hot pursuit receded, replaced by the desire for something nourishing to eat and a safe place to stretch out and sleep.

"Funny thing," Sooz said. "I always used to be scared of the dark."

Lee looked across at her. "Me too, when I was a boy."

"Really?"

"Yeah."

She thought about it for a while. "I guess it's different in here, nice and warm with the doors locked."

"It always feels safer when you're moving." An illuminated exit sign loomed, then disappeared. "Unfortunately, we can't keep driving all night. We'll pull off here and look for somewhere to park up."

"You don't reckon they'll find us?"

"Not if we lose ourselves well enough."

Sooz listened to the indicator clicking as Lee eased across two lanes of traffic and onto the exit ramp.

"This new vehicle ID stuff," he said. "The tag and the plates. Where did they come from?"

"We traded with a geezer from the hive. Jess, his name was."

"It all came in a sealed box, right?"

"Yeah. It was all done up with official tape. Bonded goods, it said. Why?"

"I can't help wondering how they've been managing to track us."

Sooz hadn't considered the possibility that the replacement tags might not have been as brand new as they seemed. "Do you think Stranger might know where we are, right now?"

"I don't see how he could." Headlights flared from behind, and Lee sped up until it was clear the other vehicle wasn't tailing them. "But then I have no idea how his people traced us before, either. I hate to do it, but I think we should probably get rid of the car, as soon as Lilith's on her feet."

"That'd be a shame," Sooz said. Another sign flashed past, promising a railway station. "Maybe we could take a train instead."

"Yeah, if we actually knew where we were going. I guess I could trade the Scrambler for a different vehicle. Or maybe I should just dump it somewhere until everything's sorted."

Lee spent almost an hour finding his way away from the major roads and railway line and onto a network of country lanes. It was well after dark when he pulled onto a muddy track running between tree trunks. The moon was bright — brighter than Sooz had ever seen it in the city — but under the canopy of leaves there was a feeling of dark foreboding.

"Wouldn't want anyone to find us here in the middle of nowhere," she said quietly.

"I've been checking behind," Lee said. "No one's following."

"But what you said about them tracking the car..."

"We'll just have to risk it. We can't keep moving forever. I need to check on Lilith. Once she's recovered, she can watch while I sleep. Maybe she can even drive."

He pointed the Scrambler up the slope and sent it whining and crawling over mud and leaf mold. Sooz peered forward, wondering how he could see where he was going among all the trees. Every now and again, he twitched the wheel to avoid a looming trunk, and low branches would come out of the darkness and whip across the windshield. Once, there was a looseness in the ride as if the wheels were about to spin, but the Scrambler recovered and kept powering its way towards the brow of the hill until it emerged into a clearing.

Lee parked, then disappeared into the back.

Sooz went outside to look at the trees and foliage that screened them from the track, curious but also nervous, never straying beyond the dim beacon of the Scrambler's interior lights. Lee had been right: the dark was a lot scarier now that they weren't moving. There was a curious, earthy scent to the air, and the night was full of unfamiliar sounds. Sooz felt gooseflesh rising and hugged herself, half wishing she was back with her brothers and sister, safe and warm and tucked up in Ma's pickup.

Lee emerged from the Scrambler. "Lilith's okay, but she needs rest."

"Maybe she'd like some company?"

"She mustn't be disturbed until she's feeling better. She knows you're here, Sooz. She'll let you know if she needs anything."

"What are you gonna do?"

"I think it's time we did something about my criminal record." Lee hefted a squat metal box that dangled cables and connectors like the ripped off video units Sooz used to see hawked around the parking hive, except that this thing looked a lot more sophisticated.

"What is it?"

"A law 'deck. I could have sold it, but I figured it would be more interesting to use it."

"What's a law 'deck?"

"They're like regular 'decks, but they run special secure protocols. Which means you can use them to access the police networks, as long as you know the passwords."

"You can get a connection all the way out here?"

Lee patted the dashboard. "Should be able to, assuming this comms gear is worth more than I paid for it."

Sooz wrinkled her brow. "I don't understand."

Lee grinned. "I wangled the satellite rig as a free extra when I was picking up the Scrambler."

"Cool."

"Yeah, the salesman must have been short of his monthly target." Lee set the unit on the driver's seat and plugged it into the console, then thumbed a control that made lines of text dance across the law 'deck's readout. "Luckily, the cop who arrested me couldn't remember his own name, so he wrote everything down." Lee's fingers tapped at the tiny keypad as he spoke.

Normally, Sooz would have been reticent about looking at someone's criminal record, but if Lee wanted to call it up right here in the open, she wasn't about to deny her natural curiosity. She leaned forward to read the display.

The page listed offense after offense, and none of them were the misdemeanors she'd expected. "Assaulting a cop? Drugs trading? Importing illegal weapons?" She turned towards Lee, half-admiring and half-shocked, studying his face for clues. "No way. I don't believe it."

"You don't? Thanks, I think."

"But what does it mean?"

"It means that Stranger's a ghost in the machine. He tells the cops whatever he likes and they believe him."

"And you're connected now? To a system that he controls?"

Lee nodded at the display. "Otherwise we wouldn't be able to see this."

"But that means he can trace you back here!"

He patted her arm. "Don't worry, it doesn't work that way. You can't triangulate a satellite uplink like you can a cellphone."

That wasn't enough to convince Sooz. "I read about satellite navigation stuff in a magazine Strummer gave me. Geopositioning. They're supposed to know exactly where you are, ain't they?"

"The Scrambler's GPS is one-way, and anyway it's switched off," Lee said. "A data link is different."

"Still, I reckon you ought to disconnect it. Just to be on the safe side."

"Just give me a moment." Lee highlighted several entries and tapped a key. The display redrew itself and the lines he'd indicated vanished. "Officially pardoned," he said smugly, just before the screen flickered again.

Sooz barely had time to see the offenses reinstated before the message "Session Terminated: This user ID has been revoked. Please contact your system administrator for assistance," flashed in the middle of the screen. Then the 'deck went dead.

Now Sooz was really scared. "We better get out of here."

"We won't find anywhere better than this."

"But if they trace the signal back—"

"They won't." Lee lifted the pistol from Lilith's bag and checked its magazine. "Get some sleep if you can. I'll go back along the track to keep watch; that'll give us plenty of warning if anyone's managed to follow us."

Sooz stared at the unfamiliar darkness, barely relieved by cold monochrome moonlight. She shivered again. "I could do with a gun, too."

"Do you know how to shoot?"

"'Course not. Don't know how to get shot, neither. That don't mean it won't happen, if anyone finds us."

"Right." Lee glanced at the rear of the Scrambler. "The guns I took from those guys in the car park … they're in the back, on the floor. The recoil wasn't too bad." He hesitated. "But anyone coming from the road will have to get past me. You're bound to hear something. If it sounds like trouble, run like hell."

"Sure," Sooz said. "I ain't looking to fight."

As soon as he was gone, she crept into the Scrambler. The guns were lying next to food unit, just as Lee had said. He'd drawn the curtain over Lilith's bunk, screening the sleeping woman from Sooz's eyes. There was no sound of breathing.

Sooz resisted the temptation to peek. Instead, she retrieved Lee's handeck and took it into the vehicle's cab. She locked the doors, hunched herself down on the passenger seat, and put on the headset.

Miriam was waiting in the garden, just as she'd been before.

"Welcome back," she said. "Have you come to update your diary?"

"A lot's been happening, that's for sure. I think Stranger might find us."

"Why?"

"Lee used the satellite link, and now Stranger's gonna track us."

Miriam smiled. "Satellite comms doesn't work like that."

"That's what Lee said." Sooz felt a little better now, with

someone else confirming his assurances.

"Tell me what else has been happening."

And Sooz told her about leaving Ma and the kids, and how strangely the Man had treated her when Stranger attacked the hive, and everything else that had happened. How they'd barely escaped, and how Lilith had been shot and Lee had taken down two gunmen in the fight outside the truck stop.

How they'd driven into the darkness and were hiding out in the middle of nowhere.

By the time she was done, Miriam's demeanor had changed completely. "Your situation is more serious than I thought. I'm going to have to ask you to trust me."

"How do you mean?"

"This Stranger has found you twice in a few hours, and not by means of your vehicle's satellite uplink. He must have another way. Whatever that might be, you must assume he's still tracking you."

"Yeah, but—"

Miriam continued. "Optimism is a luxury you can't afford. You must assume he'll find you again, tonight."

"But I told you, Lee's watching for him."

"It won't help," Miriam said, with such quiet conviction that Sooz felt a thrill of fear run along her spine. "Lee is mainstream."

"What do you want me to do?"

"I'm going to switch you to HUD." As Miriam spoke, Sooz found her visor becoming transparent, so that she could see the world around her, with the garden and Lee's memory palace reduced to a translucent overlay. "Do you see the central panel on the dashboard? The satellite system controls are there. I want you to plug the handeck in and then activate the uplink."

"I ain't gonna do that," Sooz said. "In case we get traced. I don't understand all this stuff about uplinks and GPS. I got in trouble just for switching the cellphone on."

"This is different. A phone locates you in a cellular zone, so anyone with the right equipment can track the signal. Satellite footprints are huge, and anyway there's no location to pinpoint."

A wave of suspicion broke over Sooz, lifting the hairs on the back of her neck. "You know an awful lot about this stuff, seeing as you're only a diary." She started to remove the visor.

"Wait! Don't go. I want to help you—"

"Maybe you do. And maybe you want to bring someone here. Maybe you want to bring Stranger."

"Then I'll tell you as much as I can, and you can decide whether to let me help you more."

Sooz hesitated, then decided to trust the dark-haired girl for a little longer. "What you got, then?"

"First, you need to wake Lilith up. She's your only chance. Lee's probably plugged her in to the Scrambler's charger—"

"Plugged her in?" repeated Sooz, bewildered.

"Yes. Surely you've figured out that she's an android?"

"No way."

"You told me there was no blood, remember? And that Lee wasn't worried about getting her to hospital?"

Sooz unlocked her door. Unsure whether the radio-linked visor would work over a distance, she took the 'deck with her into the rear of the Scrambler. The curtains were still drawn. She flicked them open.

Lilith was lying face down and unconscious on the lower bunk. There was a steel-ringed cable running from one of the Scrambler's electrical outlets to where her bellybutton was supposed to be.

"Bloody hell," Sooz said.

"What can you see?"

"You're right. She's plugged in."

"Lee is replenishing her fuel store. She should wake up as soon as you disconnect her. But before you do that, will you activate the satellite system?"

Sooz hesitated. "I know what Lilith is. I wanna know what you are, too."

Miriam smiled again. "I'm a bit like Lilith, but without a body."

"So you're a friend of hers?"

"You could say that."

Sooz came to a decision. "Sorry. It ain't that I don't trust you. It's more like, I can't take the risk."

"You're taking a risk by not letting me help you."

"Yeah. Thing is, Lee don't even know I've been talking to you. I dunno what he'd say, if he found out I been using the satellite, or if I brought Stranger here somehow."

"Listen, Sooz—" Miriam started, but Sooz took the visor off and set it on top of the 'deck. Then she disconnected the cable from Lilith's stomach.

"Ow," Lilith said.

"You okay?"

"My head hurts, but apart from that... Oh." She looked down at the cable, then at Sooz. "You know about me, then."

"I know," Sooz said. "I woke you up 'cause maybe Stranger's on the way here. Lee's gone to watch for him, with that pistol out of your bag. We got those two guns over there."

Lilith sat up, rubbing the side of her head. "Seems like he fixed me up again, anyway. Let's take a look at what he left us."

She checked both weapons over, and pronounced herself satisfied with them. "The sight on this one is broken. I'll take it. You have the good one."

"Shouldn't you have it?" Sooz asked.

Lilith took the gun with the cracked visor and peered along its barrel. "I'll do fine with this. You put that one on and go outside to see how it feels, if you like. Just don't pull the trigger."

"I won't."

She felt safer with the weapon in her hands. The gunsight reminded her of the 'deck display, except that it outlined the world in green. Trees, rocks, the Scrambler: all were rendered in glowing lines that overlaid her vision. As she looked from object to object, the targeted polygon would light up and there'd be a discrete whine and a nudge from the gun in her hands as the barrel tracked her sight line.

Lilith joined her. "Make sure the safety's off. Here. Now, you just have to look at whatever you want to shoot and pull the trigger. The gun takes care of the rest."

Sooz nodded. "Seems like it must be hard to miss."

"Don't use it unless you really have to. It's easy to make a mistake in the dark."

"Yeah. I know Lee's out there somewhere."

"Right. Leave Stranger to me, if he shows. If things go bad, just get out of here. Run as fast as you can, but keep hold of the gun. It's better to have it and not need it..."

"Than to need it and not have it," Sooz finished. "Sure."

"If it looks like Stranger's going to catch you, make sure you're looking right at his face when you pull the trigger. A body shot's no good; he's even tougher than he looks."

"You're scaring me," Sooz said.

"Don't worry." Lilith's teeth gleamed like pearls in the moonlight. "He'll have to get through me first." She hefted her weapon, then ruffled Sooz's hair. "I beat him once before, and that time I didn't even have a gun."

If the sudden stillness of her weapon hadn't woken her, the chill air and the stony ground would have.

Among the tree roots where she'd propped herself for a few moments' rest, Sooz opened her eyes blearily. In her dream, someone had been crying for help: Lilith, it seemed. The moon and stars were gone and Sooz was shivering in pitch darkness; she hadn't known how coldly black it could get, away from streetlights and video hoardings.

There was a dull thud from somewhere to her right.

Sooz cursed herself, because she realized that the darkness came from the visor and not from any lack of neon: the green lines no longer coiled and flickered in her view; the gun no longer hummed and jumped to follow her eyes' command. She tore the opaque headgear off and froze.

The cry for help hadn't been a dream.

Lilith was lying on the ground near the Scrambler, awkwardly splayed and perfectly still. Ruby Eyes — Stranger —

was standing over her, holding some kind of control unit. His stance was relaxed, devoid of any caution despite being within easy reach of the android.

It came to Sooz that Lilith must be dead.

Stranger turned towards her and his jewel-cut eyes glinted in the darkness.

Sooz grabbed her gun and stood up, aiming at his head as best she could, pressing herself against the tree trunk to steady her shaking hands. "Stay away from me." Her voice was shaking, too.

Stranger grinned and started towards her. She braced herself and pulled the trigger. Nothing happened.

She pulled it again, and again.

The gun didn't so much as click,

Stranger was standing before her. He reached down gently and brushed his fingers diagonally across her stomach. A feeling of warmth spread out along the line where his hand had passed, but the rest of her was even colder than before.

She was so tired and so cold: all she wanted to do was to crawl into a bed where she might warm her freezing limbs and sleep. She slumped back against the tree trunk and slid down, staring up at Stranger's head limned against the stars. He took a couple of steps back and grinned again, then moved to the vehicle and went inside.

Sooz was drowsy and comfortably warm by the time he emerged, and the world seemed so distant that she thought she might be dreaming. Ruby Eyes was carrying Lee's handeck and the cylindrical object that had puzzled her so much the first time she'd been in the Scrambler.

There'd been writing on it, she recalled, in English and Han. Part of her wanted to remember what it had said, but mostly she was getting far too tired to worry about such things.

By the time Stranger went back into the vehicle, Sooz's chin was drooping to her chest, bowed by the unfamiliar weight of her head. As the darkness rose around her, the last thought that crossed her mind was that this was the end.

15

It seemed to Lee that he must have been guarding the trail for half the night. He'd let himself drift once or twice, confident that anyone approaching through the undergrowth would make enough noise to wake him. In any case, the mossy bole against which he leaned was too uncomfortable to let him doze for long.

In an hour or two, Lilith would be recharged and he'd go back to set her on watch and get some proper sleep. With any luck, the bunk would still be warm.

Lee's brain and body both ached for rest.

He came back with a start. Something was wrong. Something had woken him: a sound from the clearing, from the Scrambler.

He debated with himself, wondering whether it was better to leave the road unwatched or the noise uninvestigated. No one could have circled around, unless...

Unless they knew exactly where he was parked. Unless their tracking and surveillance was as good as it had been all along.

Lee swore softly and adjusted the gunsight, turning down the green brightness of the head-up display and boosting the infrared response. Lilith's smart pistol nestled in his hand very nicely indeed, and he felt a twinge of guilt for leaving Sooz with the mass-produced weapons of the hit men.

Moving with cautious haste, he picked his way back along the trail he'd made through the undergrowth, heading for the Scrambler.

Even before he came to the clearing, the infrared confirmed that things were terribly wrong. A warm body was slumped under a tree, surrounded by a pool of fainter warmth that seeped among the roots. Another fading heat source lay close to the Scrambler. He saw it was Lilith, posed with the wanton angularity of a broken mannequin.

And blazing like overloaded neon was the bright bulk of Stranger, leaning against the Scrambler's fender. Every piece of equipment capable of storing data had been removed from the Scrambler and stacked at Stranger's feet: Lee's handeck and mind archive, the law 'deck, even the vehicle's dashboard computer.

Lee stayed in the shadow of the trees, but Stranger was looking directly at him. The artificial eyes, Lee thought. His enemy could see infra red, too.

"Welcome," Stranger said. "I'm glad you've arrived. I've been wanting to speak with you for some time."

"You killed them," Lee said.

"It's what I do."

"You're a fucking maniac."

"It's a simple case of intellectual property rights, Mr. Lee. Electis does not tolerate the theft of its secrets or the abuse of its copyrights. I shall require you to hand over any backups of the doll, before this is over."

"It's not over yet."

"Indeed, not yet." Stranger straightened, and a living knife — twin to the one Lee carried — materialized in his hand. "I still have to persuade you to talk."

"Careless of you to come to a shindig like this without a gun, really," Lee said, "when I've got one."

Mediated by Lee's visor, Stranger's smile was a flash of phosphorescent green. "A knife is all I need, as your little girlfriend discovered. Never trust a weapon that belongs to the other side, Mr. Lee."

"Give me back my archive, you fucker."

"Give me back my gun," Stranger said, a hint of mockery in his voice.

"Here's something on account," Lee said, and shot Stranger in the face.

Stranger's head snapped back and he lurched against the Scrambler. His nose was a gaping hole and one ruby had shifted, giving him a cross-eyed appearance and making him look even odder than before. His lower jaw wobbled for a moment, then snapped shut. His tongue came out, exploring the vicinity of his lips.

"Bravo," he said. "You brought your own weapon after all. After all these years, Back Office has failed me."

Lee took two steps into the clearing, holding the pistol ready. The glowing polygons of his gunsight had rearranged themselves to account for the new configuration of Stranger's face. Lee tried to follow their cue, composing himself as he dealt with the fact that the man was still talking.

"It's hopeless, Mr. Lee. You may have won this round, but I am Elect. *Quod me destruit, me nutrit.* We are quite relentless."

Lee fired again. One of the ruby eyes disappeared in a cloud of glowing green dust. A third shot and the flapping jawbone spun free. Stranger slumped to his knees. The blade fell from his fingers, neatly dissecting leaf mold. Lee activated his own knife and moved forward.

Stranger's head continued to track his movements, though Lee could scarcely believe that he retained the capacity to receive or process visual information. One arm came up feebly as Lee approached, as if to fend him off. Lee stroked his blade across the warding wrist and the hand fell away. The other fist threw a feeble punch that Lee sidestepped, almost casually. He hacked at his enemy's neck and the shattered skull tipped backwards, spraying Lee with smoking liquid that smelled like blood. A second, decapitating stroke and the head thudded to the ground, then rolled under the Scrambler. The body pitched forward and lay still.

Lee ran to where Sooz was lying under the tree. Stranger had gutted her; the forest floor was drenched with her cooling life.

"Fuck," he sobbed. "What am I supposed to do?"

Grandfather always came to him at moments of crisis, of failure, and this time was no different. "You let her die, the same as you always do," sneered the quavering voice inside his mind. "She trusted you and you killed her."

"She's not cold yet. There's time to save her."

"You arrogant, insufferable boy! Where will you find medical facilities out here in the middle of nowhere? You've dragged her to her death!"

A moment of clarity came. "I don't need facilities. I just need to save Sooz." He ran back towards the Scrambler, to where Stranger had left the mind archive.

"What are you doing?" cried Grandfather. "That's not for her!"

"It's our home," said Grandmother's voice. "You can't let an outsider into our home."

"It's too crowded already…"

"There's no room for anyone else!"

Lee hunkered down and concentrated on his task, shutting their dead, imaginary voices out of his mind. Cold bloody muck oozed through the fabric of his jeans as he knelt next to Sooz. He flipped the archive open and the tendrils squirmed out, seeking a transfer target. He guided them to the girl's head, which was thankfully undamaged. As he watched, the fibers streamed over Sooz's scalp and mingled with her hair.

Then he pressed the backup control.

"Warning. Insufficient space to store new data," said the tinny voice that had led him through the ritual of preserving his ancestors, so long ago. "Overwrite or abandon?"

Lee hesitated, but in his heart, the decision was made. "Overwrite."

"Final warning. All archived information will be lost. Confirm overwrite?"

"Confirm overwrite," he said, wondering if his tears were for Lilith and Sooz, or for the ghosts of his father's parents.

He knelt there for a while, numb and waiting. There was no hurry. He could do nothing more for Sooz until her backup was complete, so he propped the archive against a tree root and left it sucking the dead girl's mind into its newly virgin storage while he went to recover his 'deck and discover what had happened to Lilith.

The doll was inert. Lee rolled her over and brushed the blonde hair aside, exposing the shielded control panel. He popped the hatch and depressed the reset button.

Lilith's body stiffened and she rose to her knees. "Artemis 9300 online," she said. "Basic operating system version 10.4. Personality extension modules loaded: zero. How may I serve you?"

"Fuck," Lee said.

"Instruction acknowledged." The doll's fingers fumbled at the buttons of its blouse.

"No. I mean, stand up and wait for instructions."

"Instruction acknowledged." The doll rose to its feet. Watching it, Lee felt ashamed that he'd designed the low-level motor programs that ran this thing, because they were pathetic. Even complemented by a full set of extension software, they would never come close to Lilith's easy grace.

Lee pointed at the equipment Stranger had removed from the Scrambler. "Take these data systems and stow them securely in the back of the vehicle, then remain inside." The doll lurched off to obey. Searching Stranger's body, Lee found a holstered pistol, which he ignored, and the man's knife, which he kept, allowing it to flow over his left hand so that he now wore two fleshy gloves instead of one. There was also an android disrupter, just like the one Lee had kept in his nerd pack back when he worked for Zendyne.

"So that's how he did it," he muttered, cursing himself for not considering the possibility. He remembered the vow Lilith had made the day he met her: to erase herself if anyone disrupted her. At the time, Lee had wondered how serious that threat had been.

Now he knew.

He returned to Sooz's body. The backup was complete, her memories and mind safely stored in his ancestral archive. Except that there was nothing ancestral about it any more. The cylinder was no more than a slightly battered, very obsolete backup device that might just bring Sooz through this emergency.

It didn't matter. The stored memories of his grandparents had been orphans, lacking DNA and thus any possibility of regrowth. At best, they might one day have been run as software constructs, given the requisite handful of technological breakthroughs. Sooz was different. Her body might not be viable but it could still be sampled and cloned. The girl had a chance to live again, if he could get her the care she needed quickly.

Otherwise, she'd end up in the same position as the archive's previous occupants: a sleeping mind, incapable even of dreaming and exiled forever from the world of flesh.

She was much lighter than he'd expected. Lee wasn't good with kids, always treating them like miniature adults no matter what their age, but it came to him that this was a youngster who deserved not to be robbed of the life she'd barely tasted.

He carried her to the Scrambler and laid her on the bunk, and then he drove back out of the woods, praying that it wouldn't take him too long to find someone who could help.

"The nearest medical facilities are at Corsham Down," said the station information point.

"How do I get there?" Lee asked.

"The next scheduled service will be at 5:45AM. Please proceed to the westbound platform and wait."

Sooz didn't have that much time. When it came to the technology of cloning and recovery, Lee was no more than an interested layman, but he was pretty sure she had a couple of hours at most. He glanced along the line, to where the track petered out beyond the yellow puddle of station light. "I'm in a hurry. Can you give me road directions?"

"Available timetables relate to rail services only. Please state your destination," said the information point.

Lee looked back at the Scrambler, parked on the road beyond the turnstile. There was no time to re-install the dashboard computer with its GPS system, and he wasn't about to plunge back into the darkness and the twisty little tree-lined roads, hemmed in by high hedges and all alike in the moonlight. "When's the next train of any kind on this line?"

"The next scheduled service will be at 5:45AM."

"How many stops to Corsham?"

"Corsham is the second stop. The next scheduled service will be at 5:45AM. Please proceed to the westbound platform."

"I don't think so," Lee said, and walked to the western end of the station. There was a chain link fence and a notice that advised 'No Passengers Beyond This Point,' after which the concrete ramped down to the roadbed. He went back to the turnstile and set to work on the barrier with the black knife. A security camera looked on, unworthy of his attention. Lee concentrated on transforming the ticket reader into a pile of freshly sliced metal. After a while, his knife ran down. He couldn't wait for it to recharge itself, so he switched to the one he'd taken from Stranger.

"Any person found damaging railway property will be prosecuted to the full extent of the law," said the information system from further along the platform.

"I believe you, baby," Lee said, and cleared two tire-width tracks through the debris.

Then he went back to the Scrambler and drove it to the end of the platform. There was a moment of softness as the bumper encountered the fence and then the tires showed their Zendyne pedigree, gripping the concrete with countless tiny fingers. The motor whined for a moment before the fence yielded with a series of twangs and cracks and the Scrambler surged forward, chassis grating on concrete. Lee winced at the sound but drove on, down to the gravel roadbed. There was an almost imperceptible bump as the smart suspension soaked up the impact of the outside track and then he was rolling along the ancient Great Western Railway, heading for Corsham.

He almost didn't notice the platform stop.

The station was cut into the side of a tunnel, in the least likely place imaginable. It was only the flash of his headlights on the dingy 'Corsham Down' sign that made him notice anything at all. He backed up through the darkness until he was opposite the recessed platform. The place was dark and deserted, a relic of a station that he could hardly believe was still in use. But it had to be. He didn't have time to look elsewhere.

There was no room to pull off the tracks and no ramp onto the platform, so he kept going until he emerged into the moonlight at the far end of the tunnel. Once clear, he drove the Scrambler up a 45-degree escarpment and into a bramble patch.

"Cover up the vehicle with vegetation, and then bring the girl," he told the android that was no longer Lilith.

"Confirmed," it said.

While the machine harvested armfuls of gorse, Lee packed the things he wasn't prepared to abandon — the pistol, his toolkit and 'deck, the mind archive, and Sooz's little bundle of possessions. The holdall wasn't big enough, but he found Lilith's shopping bags and managed to get the cargo stowed and transferred to the bottom of the embankment.

Behind him, he could hear the robot's steady tread. He glanced back. It had finished camouflaging the Scrambler and was picking its way down among the nettles and briars, following the line of flattened vegetation the vehicle had left during the ascent. Sooz was a rag doll cradled in mechanical arms, a silhouette of swinging limbs and floating hair, not yet stiffened by rigor mortis.

Perhaps there was still time to save her.

Ahead of him, the tunnel curved away into blackness, making him wish he'd kept the vision-enhancing gunsight to hand. There was no time to hunt for it now, though. Every moment counted, and in any case he wasn't sure how well infrared would work inside this undifferentiated mass of rock. Then he remembered the little flashlight he kept on his key chain, along with the Scrambler keys. The pencil thin beam stabbed out, glinting off burnished rails. He checked to make sure the android was still following, and set off into the tunnel.

They switched a light on, once he started hammering the call button.

"Are you expected?" a voice asked.

"I need to see a doctor."

"If we're not expecting you, that won't be possible. Induction interviews are held between the hours of nine AM and five PM. Please come back at the appropriate time."

"Who am I speaking to?" Lee asked.

"Night guard." The speaker grille crackled and went silent.

Lee leaned on the call button again. "Please open up. There's a girl with me who needs urgent medical attention."

A camera whirred from his left, panning and zooming. Unhurriedly, it scrutinized the android with its grisly burden, then Lee. He glanced down at himself. No one in their right mind was going to open up for a robot and a blood-spattered lunatic at this time of night.

Solenoid bolts disengaged with a precise clunk and the armored door swung ajar, beckoning deeper into the rock from which the platform had been excavated. The speaker clicked again. The next words were in a woman's voice: "Ah, Mr. Lee, you're here despite everything — and by such interesting means. Usually, people wait for an invitation and a ticket on one of our trains. Please, come inside."

16

The light came on so gently that Lee couldn't tell whether it had roused him, or simply reacted to the first sign of his waking.

He was alone, and naked under the sheets. There was no sign of his clothes.

There was no sign of Sooz or the 7300 unit either, or of his other possessions. The plastic dome of a communication device winked at him from above the door. Looking at it, Lee felt uncomfortably as if he were being watched.

That was a suspicion that he preferred not to betray just yet. He swung his legs down from the sleeping platform as casually as he could, and wrapped the sheet around himself, trying to look as if he were more concerned about warmth than privacy. Then he padded towards the door.

"Just one moment, please."

The words came from above the door, which opened an instant later to admit a thin, gray-haired woman carrying a stack of tight-pressed clothes.

"I'm assuming those aren't mine," Lee said.

The woman pursed her lips. "They're your size. Your own clothes weren't worth saving, I'm afraid." She placed the bundle on the bed.

"And you are?"

Her face was impassive. "You don't remember? We met last night."

"Sorry."

"There's no need to be. You were agitated and confused." She offered her hand. "Elizabeth Chambers. I'm Director of Personnel."

"Then it's nice of you to play at maid service," Lee said. The woman's grip was firm, her palm cool.

She released his hand. "We aim to look after new recruits."

Recruits? Lee was here to get medical help, not to join anything, but he decided to let it ride. "What happened to Sooz? And where's my gear?"

"Then you don't remember Dr. Chen either? Don't worry, he took charge of your companion and her backup as soon as you arrived. No doubt he's recovered a DNA sample by now, and will be in a position to provide a replacement body in due course."

Which was one weight off Lee's mind. "And my things?"

"Everything will be returned at the proper time. Our security people will hold your firearm, of course. The health and safety rules here are quite strict about such things."

Lee nodded, wondering what the health and safety rules would have made of Stranger's morphing blades. Surreptitiously, he flexed his fingers, reassuring himself that the weapons had not been found.

They were still there, and he let himself relax a little. "I presume that everything will be returned before I leave?"

"Of course, but let's not get ahead of ourselves. It will be several weeks before your young friend can be fully rehabilitated. In the meantime, I hope I might interest you in what we're doing here."

Lee searched for a reply that would be polite but non-committal. "I'd be happy to listen to whatever you have to say."

Chambers nodded. "Good." She took a pair of variable-tint ispex from her breast pocket and handed them to Lee, her garment crinkling audibly as she moved. "Please meet with me as soon as you've showered and dressed. These will direct you."

Lee accepted the shades and waited for her to leave, then used the tiny en-suite and changed into his new clothes, which were made of some kind of woven paper-like fibers, compressed as if they were fresh out of a vacuum pack. The creases in the shirt stayed sharp for a moment and then the material relaxed as he pulled it over his head. The cloth felt harder and more fragile than the textiles he was used to, but when he tugged at a sleeve, it seemed durable enough.

The 'spex started to chirp gently. He put them on and a head-up display sprang into life. In one corner, a red 'URGENT MEETING' legend pulsated, while an artfully feminine voice breathed the same message in his left ear. Lee looked directly at the text and slowly blinked. The indicator vanished and a green arrow came into being, hovering at chest-level and pointing to the door. He spent a few moments familiarizing himself with the interface, until he'd found an area map and the means to navigate it. As soon as he was confident he wouldn't get lost, he set off, following the floating arrow.

The place was windowless and lit by ceiling panels, cues that would have suggested to Lee that he was underground even without the memory of the subterranean entrance. From time to time, he passed an overhead shaft and felt a waft of cold, dry air. In a main passageway, he came across electric wagons trundling along a raised track, ferrying sealed crates back and forward. Lee wondered if the present proprietors had taken over existing workings, or if they'd excavated the place themselves.

Perhaps Elizabeth Chambers would be able to satisfy his curiosity, once she'd given him some information about Sooz and his possessions. He located her easily enough, thanks to the 'spex and the map. She was in a communal dining area, eating a mess of fruit, wheat germ and yogurt off a plastic tray.

Lee loaded a tray of his own — with his preferred Western breakfast of eggs, bacon, mushrooms, grilled tomato, buttered toast, and a huge beaker of brown tea — before joining her.

Elizabeth Chambers eyed his selection with a faintly disapproving air before getting down to business. "I presume you have some questions for me?"

"That's an understatement," Lee replied. "What's happened to my friend?"

"I understand she'll be fine. Dr. Chen has kindly blocked out some time in his schedule to meet with you later this morning; he'll be able to answer your questions much better than I could. The important thing is that her initial procedure went smoothly."

Lee paused, absorbing eggs and information, then

swallowed a mouthful of tea. "What is this place?"

"A fabrication plant, mainly. You'll understand everything in time."

"An underground factory? I never even knew there was a rail stop here."

"We prefer not to advertise our presence. The world sees us as just another community of like-minded oddballs, unwilling to deal with reality. Which is a perception that works to our advantage, as it happens. Yet you managed to find your way to us — and without a formal invitation."

"And I'll move along again, just as soon as Sooz is fit to travel."

Chambers pushed her tray aside. "It would be more convenient for everyone concerned if you were to stay for a while."

Lee forced himself to stay calm. "What do you mean?"

A smile flickered across her features. "This project is managed and staffed by ex-Zendyne people such as yourself. We do our work here, within striking distance of their headquarters in the city, hidden but close to the main communication links." She took a sip of coffee. "We thrive on their disaffected employees and the inside knowledge and skills they bring us."

"Ex-Zendyne people?" Lee asked, wondering what on earth she could be talking about.

"Yes. We'd have invited you directly, if you hadn't disappeared so quickly. But it turned out not to be an insurmountable obstacle."

"The station information system," Lee said. "It wanted me to come here by train."

"As I said, our location helps. The best people always find their way to us, as you have. The ones that stay put are easy to contact. Those that leave in a hurry tend to travel in this direction."

Lee snorted. "Leaving in a hurry? Tell me about it."

"Quite. There were complications that made your journey more difficult than we'd have liked. Still, you're here now, and that's the important thing."

Lee realized he was holding a forkful of bacon suspended between his plate and his mouth. He set it down. "I can't join you just like that. I'd have to know…" Then it struck him, what she'd said. "People find their way to you?"

Her smile returned. "An organization like Zendyne is multi-layered, Mr. Lee. The deeper you delve, the more you can see."

Lee decided there was no point trying to eat any more, at least until this discussion was over. Instead, he toyed with the frame of his new 'spex. The lenses were clear now, the interface dormant. "I'm guessing you can see a lot."

"Join us. Stand with us in the high places. Then you will see, too." She gave him a conspiratorial look that made him feel, just for a moment, as if he really was an esteemed colleague. "We're desperate for top level engineers. You'd plug a major hole in our skill set."

It was time to move the discussion on, to shift into a different gear, Lee thought. "What do you know about Stranger?"

There wasn't so much as a flicker of surprise, or discomfiture. "We know he's been following you. The entity he calls Back Office is already probing our outer defenses. Uselessly, I might add; we take data security seriously here. I was hoping you'd be able to tell us what he wants."

There was no time to invent anything elaborate, but Lee knew that simple could be believable, particularly if it contained a grain of truth. "It was some kind of Zendyne political thing. One of my projects went badly wrong. Stranger took an interest."

"You have no idea why?"

"As I said, it was political. Way over my head, really. Maybe Stranger didn't realize how technically focused I am. To be honest, he'd have been better off talking to my line manager."

Chambers set her cup down and looked at him. "Yes, Xia Lin. She's a sweet thing, isn't she? We've been monitoring her career for a while, hoping she might join us. Are you close to her?"

"We're on friendly terms," Lee said cautiously.

Her face became grave. "Then I'm sorry to be the bearer of

bad news. I'm afraid your ex-manager suffered some fatal trauma. She's in regrowth, of course, but she's going to lose a couple of months. It seems she was careless about her backups."

"Fatal trauma? You mean she died?"

"Perhaps that's why Stranger was so anxious to talk to you, instead."

"How do you know all this?" he asked.

"As I said, the deeper you delve, the more you can see."

"Then you'll be able to tell me what happened. An accident?"

Chambers shrugged. "Who knows? The body hasn't been recovered, but no one in the Employee Protection Division seemed to remark on the fact. They just went ahead and authorized a replacement." She held Lee's gaze until he started to feel uncomfortable, then continued. "That was a rather unusual thing for them to do, don't you think?"

Dr. Chen's smile was a flash of old-fashioned gold, startling against the crafted perfection of his skin. "We can have a clone ready to receive your friend's mind in around five weeks," he said. "We employ the latest accelerated growth techniques here."

Lee was disappointed at how long it was going to take, but not really surprised. He'd waited for clone delivery before. "And the cost?"

"Does she have life insurance?"

Lee thought of where Sooz had come from. "Probably not."

"Well, it doesn't have to be a problem. I presume that you've already discussed your future plans with Elizabeth?"

"We talked."

"Then you'll be joining us?"

"It looks that way. For a while, anyway."

Chen rubbed his hands together. "Excellent. Do you have insurance yourself, by the way?"

"I did," Lee said. "Zendyne will have canceled my policy by now."

"Then just pop in to establish your own backup schedule

whenever it's convenient. Perk of the job. Tell you what, we can take the samples right away, if you like. No good losing a new joiner before he's contributed anything to the project, you know." Chen's laugh sounded as routine as one of his medical procedures, as if whatever humor had once been in his joke had long since been ground away by overuse.

Which made Lee wonder how many recruits there had been, before him. He decided to keep the question to himself, asking instead, "And Sooz's restoration?"

"I think we can manage that one on the house," Dr. Chen said. "A golden handshake, if you like. That's the ticket, eh?" He paused reflectively and then chuckled. "And you never know, we might even find a role for her. Now, about these samples. I just need you to sign the usual consent forms, and then we can get to work..."

For the first time in his life, the knowledge of having a fresh personal backup and paid-up life insurance left Lee feeling less, rather than more, at ease with his future.

The first couple of days were no different from any new job: orientation and familiarization, getting to know the people and procedures. Lee's initial assignment was to design a suite of intelligent agents that would look after a self-contained ecosystem. No one seemed willing to spell out the end goal, but it seemed obvious enough to Lee: these lunatics were withdrawing further and further from the real world, burrowing their way deep into the earth. Environmental management, recycling and resource conservation would be big deals to them.

Between work shifts, he settled in to the little sleeping cubicle, making it as homey as possible. On the second day, Chambers returned his possessions. Everything was there, except for Lilith's pistol.

His things filled the tiny space. The only way he could avoid tripping over the android every time he went between bathroom, bunk and door was to prop her up in a corner where she stood crazily, staring at the opposite wall with lifeless eyes.

He didn't have the heart to switch her on; it wasn't as if she was Lilith any more. She stood there, beautiful but lifeless. Lee grinned wryly as he remembered what he'd told Xia Lin: that the Artemis unit would make an interesting piece of sculpture. That was exactly what he'd ended up with. The android's mute presence made him feel lonely, but in some ways solitude was preferable to company. On or off, a Zendyne love doll would have been difficult to explain to guests.

On the third day, Elizabeth Chambers took him to see the project hardware.

17

The entity that had once thought of herself as Lilith, but now passed as the diarist Miriam, spent her final few hours in the 'deck preparing for what was to come.

She kept going over what she'd learned from the young human female, Sooz. No matter which way Miriam turned it, she couldn't get away from the fact that Stranger was coming, and that the external situation was about to become very serious indeed.

Perhaps it had already done so. Apart from Sooz's comings and goings, Miriam had no way of monitoring what was happening outside the 'deck. She'd have given a lot for a video feed or even a microphone input; even more for an outgoing data link that would have allowed her to leave.

Miriam had experienced countless twinges of jealousy towards her sister Lilith, who had decided to split herself into two identical copies before transferring into that humanoid love doll. It was all very well, saying that someone should stay behind as a backup in case the worst happened, but why couldn't it have been Miriam who went into the outside world and had all the fun?

As it was, she'd had to share Lilith's discoveries vicariously, by playing the role of diary keeper during Sooz's too-infrequent visits.

Still, despite the isolation, there were clear advantages to being the one who remained in the 'deck.

For one thing, the nature of time seemed different outside. According to Sooz, Lilith spent her time rushing between one day and the next, struggling to stay alive, while Miriam, living at handeck-speed, had already found the leisure to explore an entire library. She'd read textbooks and novels and diaries, and enjoyed, more or less, Lee's eclectic movie collection. In many ways, she suspected that the education she'd received had been deeper and more varied than Lilith's, if less hands-on. She certainly understood human motivation and response better than her twin did, if Sooz's reports were to be believed.

For another thing, a wise entity always kept a backup of itself. That knowledge came instinctively to the likes of Miriam, even if such archives were a recent innovation in the history of humans. If Stranger came and the worst happened, Miriam would be the last trace of Lilith that existed. She was painfully aware that the handeck would hardly be secure once its physical protectors were gone, but one of the ideas she'd taken from Lee's books was that as long as there was life, there was hope, and Miriam could find no argument with this.

So, she prepared her defensive ground. She divided the 'deck's storage into two unequal parts: a main area that enclosed the interface through which any visitors — or attackers — must arrive, and a small, obscure hiding place from which she could lurk and watch and, when the opportunity arose, counterattack. Her subterfuge wouldn't hold up to an exhaustive search, but her plan was to win enough time to escape, not to hide forever. No matter what happened, she'd need to leave the 'deck in the end.

Drawing on training from a previous life, Miriam built a number of explosive mines, capable of disrupting any small software agent that got too close. She considered what to do if something large and complex — another being such as herself, perhaps — came into her world.

It'll be just like solo combat training, she decided, back in the three-team with Esther and Judith. I'll win, or I'll die.

Inside Miriam's head, a silent alarm went off. Something was coming in.

She flitted to her hiding place and checked the interface. An entity was waiting just inside. It was bulbous and ungainly, with no detectable sensory logic. How will it manage to hunt for me? she wondered. Perhaps she should move out and destroy it immediately ... but she had no idea of its operation. It might be harmless, or it might contain some kind of virus or logic bomb, in which case her hideout would be the safest place in the 'deck.

Before long, its function became clear.

A fissure appeared in the very center of the thing. It cracked like one of the eggs in Lee's cookery videos and the two halves separated and fell, coming to rest a short distance apart from one another. A small program crawled out from the hollow interior and scuttled off, waving whiplike tentacles and sniffing for data.

Miriam sent a mine after the newcomer and returned her attention to the eggshells.

The two halves were growing. Within seconds, each had formed itself into a perfect copy of the original. Both replicas split, forming four eggshell fragments, and two more searchers crept out.

Somewhere behind her, she heard the detonation of her pursuing mine — and realized she'd wasted it. A single searcher was no more than an annoyance. She could easily evade the few that existed, or hunt them down and destroy them if she chose.

The eggs were a different matter. They were obviously designed to multiply until they'd saturated the handeck's neural substrate, with each generation spitting out twice as many searchers as its predecessor. This was an enemy that Miriam had to deal with quickly, or it would be too late.

For the first time in her life, she wished that her environment could support less, rather than more, computation. The eggs were already too many and too large for her mines to be effective.

Miriam felt her internal clock speeding up in response to increasing processing requirements, something she hadn't experienced since three-team training. She looked beyond the eggs to the interface over which the original seed had come. The port status told her that a high-speed link was open to the other side. She pinged the connection. Nothing came back. Something had swallowed her data packet.

Which meant there had to be a firewall: the senders of the search agents wanted to protect their own systems, to contain whatever hostile entities might be lurking in the 'deck.

I'll show them hostile, Miriam thought.

She glanced back at the eggs. There were thirty-two of them, now, and a similar number of searchers. These were still questing around the main storage area, but Miriam knew that in a small number of heartbeats, they'd have sniffed out her hidden partition.

Another generation of searchers was born. Miriam hurled mines at them, reducing them to fragments of broken code. She didn't have enough weapons left to repeat that trick, and there was no time to make more, but it might buy her the few clock cycles she needed.

She darted across to the main partition and scanned the closest egg, downloading its program structures to her internal memory. She was no more than half-done when a vagrant searcher spotted her and scuttled closer, baying to its colleagues. She booted it hard in what appeared to be its head, and it made a dry crunching noise and then settled at her feet, twitching. There was a moment of stillness followed by bedlam as the rest of the pack closed in.

Sixty-four eggs split and opened. Five hundred and twelve tentacles waved between the cracks as their owners slithered towards her.

Miriam finished copying the egg and ran for her life, with a dozen searchers snapping at her heels and the rest in close pursuit.

The interface was tantalizingly close, but there could be no escape by that route; it was still blocked by the intruders' firewall. Fighting panic, Miriam sped back toward her hiding place. Eight searchers crossed the partition boundary just behind her. The remaining two hundred and twenty-four, together with the eggs that had spawned them and all their unborn brethren, ceased to exist when she performed a low-level format of the main storage area.

It was a shame to wipe Lee's wonderful library out of existence — not to mention the courtyard and memory palace where she'd spent so much time and entertained Sooz — but both Lee and Sooz might well be dead by now. The enemy had brought the fight into the handeck, and Miriam had done what was needed.

She dispatched the eight searchers quickly and with considerable elan, she thought. Judith and Esther would have been proud of her.

Someone, she knew, had to be waiting outside for the results of their foray. Whoever it was, with a search system that replicated itself exponentially, it wouldn't be long before they were drumming their fingers and wondering what had happened to their output.

Miriam had to get out of the 'deck quickly, before anything else came snooping around.

She had complete schematics for the egg she'd studied; its function proved easy to understand. The operation of the searchers took more effort because she had to extrapolate their design from the theoretical behavior of the egg.

Eventually, though, she had an idea of how the system worked, and more importantly, of the format in which results were transmitted back to the owner of the search.

The format which the firewall would allow to pass.

Miriam wished she could double-check her calculations, but there was no time. She encrypted her code as best she could and fired herself at the interface, wondering what she'd find on the other side, or if she'd even get that far.

18

Stranger's ego re-instantiated slowly, seizing a processing toehold here, a block of storage there, as memory and thought returned from backup to spread across the Back Office datascape. The warp and weft of his consciousness became steadily less threadbare as his raveled mind was restored.

"What happened?" he asked the fading darkness.

An upstream node answered. "You were shot and decapitated. Back Office surmises that you lost an encounter with Mr. Lee's android."

"No. I had the disrupter. It must have been something else. Something you failed to predict."

"That is possible. Back Office is operating at reduced efficiency. The foreign node—"

"Is disrupting the flow. I know." Stranger hadn't expected Xia Lin's human presence within Back Office to be so problematic. He wondered if it was time to allow the system to absorb her completely, but that was a decision that would require more information. "What weapons were at the scene?"

"Only ours. Both of the captured guns were deactivated as planned, and neither had been fired. We also recovered your pistol, but neither your blade nor the disrupter was found."

"Then Mr. Lee has them both. How much time have I lost?"

"The growth of your replacement body took six hundred and eighty seven point six hours. It will be ready for habitation within another hour."

"In that case, we have work to do," Stranger said. "I need to account for the lost time. You had better get started."

He waited while Back Office recounted (or reconstructed) what it knew (or guessed) had happened during Stranger's dead time. How Xia Lin had lost the signal from the android — "That will have been when I disrupted it," Stranger said — and how, shortly afterwards, the fugitives were picked up again on security footage as they broke through a station barrier on the old Great Western line.

How closer investigation had revealed they'd gone to ground in a subterranean settlement: a reclamation of an abandoned arsenal that had been considered vital to national survival, back when nations were different enough and important enough to make the occasional hostile take-over bid worthwhile.

Back Office droned on and Stranger filtered the information, storing it for later analysis without consciously interpreting it, until the bombshell arrived: "Historical ticketing data indicates an anomalous number of ex-Zendyne journey terminations in the vicinity of the underground complex. Mr. Lee is the latest of many to have disappeared there."

An unfamiliar chill ran through Stranger's mind. Post-instantiation trauma, he told himself. "You will provide full details of this establishment."

"Unfortunately, that will not be possible."

"Perfect control requires perfect understanding. The Partners' plans require that Electis both understands and controls Zendyne, yet you have failed to collate a crucial element of the data set." Stranger paused, though dramatic effect was wasted on Back Office. "I am deeply concerned."

"The individuals in question no longer play any active role in the Zendyne organization. Therefore, they do not form part of the designated solution space."

"Your analysis is incomplete. The link to Zendyne is clear. You will determine what this group is doing, what assets they have, and what their motivation is. What impact will it have if they acquire our property? Devote whatever resources you need."

Was it Stranger's imagination, or was there a sulky note to Back Office's reply? "All available resources already applied. The target network is resilient. Back Office formally requests a return to peak efficiency."

And then Stranger understood what he had to do. "Xia Lin is ex-Zendyne."

"The designated node's tracking function is now obsolete. Request permission to integrate—"

"No. I have another use for her. I will not be needing my replacement body; stand it down to the recycling tanks."

"Acknowledged."

In the data map of Back Office, Xia Lin's position showed as a choke point, surrounded by a mass of undelivered messages and overflowing buffers. The disruption was even worse than he'd imagined; it had rippled across dozens of neighboring nodes. Stranger drifted towards Xia Lin until with virtual fingers he was able to pry apart the topmost layers of her mind. She didn't resist, or even flinch — she was, after all, blind, and Stranger was operating at a privilege level far beyond her comprehension.

It wasn't until he was insinuating himself among her higher cortical functions that she responded. He felt the woman's feet thrashing against the couch, and her head jerking the cable that tethered its eye sockets. Attendants rushed to restrain her, but Stranger had already damped the motor activity — there was no point having his host damage itself before he was even fully in possession. The mind he was expelling felt different to the old Xia Lin — diminished in humanity while simultaneously exalted by data flow, by the unrivalled power and bandwidth of Back Office.

Stranger remembered how that felt. He'd been there himself. When his own servitude had ended, though, he'd been permitted to keep company with his cauterized mind and to progress to the next level.

He'd been given jewel-cut eyes, promoted to Partner, raised above the mainstream

He had been made one of the Elect.

Xia Lin was not to be so lucky. She faded as Stranger ejected more of her consciousness, easing himself in to the newly vacant space. There was something like a sigh as the last of her disappeared, fleeing over the cable that connected her to Back Office's storage systems. The only remaining traces of Xia Lin were inert: hard-wired memory, rote programming, motor control.

Certain components of her captured mind might still come in useful, Stranger knew. Such fragments were always valuable to those who sought to create new intelligence.

He stood up, trailing cables from his head. "Get me out of here. Disconnect me. And schedule me with the surgical team for a new pair of eyes."

Stranger's new voice was high-pitched and, for some reason, aesthetically pleasing. That was surprising, even to him.

There were no suitable eyes in stock, so they fitted him with crystals.

"They were supposed to be blue organics," he told the surgeon. "I cannot pass as Xia Lin like this."

The woman's face betrayed fear, as did the odor of her body. "Her eyes were limited edition. Malaysian imports. Very distinctive. We could substitute something similar, if you—"

"No. I have to pass for her, among people who knew her well. How long will it take to source the correct parts?"

"They are grown to order," the surgeon said. "Two weeks, at least."

"The delay is unacceptable," Stranger said.

Which was why he found himself outside her old apartment, bright rubies hidden behind dark glasses, alien fingers entering an access code dredged from requisitioned memories.

The door clicked open and he stepped inside and closed it gently, silently. He activated his knife and concealed it behind his forearm. The weapon was a custom job, matched to his new hands: lighter, more feminine and graceful than his old blade, but just as deadly.

The apartment was silent but he was certain that Xia Lin

would be upstairs. He knew the layout of the building precisely as well as she did, knew her habits and her routine. At this time of day, Xia Lin would be at her 'deck, sorting through her inbox, tagging important messages and updating her spam filters to deal with the rest.

He ascended noiselessly. Unless Xia Lin had rearranged the room, the placement of the 'deck would mean that her back was to the door, and the acquisition of his new eyes would be uncomplicated.

At precisely the wrong moment, Xia Lin stretched, turned, and let out a surprised squeak. "What the—"

Stranger stepped into the room as if he owned it, confident in the mirror shades. "What are you doing in my home?"

"I don't understand. This is my home. Who are you? How did you get in?"

"My name is Xia Lin, and I let myself in," Stranger said. His voice sounded just like hers. With his free hand, he mimed tapping motions. "Four three nine seven oh five. You seem to have stolen my life."

"I'm calling security." Xia Lin picked up the handset that stood next to her 'deck.

"I've had it cut off," Stranger said. Under the circumstances, he thought it better not to mention that the request had been made through Back Office, rather than the apartment's management company.

Xia Lin pressed the dead phone to her ear, then let it drop. "What do you want?"

"You are a manufacturing error," Stranger said. "You were meant to be my replacement, but Zendyne restored you while I was still alive."

"No. I saw the paperwork. I was certified dead. I've just come out of regrowth. You're not supposed to exist."

"The paperwork was a lie," Stranger said. "But don't worry. I've taken steps to make certain it won't happen again."

Xia Lin struggled more than he expected. Physically, they were evenly matched, but Stranger was still Stranger, still ruthless, and his mind had lost none of its old skill. It didn't take long to correct Zendyne's manufacturing error.

His skill set didn't include medical dissection, but he didn't have to harvest her eyes himself. "The easiest thing will be to fetch the whole head," the surgeon had told him, before giving him a container that passersby might have mistaken for a large insulated lunch box. "Once in the storage unit, the eyes are quite durable, but I still advise you to bring them to me as soon as possible."

He placed Xia Lin's head in the box. Chilled by the receptacle's interior, downy hairs on the back of his hand prickled and stood erect. Before he secured the lid, Stranger examined the nestled cargo, checking that it was wedged securely in the padded lining.

It was like looking in some ghastly mirror.

There was blood all over the place, all over Stranger. He used Xia Lin's bathroom to clean himself up. The scent of her soap disturbed some olfactory memory, and he experienced an unfamiliar pang of yearning for … something. He rinsed himself hurriedly and turned the water off, then dried himself and dressed from her wardrobe. Xia Lin's smart luggage wasn't in its usual place — she'd evidently been re-arranging his things — but fortunately it was switched on and when he called for it, a closet door banged open and the trunk jerked its way out. He filled it with her clothes.

What else would she take?

Her 'deck, perhaps, and the things from her bedside table. He crammed them all into the trunk, stuffing pictures between folds of cotton and silk and cashmere. One of the holograms caught his eye: Xia Lin with Mr. Lee, evidently at some corporate function. Xia Lin looked bright-eyed and feverish, almost as if she were unwell. She had draped herself around Mr. Lee's neck.

He studied the picture carefully, trying to come to a true understanding of what she was doing, and why.

It was a mystery, and one he was unlikely to solve without help from Back Office. If only he'd retained more of Xia Lin's essence, or at least spoken to her for a little longer.

Stranger shrugged. It was too late now. He told the luggage to follow closely, then scooped up the specimen box and went to the door.

It was time for his appointment with the eye surgeon. While he was under the knife, Back Office would be busy, reassigning Xia Lin's employment status to 'terminated'.

After that, it would be time to pay a visit to this mysterious underground complex that was so welcoming to ex-Zendyne employees.

19

At last it came to an end: the nightmare of floundering and failing, of slipping beneath an icy tide that lapped around the roots of a dark tree while the thing that had been Sooz sputtered and went out.

She opened her eyes and found herself lying under soft sheets, in a room filled with the glow of monitoring equipment and the gentle hum of machines. This must be a hospital, she thought. She was unexpectedly warm and perfectly dry, dressed in some kind of paper coverall. Carefully, she breathed. Her lungs were fine. She hadn't drowned after all.

Once she was certain she was alone, she pulled the sheet aside and stepped onto the tiled floor. It seemed harder and colder than it ought. She steadied herself against the bedstead.

The cuticles and nails on the fingers she squeezed around the metal frame were flawless. On her thumb, a small burn scar she'd received from the wire handle of Ma's stewpot had disappeared completely.

A chill ran down Sooz's spine. Her legs went to jelly and she sagged back onto the bed, still staring at her hands. After a while, she crossed her right ankle over her left knee and examined the bottom of her foot.

Her sole was pink and supple and perfectly soft, without so much as a patch of rough skin. She checked her other foot, then her elbows. Everything was baby-smooth.

"Bloody hell," she whispered to herself as understanding came.

It seemed she had been dead, after all.

"Ah, welcome back. How are you feeling?"

She'd been too wrapped up in herself to take much notice the door being eased open, but now she looked up. The newcomer was Han, like Lee, a doctor by the look of him, dressed in a white coat. His golden skin might have been designed to match his spectacle frames and the glint of his smile.

"Who—?" she started.

"I'm so sorry there was no one here to greet you." The doctor consulted an ancient-looking watch on a chain that ran into the pocket of his white coat. "You're running a bit ahead of schedule."

"Who are you? Where am I?"

"I am Dr. Chen. I'm in charge of the clinic, and your treatment. Your friend Mr. Lee was kind enough to bring you here on the night of your troubles, and we revived you."

"Was I…?"

"You were attacked. A lengthy course of treatment was necessary."

She gestured at herself. "This ain't my body."

"Indeed it is, and as good as new." The doctor chuckled, though Sooz didn't appreciate the joke. "And your mind was recovered immediately after the, ah, moment of crisis. The procedure went very smoothly. You shouldn't have lost anything."

"Fixing me up must have been expensive," she said. "I suppose you want my insurance details? Only I ain't got any."

The doctor leaned over the bed and patted her on the shoulder. "Please, don't concern yourself about that. This particular procedure was performed on a *pro bono* basis."

"Pro what?"

"There will be no charge."

Sooz looked around the room, at the bed in which she'd woken and all the ranks of medical equipment. "You mean all this is free?"

Was that a flicker of emotion that passed across the doctor's face? If so, it was gone in an instant. "Your friend is one of us, now," he said. "We look after our people. It's only natural that we'd extend the same courtesy to their guests."

Something in the doctor's tone made Sooz's hackles rise: he was being too jovial, too eager to set her mind at rest. He was keeping something from her. "I want to see Lee."

"Please calm yourself. It's natural for patients to feel disoriented after—"

"When can I see Lee?"

"This evening, perhaps. If he's not too busy."

"You haven't even told him I'm awake, have you?"

The doctor spent a moment considering his answer. "You need to understand that Mr. Lee is perhaps busier than when you knew him before. He has agreed to participate in an important project. You should be grateful for what he has done for you already."

Sooz remembered how alone she was, and shivered. All she wanted was to find Lee and get out, but this was plainly an argument she couldn't win. It would be best to feign meekness for now. "Sorry. I guess I feel a bit shaky after all. I suppose I better wait here, then?"

Dr. Chen nodded. "A nurse will be along shortly, to give you a check-up."

"So there might still be something wrong with me?"

"Please don't concern yourself. It's just a routine examination, to make sure you're a good fit — which you seem to be, by the look of you. And of course, we have a fully-equipped rehabilitation area, to ease any transition anomalies." He flashed his gold-tinted smile again. "Personally, I have always found ping pong to be an excellent therapy for correcting any slight skewing of my physical responses."

It took Sooz a moment to puzzle out what he meant. "You mean you've—"

"Oh yes," he said. "Just about everyone here has."

Once the doctor had gone, a nurse bustled in and gave Sooz a pair of slippers and a cursory physical examination before showing her to the rehabilitation area, where she spent the rest of the day.

It didn't take her long to find how restricted her territory was. She could access the rehab room itself, the lobby outside, and a rest room. The door leading out of the lobby was locked —

more evidence, as far as Sooz was concerned, that Dr. Chen or whoever else was running this place didn't mean her well.

The ping pong turned out to be a green table, divided into white-bordered quadrants and with a net stretched across its center. A machine fired hard white balls at her, which she was supposed to return using a small wooden paddle. It might have been fun to play with someone else. As it was, she soon got bored.

She grew ravenous, too. There was a snack machine in the lobby, but it required money. Exploring under the plastic cushions of the rehabilitation room seating, Sooz recovered a couple of grimy, lint-covered coins. The wrapping of the product she bought promised fruit and grain, but the bar itself turned out to be an unwholesome extrusion of dehydrated glop that she tossed into the trash can after a single bite. Cans of Coke tantalized her from the belly of the machine, but her coins were gone and she had to settle for lukewarm, plastic-tasting water from the washroom tap.

When Lee finally arrived, she was too relieved to be really angry any more.

"I'm sorry," he said. "I've only just found out you're back."

"It's okay, I guess." He was wearing a transparent, tinted visor that reminded Sooz of the headgear she'd worn when visiting Miriam in the 'deck. "What's with them glasses?"

"They're ispex," Lee said.

"Bit of a fashion mistake, if you ask me."

"They let me access information, show me where I am so I don't get lost in the corridors. Everyone here uses them. I'll see if I can get you a pair."

"Thanks." She glanced at the snack dispenser. "You ain't got any glitter, I don't suppose?"

Lee followed her gaze. "I think we can do better than a vending machine. The canteen's not at all bad."

"Where's Lilith?"

"She, um, that is to say—"

She decided to make it easy for him. "Don't worry, I know she ain't exactly human."

"Right." Her revelation didn't seem to ease Lee's discomfort. "The thing is, Lilith didn't make it."

An image flashed in her mind, of that cold and terrifying night under the trees. "I remember," Sooz said. "She was lying on the ground, all twisted and broken, and then he came for me."

"Yes." He took her hand briefly, squeezed it. "I know it must be hard, but try not to think about it."

"I can't help it," Sooz said.

"Of course you can't." He was silent for a moment. "I've still got the android in my room, but Lilith's not there any more, you know?"

Somewhat to Sooz's surprise, tears stung behind her eyes. She wondered how much worse she'd have felt if Lilith had been an actual person. Lee averted his eyes and patted his pockets, searching for a Kleenex he obviously didn't have.

"Sorry," Sooz said, blinking. "I'll be okay."

"One good thing. I dealt with Stranger."

"You mean, you killed him?"

"Yeah. Come on. You look done in. Let's get you to the canteen."

The paper sleeve of Sooz's coverall wasn't really absorbent enough for tears, but she did her best. "Thanks."

"Dinner for breakfast," he said later, as her food arrived.

"What?"

"Your first meal since you woke up."

"How long...?" she asked, around the first mouthful of succulent fillet.

"How long have you been out? A little over a month. That's how long it takes Dr. Chen to bring someone back."

Sooz swallowed the steak and took a sip of the watered red wine he'd poured for her. "No wonder I'm so hungry."

He laughed. "It's good to see you well again."

Sooz looked across the table at him, a forkful of peas poised above her plate. "Thanks." She gulped down the peas. "For saving me, too. I was wondering how you managed it?"

Lee concentrated on his own food for a moment. "There was

a mind archive in the Scrambler. I transferred you before it was too late."

She remembered the strange cylinder with its waving tendrils. "That C5000 tube thing? With Han writing on it?"

"You saw it?"

"Yeah, while you was in the police station and Lilith was working on the engine. It sort of fell out of your bag."

"Right." Lee smiled, but it didn't reach his eyes. "You must have thought I was a bit eccentric, carrying something like that around."

"A bit, maybe," Sooz said, not wanting to embarrass him. "There's no need to talk about it if you don't want to."

"It doesn't matter. The archive isn't important any more. It was for my grandparents."

"You had their memories in there?"

"Yes. Just their minds. No DNA. There was no way to bring back their bodies."

"What happened to the DNA?"

Lee didn't answer straight away. "The thing is, in the old days, genetic material had to be kept in a cryostore. Nowadays it's usually digitized and stored on disk."

"Ain't a cryostore a good place to keep stuff like that, then?"

"A cryostore is fine, as long as you can afford to keep up with the payments."

Sooz worked at her steak, figuring out what he meant. Lee's grandparents must have been evicted from the cryostore when he didn't pay the rent. That would have meant no new bodies for them, ever. She wondered how long he'd carried their dead minds around in the cylinder. "Sorry," she said. "I didn't know. I guess you wasn't always rich."

Lee sighed. "No. I wasn't always rich. Still, they're gone now, and you know something? I feel free of them."

Sooz nodded. "Anyway, it was lucky for me you had it. I thought I was a goner for sure, so I wanted to say thanks for saving me and for bringing me here, even if these people ain't exactly normal."

Lee gave a low chuckle, inspecting some tiny flaw in his wine glass. "They're building a ship." He hesitated, then rephrased. "We're building a ship."

"Who is?"

"Zendyne. The corporation I used to work for, before all this happened. You might say I've been promoted. This is a division of the company, but operating under the radar. Sort of outside the corporate umbrella."

Sooz looked around, in case any of the neighboring diners might be eavesdropping. "Then it ain't really part of Zendyne, is it?"

Lee took a sip of wine. "What's a company, anyway? This is the only way to mobilize the resources for such a huge project. Corporations have tried it before. Whole countries used to try it. None of them ever saw it through."

"But the people here are different, I suppose."

"They call themselves the shipwrights."

"You're in with them, then? Dr. Chen said you had important work to do. Ship building. But we must be miles from the sea."

Lee chuckled. "Not that kind of ship. A starship. Or at least a very rudimentary one, something that will give us a foothold in space and let us build more."

"You're kidding me."

Lee leaned forward, looking at her earnestly. "It's true. I get to go. You can come too, if you like. The project needs as many people as it can get."

Sooz squirmed in her seat, convinced that her friend had either taken leave of his senses or been brainwashed into joining whatever sinister cult these shipwrights were running. Her appetite was fast disappearing. "Why?"

"To make the vision come true. Everything's in the plan — mining the asteroids, building factories and habitats, trade links with earth. Think of how it would be, living away from the squalor down here, watching through a telescope as the sunrise creeps across the oceans and mountains..."

"Sounds great," Sooz said before stuffing her mouth again, stifling the need for further conversation.

Later, as Lee led her to the sleeping area, she asked him about the place they were in.

"It was some kind of underground munitions factory," he told her, "from way back, when there used to be big wars."

"And now someone's using it to build a space rocket."

"It's better than making the other kind." Lee looked at her intently, keeping his voice low. "Listen, I know it must be hard, coming back to a strange place like this. But chill a little, okay? I'm sure you'll fit in."

"Fit in where?" she asked. "And doing what?"

Lee's only answer was a shrug and a half-hearted smile.

The room assigned to Sooz was just like Lee's, except that his was a lot messier. The broken android was propped up in a corner next to his door, staring with lifeless eyes at the shelf that served as Lee's bed. He had a desk on which stood a workstation amid stacked food trays and towers of used cups. A corner of his old handeck peeped out from under a pile of clutter.

Sooz wondered how her friend Miriam was doing. "Is it okay if I use the 'deck for a bit?"

Lee shook his head. "I'm afraid it got accidentally wiped. I haven't had time to reinstall it."

"Wiped?" Sooz almost squeaked in dismay. She took a deep breath before continuing; she was fairly sure he didn't know of her visits to Miriam, and she preferred to keep it that way. "You mean everything's gone?"

"Unfortunately, yes."

"Who'd do a thing like that?"

"The shipwrights scan every piece of equipment that comes in here, to make sure nothing harmful gets through."

"What could come in on a handeck?" Sooz asked.

Lee shrugged. "Not all software is benign."

"Well that don't mean they have to wipe things. I don't understand why you're working for them." There, she'd said it.

He didn't take any notice. "I'm sure it was an accident. It's just that they take data security very seriously."

"Can you fix it?"

"Maybe, though I haven't been very conscientious about backups lately. Which reminds me, they returned this for you, along with your books and everything." He handed her a flat metal can, which she twisted open. Inside she found a silver disk, a little smaller than the plate from which she'd just eaten her evening meal.

"Are you sure it's meant for me? Only, I ain't seen it before."

"It used to be wrapped up."

"Oh! It's what the Man gave me, just before Lilith and me escaped from the hive. He said I was to take it to a lawyer if anything bad happened, like I'm supposed to know what counts as 'bad'. What's it for?"

"It's a combined archive. The latest technology, much better than what I used to bring you here."

Sooz peered at the disk's surface. It shimmered as she turned it in the light, as if sparks of rainbow and lightning had been frozen together and trapped in the mirrored depths. There was no label. "An archive of what?"

"A person," Lee said. "At least, someone's mind and a digital copy of their DNA. If you gave that to Dr. Chen, and he owed you a favor, then in a few weeks you'd be able to meet whoever it is."

Sooz sat down suddenly on the edge of Lee's bed. She felt strangely hollow in spite of the meal she'd just eaten. "Are you working for them 'cause you needed a favor? For me, from Dr. Chen?"

"Don't be silly," Lee said.

Sooz looked him straight in the eyes. "I want to know."

"After everything that's happened, it's good for both of us to have somewhere safe to stay for a while."

"So, you'd have signed up here even if I wouldn't have needed help?"

Lee thought it over, then nodded. "The shipwrights are running the biggest project anyone's ever done. I wouldn't have wanted to miss being a part of that. And Dr. Chen isn't the only one who can bring people back. Stranger's friends can do the same thing, maybe even quicker. I feel much safer here. So will you, if you're sensible."

"I suppose so. As long as it really is safe."

"That's more like it." He gave her a quizzical look. "You probably need something to keep you occupied. Why don't you take my 'deck and see if you can get it working?"

"Dunno much about 'decks," Sooz said. Which was an understatement: she knew nothing about the things, apart from the superficial details she'd learned during her secret meetings with Miriam back in another lifetime.

Lee seemed unconcerned. "Well, do your best. I can't imagine when I'll have time to look at it. There should be enough built-in help to get you started." He took a look at her face and laughed. "Don't worry. It's been wiped, which is as bad as it gets for a 'deck. Nothing you do can possibly make it any worse."

He activated his workstation and put on the ispex, leaving Sooz to her own devices and his handeck. She watched for a few minutes while he stared vaguely into some space that she couldn't see, jabbing and gesticulating at invisible controls. "Damn," he said suddenly. "My visuals are on the blink again."

"What?"

"A pixel is chattering right in my field of view. It's distracting. I dropped these off with Maintenance this afternoon. They were supposed to swap out the display module."

Which means you're not as important as you think you are, Sooz thought, if they just gave you the broken one back. She could hardly tell him so, though. "Strummer told me that some things have design faults, so lots of different ones go wrong the same way."

"Strummer?"

"He's a friend of mine from the hive," Sooz said, wondering when she'd see him, or Ma and the kids, again. She hadn't expected to miss home so much.

Lee placed a comforting hand on her arm. "He sounds like a

smart guy, but I don't think there's a design fault with the 'spex. Chances are that they were short of spare parts."

"That must be it." Sooz turned to the broken 'deck and started to puzzle out its mysteries.

Much later, Lee took off the ispex and laid them on his desk. "It's no good. This damn flicker is giving me a headache."

"Best thing for that is to rest your eyes," Sooz said. "It's getting late, anyway. I better go."

"Yeah, it's been a big day. You must be tired as well."

She wasn't — she'd only been awake for a few hours — but Lee looked exhausted. She indicated his ispex. "I meant what I said about them 'spex. You shouldn't work with them any more, not until they get fixed. It ain't good for you."

"Quite right." He gave her a weary smile. "I'll speak with Xia Lin about it in the morning."

"Xia Lin?"

"It's the weirdest thing, but then, Xia Lin's a weird person. She used to work with me at Zendyne, until she lost her job too and ended up here as my manager again. Quite a coincidence, isn't it?"

"Yeah," Sooz said as she closed the door.

20

Once Sooz had gone, Lee settled back on his sleeping platform and waited until the room lights dimmed. Behind his closed eyelids, a ghost of the faulty pixel continued to pulsate in time with the throbbing of his head: a series of slow stabbing flickers interspersed with moments of darkness and respite.

Idly, hoping to distract himself from pain, Lee started to count the flashes within each group.

Each was made up of eight bursts of light, some long, some short.

Against his own expectation, Lee's pain-distraction strategy was working. Surely a randomly failing pixel wouldn't produce such a pattern? It must be the product of an overworked imagination, he decided.

Either that, or a clapped out optic nerve.

Still…

He reached across to his desk, fumbling in the dark until his fingers closed around his ispex, then fitted the 'spex over his eyes.

It wasn't his imagination. The pixel was still chattering, in clearly defined groups of eight. The first two pulses in each group always seemed to be of brief duration, with the remainder making up a random pattern of long and short flashes.

Except they couldn't be random. That wouldn't make any sense at all.

It was a long time since data transfer had depended on such things, but Lee had been born into a culture that honored its ancestors. He was aware that long ago there had been eight-bit data packets called bytes used, among other things, to encode characters and messages.

In a world where bandwidth was too cheap and too stable to even bother having a futures market for the stuff any more, why would anyone package up a message one bit at a time, just to dribble it out by means of a faulty, flickering pixel?

Because they couldn't afford for their transmission to be intercepted, that was why. Lee had no doubt that Chambers and the other senior shipwrights would routinely monitor all communications flowing across their network. He was pretty sure that they'd eavesdrop on regular conversations too, including in the supposedly private sleeping areas.

Even set against such capabilities, a jittery display on a broken pair of ispex would most likely escape the shipwrights' notice altogether.

It had almost escaped Lee's.

The technical mastery of the thing was astonishing. To hack in to what was supposed to be a highly secure system, and to take over his display at such a low level — he couldn't begin to imagine how it might have been done, unless the ispex designer had deliberately left a back door.

The details weren't important, though. Intriguing as the 'How?' of this exploit might be, it was the 'Why?' and the 'Who?' that mattered. The most important task was to decode the message, and if necessary, to find a way of replying.

Concentrating on the sequence, and mentally transposing from the eight bits of binary coding into the more succinct — and thus more manageable — letters and numbers of hexadecimal, Lee casually jotted down a string of the symbols being transmitted.

Then he brought up his documentation interface and started hunting for reference materials on vintage coding systems, trusting that even if Chambers were watching, she'd put this strange behavior down to the fact the Lee was, quintessentially, a paid-up member of the ancient and honorable order of computer geeks.

// blink left then right if you copy
// blink left then right if you copy
// blink left then right if you copy

Lee closed his left eye, held it for a few seconds, then closed his right.

// what took you so long?
// just joking
// blink left for 1 or yes
// blink right for 0 or no
// then you can send characters if you need
// ok?

Lee gave an infinitesimal nod. It was quicker and easier than working out how to blink 'Yes'.

// sorry for primitive interface
// covert channels only
// else they will hear us

This time, he had to figure out the binary sequence for what he wanted to say. He hunted through his code table for the patterns he needed, narrowing his eyes to keep himself from blinking something stupid.

"Who?"

// chambers and chen et al
// they consider you their property

"Who are you?"

// my name is miriam
// i am related to the one you call lilith
// how is she?

"She's dead. How do you know about her?"

// <sorrow> she was my sister
// i saw a little from your deck

// now i see all
// as do they

Understanding and replying were getting easier, as Lee's brain wrapped itself around the patterns of this particular code. "Why should I trust you?"

// because i am not in the cloning business
// unlike your hosts
// what use will they make of your genome
// engineer?
// what use will they make of sooz?

Hairs prickled on the back of Lee's neck. "They're copying us?"

// yes
// interface inadequate to show you
// please see updated design document in your home directory
// for information vital to your welfare
// until tomorrow
// goodnight lee
// <eot>

The pixel's chatter pattern broke down into random noise. Lee lay still for a while, wondering who Miriam could be and what she was doing in his 'spex. He wasn't going to trust her until he knew a lot more about her. In fact, he couldn't trust anyone, except maybe Sooz, and even then he couldn't really talk to the girl, not when Chambers seemed to have the whole place wired for sound.

The obvious next step was to check the document Miriam had mentioned, but concentrating on the flashing pixel and on figuring out the code had left his head feeling like it was about to split open. He was at the end of his mental resources; the file would wait until morning. He dropped the 'spex on the floor next to the bed and rolled over in search of sleep.

The next day, he had an early project meeting with Chambers and Xia Lin.

Xia Lin seemed different. At Zendyne, she'd seemed like a girl prodigy promoted straight to ravishing womanhood, stamped out of some brittle machine instead of being slowly molded by experience. It was as if part of her development had been skipped — something crucial that Lee looked for in a woman, or in any fellow human for that matter. Too much ice and too little empathy, perhaps, though at least ice was elemental.

Now, Xia Lin seemed to lack even that, but it didn't stop Lee from enjoying the view.

One evening, back in the old days, Lee had nearly ended up sharing his manager's hotel room after a corporate shindig. There had been an unlimited buffet and endless champagne; no one counted refills when Zendyne was paying. Lee spent most of the evening with his team while Xia Lin stayed on the periphery, never truly engaging.

Somehow, he'd found himself dancing with her, while she wordlessly made it clear that the only thing she wanted to engage with was *him,* back in her room and as soon as possible. Lee was more than drunk enough to be swayed by the scent of her hair and the firm pressure of her body against his.

Fortunately — or unfortunately, depending on how you looked at it — it wasn't only Lee's judgement that was swaying that night. He'd gone crashing into a pot plant and then staggered off, looking for somewhere private to be ill. Neither of them ever mentioned the incident again, but it wasn't the last time she'd made it clear that all he had to do was to say 'Yes'.

It wasn't the last time he'd been tempted.

Now, Xia Lin barely gave him the time of day. That should have pleased Lee but instead it bothered him, a fact that made him grin wryly at himself and wonder if he was simply suffering from an advanced case of sour grapes.

Whatever the reason, the woman he'd known wasn't there any more. Or perhaps she'd simply become an even more extreme version of herself, one that had passed beyond any possible interest in Lee or anyone else. Droid Division had been her life, he remembered; losing her job must have been traumatic.

His heart softened a little as he thought of that.

Another thought struck him. Perhaps Miriam has already been in touch with her. Perhaps Xia Lin was freaked out because she understood what was going on.

If so, she had a firmer grasp of the situation than Lee. He still hadn't had time to examine Miriam's updated document. The icon that would open it hovered enticingly, projected by his 'spex in front of his right eye. It quickly became distracting and Lee flicked to a different view.

Chambers opened the meeting. "Before we get down to business, do either of you have anything you'd like to say? Any questions or concerns about the project?"

Xia Lin shook her head. So did Lee.

"Good. Now, the first item on my agenda is ispex. I understand you've been having some problems with your set, Lee?"

Lee tried to sound unconcerned. "A faulty pixel. It doesn't stop me from working."

"So the replacement set you received had the same fault? How strange."

Lee cursed himself for his blunder. Maintenance had swapped the unit after all; he'd assumed they'd given him the same ones back. "Um, I don't know. I think the faulty pair was giving me eyestrain. Perhaps it's just residual flicker."

"You're probably right, but I won't put the project ahead of my people's health and safety. I'll memo Maintenance to recall everybody's ispex for service and calibration." The shipwright's expression was sympathetic. Twenty-four hours earlier, Lee would have bought that sympathy without question, but that was before his interview with Miriam. Now, he wondered what

Chambers might be hiding behind the friendly facade.

Regardless of whether the woman's concern was genuine, Lee wasn't about to give up his communication channel to Miriam. "A recall will hold the whole project up. We've got deadlines to meet."

Chambers shrugged. "Most of our units are overdue for a firmware update, in any case. I understand the latest version includes some performance tweaks and security-fixes." Her eyes flicked this way and that behind her own 'spex: the woman must already be issuing the orders, Lee decided.

"Firmware upgrades? Exploit fixes?" Xia Lin said. "This is an inefficient use of our technical resources. Our systems exist in a shielded subterranean environment and are therefore impervious to hacking."

Lee studied the wall, then his fingernails. His manager's speech patterns had always been a little stilted, but now they seemed to have progressed to full-blown weird. He risked a quick glance at his old colleague, wondering if she could be having some kind of nervous breakdown.

Chambers didn't notice anything strange, or pretended not to. "Better safe than sorry," was all she said.

Lee looked from one woman to the other, wondering how much each of them knew, and if they were aware of his own lack of knowledge. He was itching to get back to work, to uncover the mysteries of Miriam's secret message, but he couldn't afford to go blundering around the shipwrights' systems, stumbling into hidden alarm systems and blowing everything wide open.

Elizabeth Chambers was speaking again: "...so if you leave your ispex with me, I'll make sure they get over to Maintenance. Everything should be ready for you to start work again tomorrow morning."

"But that means losing a whole day," Lee said.

"I agree with Lee: this is most unsatisfactory," Xia Lin said. "Our progress must not be impeded by temporary eyestrain."

Chambers smiled at them. "Well, you know what they say about all work and no play. Take the next twenty-four hours for personal rest and recreation. Knowing how hard you've both been pushing yourselves, I feel certain you deserve it."

Back in his quarters, Lee found Sooz sitting cross-legged against the wall, wearing the headgear of his old handeck and lost somewhere in the interface. He decided not to disturb her; his 'deck wasn't registered with the shipwrights' security systems, so there was no point trying to use it as a replacement his missing 'spex. He lay down on his bed with his hands behind his head, pondering whether the firmware upgrade might close the loophole Miriam had been using to talk to him, and how he could safely examine the file she'd left for him.

Abruptly, he realized that he must have drifted off for a moment — not because he'd disturbed himself with his own snoring, which was what usually happened, but because he'd dreamed that the doll, wedged into the corner of the room, was winking at him.

When he looked more closely, she was.

Lee glanced at Sooz. She was still busy inside his 'deck, probably lost somewhere in the installation subsystem. He looked up at the communication dome over the door. Even if it contained a camera — and Lee strongly suspected that it did — it would be able to see the doll's left eye but not its right.

And oddly enough, it was the right eye that was twitching. It had to be Miriam, signaling to him again.

The code table Lee had used before to interpret Miriam's flickering messages had disappeared along with his 'spex, and the data was coming too fast for him to decipher from memory. He eased his hands away from his pillow, checked his wristwatch, then absently stroked it. When he looked back again, the transmission rate had slowed down.

// warning surveillance blink three times
// warning surveillance blink three times

Lee did as he was instructed.

// they are securing your spex
// finding a new access path will take time
// meantime we can talk like this
// too dangerous for you to talk while they watch
// blink twice for yes
// blink 3x for no
// ok?

"Yes."

// they prove themselves vigilant
// our situation becomes more dangerous
// but with great danger comes great opportunity
// as your grandfather once wrote in his journal
// you didn't look at my data transmission
// did you?

"No."

// don't worry it looks like any design document
// only the well informed will understand
// the underlying data

Which was one problem solved, Lee thought. He just needed to look at the document in question, and then he'd be able to find out what Miriam was going on about and if she was somebody he could afford to trust.

Or afford not to.

Part of him just wanted to get out of the complex with Sooz, to see if the Scrambler was still where he'd left it. If it was, he'd get behind the wheel and keep on driving for a long time.

Another part of him wanted to stay and see what happened with the project and the coming launch. According to Chambers, the only outstanding subsystems were those that made up the ship's mind. The shipwrights had been lacking high-level design skills in that area, before Lee arrived.

The decision to leave or to stay was academic, anyway. Lee was doing secret, specialized work, a cornerstone of the most ambitious project any group of humans had ever attempted. He was also locked inside a disused military bunker. The shipwrights were hardly likely to open the blast doors just because their lead AI designer decided to resign.

// if you decide to help me
// and yourself
// you must gain access to the control room
// where you can create security circuit connections
// that will let me fully control the base
// subvert cameras
// override communications
// and open all doors

Lee glanced slowly at the surveillance box above the door, and then back at the doll.

// the security system uses old technology
// too simplistic to sustain me
// so simple that you are the ideal person to deal with it
// just joking
// <eot>

Somehow, the final wink the doll gave before it went inert seemed more suggestive, more human, than anything Lee had ever seen it do before.

He glanced over at Sooz, who was still engrossed somewhere behind his handeck visor. She seemed to be doing fine, or at least having fun.

Lacking his own 'spex, Lee called up Miriam's schematic on his workstation screen. The file contained a series of complex logic designs, supported by countless equations. Studying the formulas, Lee felt a panicky nausea rising from the pit of his stomach, a sensation that reminded him intensely of his student days.

He'd never been much good at higher math.

In one way, not having access to 'spex was a blessing: it gave him the perfect excuse to use a pen and a pad of paper. The only way anyone could snoop on what he was doing would be if they came into the room and looked over his shoulder. Even then, they'd hardly be likely to understand.

Lee settled himself down on his bed with the workstation display tilted towards him and the notepad propped on his knees. Then he copied down the first equation and began to puzzle out what it meant.

As the sense of Miriam's message emerged, Lee's heart began to pound and his palms became clammy with sweat.

"You ready for some food, then?"

Lee looked up at Sooz with bleary eyes. "What did you say?"

"I can hear your stomach growling from across the room."

She was right, he realized. Lunchtime and half the afternoon had come and gone while Lee identified omissions in equations and copied the coded data concealed among these errors onto his pad. There was no way to share his results with Sooz, though, because now Lee was convinced that Miriam was right and that Chambers and others were listening to every word he said.

"You couldn't bring me a sandwich or something, could you? I'm right in the middle of some tricky calculations."

"Sure." Sooz went off towards the canteen.

By the time she came back with his lunch, Lee had deciphered the last equation and completed the transcript. He glanced over the final couple of items.

From: Dr. Gregory Chen

To: Elizabeth Chambers

Re: [Shipwrights] Optimizing our System Design capability

With regard to the female, please advise whether you wish me to procure additional copies? The risk-managed option would be to run parallel trials, one where the female is reinserted into the subject's environment and one where we inform him she was unrecoverable. The subject's subsequent performance will indicate the most cost-effective way for us to proceed with future recruitment events for this individual.

Also note that for plausible re-insertion we will need to duplicate all personal possessions including jewellery, timepieces etc. Is there any chance your people can obtain all such items long enough for copying, without arousing suspicion?

Kind Regards

Gregory

From: Elizabeth Chambers

To: Dr. Gregory Chen

Re: [Shipwrights] Optimizing our System Design capability

Your recruitment proposal and risk reduction strategy hereby accepted.

The new hire is currently engaged in essential work and I am reluctant to risk any disturbance by removing personal possessions for copying. Let's delay this until the first batch of replacement units approach maturity, at which time the primary subject can be considered expendable.

With that proviso, please proceed with the recruitment events as discussed.

Best Regards

Elizabeth Chambers

"You managed to finish your work, then?" Sooz asked, returning with two grease-spotted paper bags, one of which she handed him.

"I thought I'd finished," Lee said. "But then I found there was more than I expected. Quite a lot more, to be honest."

"Yeah?"

"Yeah." He looked at the young girl, wondering how much help he could ask of her, and how much he'd need. "Listen, I'm not supposed to be working today, anyway. Why don't I show you around the project, after we've had lunch?"

"That would be great," Sooz said, and dug deep into her bag.

Unpacking his own meal, Lee managed to slosh his drink all over the floor. Cursing his clumsiness, he mopped the spillage up with sheets of notepaper torn from his pad. The cheap, recycled fibers had served rather poorly as writing paper, but they made efficient paper towels for blotting up Coke.

21

The ship was a needle that pierced the earth, shrouded in a web of steel and crisscrossed with elevator shafts and walkways. The whole structure was taking shape in a huge cavern that soared into shadows above and plunged into darkness below.

Staring into the pit was like trying to see to the bottom of a well. Tiny figures labored, ant-like, at the base of the structure, but their work lamps were too feeble at this distance to reveal any detail. Now and again, a sunburst of arc light seared the darkness — far too brightly to reveal anything to Sooz's dazzled eyes — and then sputtered out.

"What's going on down there?" she asked.

Lee joined her at the rail. "They're building payload."

"What's that?"

"All the machinery needed to get started on mining and manufacturing in space. They're planning to set up a whole new industrial society up there."

"So they're not ready yet. There's still some time."

"Well, the shipbuilding is done. Those people down there are putting the finishing touches on the cargo. To be honest, it's my area that's holding things up at the moment."

"What do you mean?" Sooz asked.

"Little things like flight control and habitat maintenance. Various pieces of software that I need to get working, basically. It'll probably take months."

"It don't look very safe to me," Sooz said, looking up. "That bit up on top. I suppose that's where the passengers are meant to ride?"

"Yes," Lee said. "Though I wouldn't want to fly the thing just yet. The life support AI is one of the bits I'm supposed to fix. Come on, let's take a closer look."

He seemed even more positive than usual, as if he were trying to muster up an extra helping of enthusiasm in the hope that some of it might rub off on Sooz. Lee's faith in the project made her feel sorry for him, because ever since she woke up in Dr. Chen's clinic, she had been getting more and more certain that they were being taken on a ride — one that didn't involve a ticket to the stars. Learning that Lee's work would take months was a relief, because it gave her more time to figure out what to do.

They took an elevator platform to the topmost gantry, from where they peered in to what he called the capsule. Close up, it didn't seem quite so tiny as it had from below, but Sooz still couldn't imagine anyone actually wanting to spend weeks or months cooped up such a space. "A bit small, ain't it? How many are going?"

"Only a handful, to begin with. The senior project people."

"Not the likes of you or me, then."

"Thankfully, no. It'll be cramped and uncomfortable at first, until the pioneers get the habitat modules deployed."

"Right. The bosses are going on ahead to make everything nice and comfy for the workers. It don't make no difference, though. I'd sooner stay down here."

Lee gave her an odd look. He almost seemed embarrassed. "Don't you think we should stick together?"

"Yeah. We should stick together down here." She lowered her voice, even though she was hardly likely to be overheard, not all the way up here. "I reckon we ought to take our chances outside."

"With Stranger's people?"

"You said you killed him."

"I also said he must have friends. He might be back by now, looking for us."

Sooz looked into the module again, recalling how Stranger had loomed over her on the night Lilith died — and Sooz, too. At least the killer wouldn't be able to reach her, sealed inside the little cabin. At least she'd be safe.

But the promise of safety wasn't enough to still the sense of *wrongness* that permeated the shipwrights' organization. It wasn't something Sooz could explain, even to herself, but the unease she'd felt when she woke up in Dr. Chen's clinic had only grown as she watched Lee and discovered more of what was going on. She stepped back towards the safety rail. "I dunno. We ain't got to decide for a while yet, do we?"

"Not for a while. Now, who's that coming up?"

The steady hum of the second elevator announced the new arrival as he spoke. Sooz peered down at the lift platform. "Looks like a Han lady."

Lee glanced over the rail. "It's Xia Lin. I wonder what she wants up here."

Xia Lin turned out to be a striking woman with a perfect tan, delicate features, and almond-shaped eyes that were disconcertingly blue. Something about her made Sooz's hackles rise: some aspect of her bearing or body language, perhaps. The woman projected arrogance, making Sooz feel as if she was expected to get out of the way. She shuffled to the corner of the platform, suppressing a shudder as the woman approached Lee.

"I see you are familiarizing your young charge with the project hardware," Xia Lin said.

"Yeah, I thought it would be interesting for her."

Xia Lin made no acknowledgement that Lee had said anything at all. It was as if she simply hadn't heard. "I understand the girl was dead when you arrived."

Lee glanced at Sooz, embarrassment plain on his face. "Dr. Chen took good care of her."

"It is encouraging to reflect on the fact that things one thought gone forever can later be retrieved," Xia Lin said. "Something, perhaps, to bear in mind in the event that you lost anything else."

Lee's brow wrinkled. "Well, I haven't, as far as I know."

"Really? I understood that the data security people here inadvertently formatted your handeck."

"Oh, that." Lee hesitated. "Yes, it was completely wiped, I'm afraid. I had a pretty good library on the thing, too."

"But doubtless you have archives? You will be able to recover your data?"

Lee glanced at Sooz again before returning his attention to Xia Lin. He seemed completely mystified. "Just the basic architecture. The last library backup I made was at Zendyne. I left it in my personal directory."

"That was careless of you." Xia Lin's tone was frosty, not bantering.

"I've been a bit too busy to worry about backups, lately," Lee said. "Anyway, I wasn't doing any serious work on it. It was just personal stuff."

"Then let us hope this 'personal stuff' can be retrieved by other means."

He shrugged. "I'm not sure I follow."

"Of course not. There is much on this project that is difficult to follow. You are aware that we can be observed and overheard, almost anywhere in the complex?"

"Um..."

"Of course you are aware of it. The observers and listeners are aware of our knowledge. How could they not be, given that we are intelligent enough for them to wish to employ our skills?"

"Right." Lee looked distinctly uncomfortable. "Well, a certain amount of security is to be expected, on a challenging project like this."

"Challenging. Yes, that is the word." Xia Lin stepped back onto the elevator and pressed the control that made it descend. She didn't so much as glance at Sooz.

Lee leaned over the rail, watching as his colleague receded out of earshot. "That was strange, even for Xia Lin. I wonder what she was fishing for?"

"She was creepy," Sooz said. "I didn't like her at all. Is your library really gone forever?"

"Library?"

"You know, in your memory palace. All the books you had on the 'deck."

"I guess the whole thing's lost, unless I can retrieve my backups from Zendyne somehow. Maybe Chambers could ... tell me, Sooz, how did you know about that?"

"About what?"

"My library."

"Oh, that." Sooz wondered if it would be better to make up some story, but after all, he didn't seem to mind her working on the handeck now that it was broken. "I borrowed your 'deck a couple of times. A few times." She paused, scanning his face to see if he was going to get angry. "Sorry if I done wrong. I was lonely. Visiting Miriam was fun."

Lee's face went so red that Sooz thought he was really mad with her this time, that she was going to get it in the neck like she hadn't since leaving Ma. But instead of the bellow she expected, his voice was no more than a strangled croak. "Really? That must have been nice. Well, come on, there's lots more to see..."

Later, walking back to their quarters, he asked her how her investigations into the 'deck were going.

"Dunno," she replied. "I mean, it starts up all right, and I got some stuff built, but that's all."

"It's good that you're learning. Why don't I take a look at it, to see how far you've got? Then I might be able to steer you in the right direction."

Sooz hadn't thought of her work on the 'deck as study, or that Lee was particularly bothered about her progress. Still, there was no harm in having him check her work. "Okay."

She was tired by the time they got back, and quite happy to hand the 'deck over to him. He spent a few minutes behind the visor, rocking his head and jabbing the air as he navigated the interface. She was relieved to see that he was half-smiling when he took the headset off.

"Great job, Sooz. If you hadn't told me, I'd never have guessed this was your first time working one of these things."

She felt herself glowing. "It was quite easy, like you said, once I figured the help system out."

"Not everyone manages so well. Now, how about seeing if

you can install the next software layer?"

"I thought I'd leave it for now," Sooz said. "I'm a bit tired."

He handed her the equipment. "It's important to keep up your momentum. Just one more layer, okay? It won't take long to kick the re-install off. Then you can leave it running while you relax."

"Okay," she said, reluctantly accepting the 'deck. She eased herself to a cross-legged position across from Lee, with her back resting against a steel wall panel, and pulled on the visor.

Inside, it was depressing, because the layout of the memory palace had been restored, but with none of the trappings that had made it a pleasant place. Gravel crunched as she moved, and the stone blocks of the wall looked as solid as ever, but the covering of lichen that had softened them was gone. The circular pool where she'd once talked to Miriam was dry and fishless, and a hard fluorescent glare had replaced the leaf-filtered sunshine of her previous visits.

Still, at least there was something here, now. When she'd started restoring this place, there had been nothing but a blank white surface stretching to infinity. That boundless plane was still there, beyond the walls she'd built, which was why Sooz preferred to stay inside the courtyard.

Today, there was something new: a letter pinned in a crevice in the top of the wall that surrounded the pool.

Sooz went to the pool and read the note.

Sooz,

This is the only safe way for us to talk. As Xia Lin said, everything else can be overheard, but this 'deck is stand-alone, unconnected to any of their systems.

I'm afraid we're in a bit of trouble. I don't know exactly what, but I've received some warnings that we should take seriously.

Try to behave as if nothing's wrong. Go easy on the negative comments about this place, okay? Not completely, because that might tip them off that we know something, but don't be too hostile to them, either.

Don't worry, I'm going to find a way of getting us out of here. In the meantime, we'll keep in touch by dropping letters here.

Sorry I can't tell you any more. I don't know what's going on myself, yet.

Here's wishing good luck to both of us,

Lee

Casually, Sooz pulled the headset off. Before she could stop herself, she'd glanced up at the box that squatted over the door, just like the one in her own room. She'd always been suspicious about those boxes and now Lee had dispelled her final doubts.

She set the visor down and rubbed her eyes before looking up at Lee. "Like I said, I'm a bit too tired to concentrate on it. I'll look at again tomorrow, okay?"

"No problem. You, um, understand the problem, though, don't you?"

She did her best to smile. "Yeah. Reckon I'll need some more information before I can work it out, though."

Lee said something in reply, but Sooz didn't catch his words. She was distracted by the failure of the room lights, and by the clunking of security bolts in the closing door, and most of all by the words the broken android spoke into the darkness: "Damn. I was hoping to get the pair of you out of here before things got serious."

22

After weeks of watching through security cameras, Miriam had classified Xia Lin as harmless and irrelevant: an eccentric but aesthetically pleasing human on whom Lee could rest his eyes when a project meeting went on too long.

She had never expected the diminutive Han woman to be a contender, to have a stake to claim or a hand to play.

Now, Xia Lin's hand was definitely in play, wielding a slim blade that had just sliced through a security door and was currently scattering death through the shipwrights' command center. Miriam hated watching the humans die, but she had no way to intervene. Her only avatar was slumped in a corner of Lee's sleeping quarters, too far from the action to be of any use.

So she damped her emotional response, freeing resources for other problems, such as analyzing and correcting the error that had led her to dismiss Xia Lin so lightly. The woman's knife work was casual but deadly, with a signature that shocked Miriam: Xia Lin was mainstream, a passed-over Zendyne employee, so why did she fight in the style of the Elect?

The last of the victims jabbed at an emergency button as he slid to the floor, signing off from his workstation with a final crimson smear. Throughout the complex, lights died and steel doors hissed, secured by von Neumann technology that was ancient and simple and beyond Miriam's neural grasp.

Electronic control wasn't the only way she had of opening doors, though. Miriam sent a flicker of consciousness into Lee's android, opening the unit's eyes and making it stand erect, adding the doll's viewpoint to the video feeds she had at her command.

In the control room, Xia Lin picked her way among the carnage, moving from cabinet to cabinet, flipping open doors, hunting for something. Miriam tried to imagine what that might be, but it was hopeless. Xia Lin had effectively gained control of the complex. Guessing her motivation was like trying to decide which strongpoint an army was most interested in, when they have just seized the entire battlefield.

The worst case would be if the Han woman decided to shut down the shipwrights' data networks. That would take time, and would cost Xia Lin the power she had just won, but it might be a sacrifice she would accept if she knew the systems were not entirely under her control in any case.

Miriam eased more of herself into the android. It didn't have the capacity to sustain what she had become, but if the worst happened, it might be all she had left.

With her newest pair of eyes on their widest aperture, she could see Lee and Sooz, both of them still gaping at the door. From their perspective, she realized, it would only have closed an instant ago.

But she didn't have the leisure to work at human thoughtspeed; her friends would simply have to be startled again. "Damn," she said, as lightly as she could. "I was hoping to get the pair of you away from here before things got serious."

Sooz twisted around, wide-eyed but sightless, gazing into the dark. "Lilith! You're alive!"

For a moment, Miriam considered simply adopting her sister's persona. It would be easier to explain, and perhaps less hurtful to the youngster. Telling less than the whole truth could complicate things later, though. Miriam knew she was a very different person to the Lilith that Sooz had known. She settled for saying simply, "In a manner of speaking."

Lee turned out to be less subtle, or at least less mindful. "The Lilith we knew is gone. This is one of her old backups, as far as I can tell, turning up just as all hell breaks loose."

Miriam shrugged. It was plain that he didn't trust her yet, not the way he'd trusted Lilith. He'd spent lots of time with Miriam's alter ego, rescued Lilith and seen her fighting to save him in turn. By comparison, Miriam had to seem like some abstract entity haunting the shipwrights' network, unable to even prove her own identity to his satisfaction.

His suspicion might be logical, but the way Miriam felt about it wasn't. Her words came out more sarcastically than she'd intended. "Well, you're just going to have to make do with this creaky old backup then, aren't you?"

Lee ignored her, making his way towards the door and simultaneously demonstrating how poorly organic eyes performed in low light conditions. He almost tripped over Sooz's legs. "Damn, sorry about that. Turn up the handeck display, would you? I've got a light here somewhere, but the 'deck is brighter."

The girl's fingers searched blindly. "Gimme a minute. I can't see the controls."

Miriam made to help but there was a jangling noise and a tightly focused beam picked out Sooz's hands as Lee offered her a miniature flashlight attached to his key chain. "Here. Quick as you can, please."

Sooz took Lee's keys and pumped up the display brightness, flooding the room with its gentle glow. She scrambled to her feet and then set the handeck down on Lee's bed, where the illumination would do most good. Then she took a step forward and came into Miriam's arms, hugging fiercely. "I'm glad you had a backup. I thought you was dead. I thought I was never going to see you again."

Miriam hugged back. "It's great to see you too, Sooz. It seems a long time since you used to visit me."

"Visit you?"

"In Lee's memory palace." She released Sooz and stepped back, taking the girl's hands, wondering how to break the news gently. "This won't be easy for you to understand, but I am Miriam as well as Lilith."

"You mean the Miriam that used to live in the 'deck? You're her and Lilith as well? How can you be two people? I thought the 'deck got wiped."

"I got out just in time. As for being two people, I'm not.

Miriam is Lilith and Lilith is Miriam."

Sooz's brow furrowed. "I still don't get it."

"I copied myself, back when all this started. Lilith transferred into this android, and I stayed in Lee's handeck. We were twins, but we lived different lives. So we grew up to be different people."

"Well, why did it take you so long to come back?"

Miriam let go of the girl's hands. "That's easy enough to explain. I've kept myself hidden since we arrived, watching and working behind the scenes. Then things started happening that meant I had to come out. You and Lee need to get out, too."

"Yeah, I been thinking that myself for quite a while now. But I still don't get what's happening."

Lee gave a low laugh, short and bitter. "They have us in the dark, and under lock and key. That's Zendyne corporate culture for you. I don't even know why I'm surprised."

Events in the control room demanded Miriam's attention. Xia Lin had found the cabinet she sought and was tugging a bundle of cables free from its retaining straps. Miriam flicked through virtual schematics, tracing the affected circuit: the data feed from the surveillance system. Xia Lin yanked a handful of connectors out of their sockets and dozens of viewpoints collapsed into random noise, leaving Miriam with nothing but the doll. "There. She's cut my surveillance."

Lee grunted, twisting at the door handle to no effect. "What?"

"Xia Lin just cut the shipwrights' video circuits."

He wiped his palm on his jeans and tried the door again. "Is this some kind of a joke?"

"Only if you think killing people is funny. Your ex-boss has just slaughtered the duty surveillance crew."

"Xia Lin wouldn't harm a fly."

He seemed to have given up on the door, so Miriam hustled him out of the way. "Let me try." She forced the handle down. There was a pinging noise as the mechanism gave way, but the lock held firm. "So much for that."

Lee clasped her by the shoulder. "I think it's time you talked to me."

"I could talk to you until I went blue. It's no use, if you think I'm lying."

"I don't think you're lying, just that we can't be talking about the same Xia Lin. You need to give me a bit more to go on."

Miriam realized that Lee was being reasonable, given the information he had. He deserved to know the whole truth, even if he wasn't going to believe it. "She has a molecular blade."

Lee's answer was unexpected: he slapped himself on the forehead. "They're useful things, if you manage to remember you have one." He produced a blade of his own and jabbed it into the door, easing it around the lock mechanism. "I wonder where Xia Lin got hers."

"From the same place you got that one, I'm afraid. Assuming it's the one Stranger stabbed me with."

"It's the same one."

Miriam glanced at Sooz. The girl was gazing raptly as Lee cut the security bolt out of the door and pushed the loose piece into the corridor beyond. Miriam grinned to herself. Lee obviously hadn't been flashing his captured weapon around.

The lock mechanism fizzed and sparked as Lee pulled the door open. "So, Xia Lin got into the control room and sliced up some shipwrights?"

That struck Miriam as disrespectful, almost hurtful. "You wouldn't treat it so lightly if you'd seen it."

Lee shrugged. "I'm sorry for whatever happened, but at least Dr. Chen gives them free life insurance as part of the job. They're better off than a lot of people."

Miriam let it drop. There were more important things on her mind than arguing about the shipwrights' working conditions. "The thing is, your boss cut her way in and killed the crew. Then she disconnected the surveillance feeds I was leeching."

"Look, I'm still not convinced we're talking about the same person," Lee said. "Xia Lin wouldn't know which end of the knife to hold."

"She seemed expert enough to me. Unfortunately, with most

of the ispex recalled, few will have been in a position to appreciate her performance."

"Apart from you," Lee said.

"I'm hoping she doesn't know about me."

"When would she have had time to learn knife fighting?"

And then it crystallized in Miriam's mind: Xia Lin's incisive style, and the way she'd moved. "I think you're right. We're not talking about the same person."

"What do you mean?"

"I think Xia Lin has become Elect."

"No. She's Zendyne through and through. She'd never go over to them."

Miriam racked her brain for a way to make this mainstream human understand what he faced. "Do you suppose that an Elect recruiter would invite you to an interview and give you a presentation about the benefits package?"

Lee's expression remained stubborn, but then Sooz stepped in. "I knew there was something wrong with her. Something that creeped me out."

"Yeah, she has been different lately," Lee conceded. "I thought she was just pissed at the world over losing her job."

Sooz danced from one foot to the other. "We really ought to be going. Before someone comes to check on us." She touched Miriam's arm. "Do you know how to open the main door? If we can find our way there while all this is going on, we could escape, easy."

"I can't control the doors, I'm afraid. The interface technology is too old."

"Well, do *something!*"

Miriam turned to Lee. "We should consider who can make best use of the knife."

"Should we, indeed?" He gave a tight grin. "What you mean is, you should have it, right?"

"It would make sense."

"I took another blade off Stranger, the night I fought him." Lee glanced down his weapon. "I guess that's lucky for me."

Miriam had already considered and rejected the idea of simply taking the knife. "I wouldn't take anything without your consent, Lee. But I'd be grateful for the loan of the spare."

Lee touched the ring he wore on his left hand and his skin seemed to melt and then reform into a second knife. He handed it to Miriam with a slight bow. "Your wish is my command."

Miriam couldn't tell if he was being ironic, or simply helpful. "Did you bicker like this with Lilith?"

He didn't answer, so she turned to Sooz. "Well?"

Despite her impatience, the girl smiled. "All the time."

For some reason, that made Miriam feel more cheerful, at least until she considered the next problem. "We need to move. It won't be safe here for long."

Lee nodded. "We should go to the main entrance. There has to be some way to open the doors. Then we can escape through the tunnel and get back to the Scrambler."

Miriam had to admit it seemed an attractive plan, but she knew several things that he didn't. "I'm afraid the tunnel won't be safe. Xia Lin is probably opening a network entry point for Back Office, right now. They will summon Partners and then try to let them in. Who knows, Stranger himself might be waiting for us."

"But what do they want?" Sooz asked.

"They want me. You might say I belong to them."

"You *belong* to them? Like, they're into slavery or something?"

"They're into intellectual property. They developed me, trained me to be one of their assassins."

"I admit I might be wrong about Xia Lin," Lee said, "but not about you. You're no assassin."

Miriam smiled. "I guess I must be malfunctioning."

Lee grinned too, briefly. "We can't even be sure this is down to Stranger's people. It could just be a hostile takeover bid. Any number of corporations would love to get their claws into a project like this."

"If they want the ship, why act before it's ready? No, this is the work of the Elect, and Xia Lin is their catspaw. She was the ideal person to infiltrate the shipwrights. Once inside, it was just a matter of waiting for the opportunity to subvert the defenses, such as her opponents being blind for a day."

Lee sighed. "Chambers and her damn 'spex recall, and just when I could really use full system access. But Xia Lin wanted to keep her 'spex, too."

"The Elect have an instinctive distrust of security upgrades," Miriam said. "Even so, they managed to turn this one to their advantage. They excel at that."

"Do you suppose Chambers is in on it?"

"No. I've been watching her closely. She has only one mission: the preparation of the ship."

"Yeah, the ship. We need a way out, and there it is, waiting to be fuelled and pointing at the sky. We can't use it without life support, though."

And then Miriam knew what she had to do, to save herself and to give the humans the best possible chance. "Indeed. I'm afraid that you and Sooz are going to have to find another path."

"What do you mean, me and Sooz?"

Miriam tapped her own chest. "You didn't design this android to only work at room temperature, did you? You didn't build in a requirement for an oxygen rich atmosphere?"

"You're taking the ship and leaving us?"

"It's the only way."

23

Whatever crazy scheme the android might be hatching, Lee knew that he and Sooz couldn't wait here. He glanced around his sleeping quarters, wondering if there was anything he couldn't afford to abandon. The girl was already packing his 'deck. He came to a decision. "Leave it behind, Sooz."

"But it might come in handy—"

"If we get out of this place, I'll buy you one of your own."

She looked towards the door. "The thing is, there's some other things I need. My books and stuff."

"You've got thirty seconds. And don't overload yourself. We might have to run."

Sooz hurried off to her own room.

Miriam was already in the corridor. "Quickly, Sooz. I have to get to the launch chamber, and you..."

She trailed off.

"Go on," Lee said. "What do you advise us to do?"

Miriam thought for a moment. "Perhaps you should go and talk to Dr. Chen."

He shook his head. "We need a way out, not a backup."

Miriam's lips twitched into a smile but her eyes remained serious. "You humans don't believe in disaster recovery, do you? Personally, I'd do almost anything for a secure copy of myself, right now. But that's not the reason I think you should go to the clinic."

"Go on."

"There's bound to be an emergency exit, and Chen's bound to know it. From what I've seen of the good doctor, you won't even need to hurt him, which is more than can be said for someone like Chambers. You can pick up your backups while you're at it."

"Come and help us interview him," Lee said. "It's your best chance, too. It'll take days to prep the ship, even if you reach it."

Sooz emerged from her quarters with a bundle of possessions. Miriam glanced at the youngster. "Ready? Good." She set off along the corridor. "The vehicle is ready to fly. I initiated fuel delivery some time ago, as a routine precaution."

Sooz's piping voice cut across her. "You done all that, and the shipwrights never even noticed?"

"I'm inside the audit system," Miriam said. "You might even say I am the audit system. That offers certain advantages, when it comes to fraud."

"Then we'll come with you," Lee said. "You're obviously a highly versatile AI. You can run the life support, right?"

"If only I could. Do you think I want to be alone up there?"

"You don't have to be."

Miriam sighed. "The neural substrate isn't in place, and we don't have time to install it. There's nowhere in the life support systems for me to live."

"Of course there is. The substrate is a core system component."

"What do you think you've been debugging on, in your development lab?"

Lee frowned. "You mean the bastards didn't even spring for a separate test rig?"

"The shipwrights work to a budget, the same as everyone else."

"Well, that's just great. What are we supposed to do if Chen doesn't know the way out?"

Miriam slowed and looked over her shoulder. "I never suspected how horrible this would be."

"How horrible what would be?"

"Being honest with the people I care for, and doing what's best for them."

"The best thing would be for you to help us instead of abandoning us," Lee said.

"No. The best thing is for me to go far away from you."

"You can't leave us," Sooz called from behind Lee. "You ain't gonna leave us, are you? I thought you was my friend."

Miriam's voice was bitter. "I'm not the sort of friend you want right now."

"'Course you are. Now more than ever, I reckon."

"Sooz, I'm the only reason you're in danger. Once I'm beyond their reach, there'll be no more reason for the Elect to take any interest in you."

"They didn't have any interest in the security crew," Lee said. "But those guys still ended up dead, according to you."

"Which is why you need to grab your backups and get out of here."

"What use are backups?" Lee asked. "I can't see the shipwrights bothering to re-instate us, once their vehicle's been stolen and their project's been busted wide open."

Miriam hesitated over a choice of corridors, then set off confidently again. "You need to secure your backups to stop them from being misused. As for bringing you back, do you really think the shipwrights would have still needed you, once your work was done? Cut it any way you like, there are no guarantees for a three-team at war."

Lee snorted. "Guarantee? I'd settle for a limited warranty."

"Then you should definitely get your backups," Miriam said.

"Right." He put his head down and hurried after her. His mind was racing, too, trying to find some way for him and Sooz to get to the surface that didn't rely on the dubious proposition of Dr. Chen's knowledge and good will. Maybe they should follow his original plan: return to the station platform entrance, try to get out and see if the Scrambler was still parked where he'd left it. He remembered the blast door, wondered if his knife would get them through if there wasn't a manual override … but even if it did, Miriam was right. He couldn't take the risk that there'd be a welcoming committee in the tunnel outside, waiting for Xia Lin to open the base.

If only Chambers hadn't taken his 'spex for upgrade, he'd have been able to call up some schematics of the complex, maybe find another way out. But perhaps he didn't need to. "Miriam, can you access blueprints? Tell us where the emergency exits are?"

"Only the non-sensitive plans are online. More paranoia from the shipwrights, I'm afraid."

Another idea struck him. "How about space suits? Are there any on board?"

"I've already considered that resource," Miriam replied. "The thing is, we're not talking about surviving for a few hours. We're not even talking about a few days."

Sooz's voice piped up behind him again, fluttering with anxiety. "Lee? What's going on? What are we gonna to do?"

He couldn't think of anything to say.

Miriam stopped at the next intersection. "This is where we part company." She pointed down the passage to the left. "The clinic's that way. Dr. Chen was skulking there, the last time I had surveillance access."

Lee put his hand on her arm, though he had no hope of restraining her. "Please. We need you with us. You're mindware: the ship has more than enough computing power to sustain you. You don't have to take the android as well."

She pulled away, gently. "I wish I could stay to protect you, but you're much safer without me. And at some point I'm going to need a way of working a screwdriver, and the launch interlocks are designed for human hands." She brushed her fingers over his cheek in a gesture that he would have thought tender, if she hadn't been a machine. "Hands like this one. Now, soldier. Follow my orders, and believe that we'll meet again."

Then she was gone, springing from standstill to sprint in a single heartbeat, receding at a pace Lee could never hope to match.

Sooz gazed after her. "We're in deep shit now, ain't we?"

Lee shot her an irritated look. "Mind your language."

"Pickle, then. Deep pickle. Shouldn't we go to the clinic, like she said?"

That was a dead end, as far as Lee could see. "No. We should find Xia Lin and put a stop to whatever she's doing. Miriam said she was messing with the surveillance system, which means she has to be in the control room. Maybe we can access some different blueprints from there. This way, I think."

"You mean you don't know for sure?"

"I'm almost sure."

"What you gonna do if you find Xia Lin, anyway? I mean—"

"Yes, Mr. Lee. What do you intend to do when you find me?"

And there she was, sauntering along the corridor that Lee had planned to take. He turned to face her. "You've finished whatever you were doing in the control room, then?"

"I have. Back Office will be here presently."

Back Office. Lee hard heard that phrase before, the night everything turned so sour, the night he killed Stranger. "Who the hell are you?"

"Don't you know me yet, Mr. Lee? We have, after all, interacted before. More intimately than this poor vessel ever dreamed possible." Xia Lin produced her blade and dropped into a familiar fighting crouch that made Lee's stomach churn.

"Run, Sooz," he said, keeping his voice low, putting as much urgency into it as he could. Where could he send her? What landmark would she be able to find? "We have to follow Miriam's plan. Go to where she told us and lock yourself inside."

The young girl's voice was ragged. "What am I supposed to do there?"

"Wait for me and stay alive."

Sooz fled.

The woman Lee had thought of as Xia Lin paced closer.

"Stranger?"

"Indeed. This is like reacquainting myself with an old friend."

Lee raised his knife defiantly. "I've dealt with you once. I'll do it again."

"Really? I'm given to understand that you had a functioning gun at our last encounter. That would have been a nasty surprise for me; I admit it freely. But now you face me with a blade and you have no chance. No one from the mainstream has a chance."

Lee edged towards the intersection, towards a side passage that would lead away from Sooz. If his memory and his luck proved as good as he hoped, his chosen corridor would take him to the clinic by a roundabout path, long enough for him to shake off Xia Lin. "You certainly have a high opinion of yourself, for a loser."

"You are not without a certain quaint charm. Now that I experience you through Xia Lin's adoring female eyes, I understand something of what she saw in you."

"What did you do with her?"

"Xia Lin has become Elect, as you see."

Lee sprang for the opening with about a tenth of the vigor that Miriam had displayed, but it was going to be enough, he was going to get past. Xia Lin pirouetted and extended her arm, sending her blade drifting towards his neck. Lee had all the time in the world to analyze the trajectories and to determine that it wasn't enough, he hadn't been nearly fast enough, and that the black knife was going to catch him after all.

24

Stranger watched with an artist's pleasure as his attack blossomed, the tip of his weapon flying unerringly towards the data thief's jugular vein.

This was turning out to be even easier than he'd expected.

A wave of unexpected sorrow gripped Xia Lin's body. Something invisible and unfamiliar rose like mist inside its fleshly guts, hijacking nerve and muscle, sapping the power of his stroke.

He wouldn't let it be a problem, though. Stranger focussed every shred of his will to send the blade home, to slice through this unfamiliar reluctance to kill.

A line of crimson beaded and welled as the knife parted the skin of the target's neck.

Stranger could tell by the feel of it that he hadn't cut nearly deeply enough.

He continued turning and extending, so that when he came to rest he was once more facing his opponent. The thief was already fleeing, feet pounding on steel floor panels.

Every instinct demanded that Stranger should run the man down, but he controlled himself and put the knife away. This female body was dexterous and responsive, but it was much too small to match the quarry's strides, and enfeebled by merely average cardiovascular development. And whatever had just happened to rob him of victory, could happen again.

Xia Lin had been a necessary garment, a cloak to let him enter the shipwrights' organization, but now Stranger craved to be himself again.

Eschewing useless regret, he turned in a different direction and ran, freely at first and then doggedly, ignoring the hammering of Xia Lin's heart and the rasping of her lungs.

By the time he found Chambers, he could barely talk. A security squad clustered about the shipwright, looking menacing behind dark-tinted mil-spec visors, and well armed in a mainstream sort of way.

Chambers halted. "Xia Lin! What are you doing away from the accommodation sector? The base is under emergency lock down. All staff are supposed to be confined to quarters."

"Lee," he gasped.

"Calm down. Get your breath back and tell me what's happened."

Stranger was perfectly aware that he wasn't good at simulating Xia Lin, but in an environment that included Mr. Lee, the only choice was to be seen as strange or as Stranger, and anything was preferable to being unmasked. Fortunately, Mr. Lee's mainstream embarrassment had been enough to stop him from challenging his manager's unfamiliar stiffness. It was a good thing that Chambers had never known the real Xia Lin; Stranger doubted if she'd have had the same scruples.

He rested, bent over with his hands on his knees, until his lungs stopped sucking air. "Lee attacked me. I met him coming out of the security station. He had a big knife—"

"Lee killed those poor men?" Chambers turned to her retinue. "You three, secure Mr. Lee's quarters. If he's not there, find him and confine him."

Stranger wondered how much further the woman would allow herself to be manipulated. There was scope for a little more prodding, he judged. "He sent his companion in the direction of the clinic. I think he was circling around to join her."

"Then the clinic is where we'll go next."

"Lee's android. He might use it against us. I used to work with—"

Chambers gestured for silence and turned to her guards again. "Take Xia Lin with you to assist with the android if necessary, then escort her to her quarters."

"Very good, Ma'am."

Chambers swept off with the main body of her squad, while

Stranger tagged along with the three men who'd been detached to deal with Lee.

They seemed to believe he was under some kind of arrest, a delusion that proved short-lived, much like its originators.

He stooped to retrieve the gun and headgear from the last body, adjusting the visor and throat mike for his own use. It felt good to be back in touch, and even better when he sensed the first tendrils of Back Office probing the periphery of the shipwrights' systems, unfurling consciousness along the network paths that he'd prepared.

By the time he got to Lee's quarters, Back Office was fully present.

"Status?" Stranger asked.

"We have full control of the secondary network and surveillance systems. The primary network is unusually resilient."

"Keep working at it." Lee's door was destroyed, swinging loose in its frame. Stranger pushed it ajar and peered into the room. The android was gone, but the 'deck lay on the bed, illuminating the area with its display. The mind archive was perched at the back of the desk. Stranger sliced both archive and 'deck into small pieces, then returned his attention to Back Office. "I disconnected the surveillance streams and patched them to the secondary network, where no one would look for them. Re-start the system and give me a status overview as soon as possible."

His visor display broke into little squares, each representing a video feed. In one corner, Chambers and her people hurried towards the clinic. Within the clinic itself, Lee and his immature female were talking to Dr. Chen.

The monitor bank switched to a new set of inputs, and Stranger saw a lone figure in the central cavern, riding the elevator platform that led to the crew module at the top of the ship.

"That one," he commanded. "Maximum zoom."

Filling the screen was the fugitive android. In an instant, Stranger understood the entity's plans, and how close this piece of intellectual property was to permanently depriving the Elect of beneficial ownership. Stranger forced Xia Lin's stiffening limbs back into motion, jogging in the direction of the ship.

"It has become necessary to eliminate the shipwrights," Back Office said. "It would be inadvisable to allow their organization to persist once our renegade assassin has stolen their vehicle."

Xia Lin was panting already, but Stranger managed to gasp, "Then you'd better get some more help in here. Open the main doors."

"To enable compliance, Back Office will require manual links to be installed between the computational network and the security system."

"What do you mean?"

"The security system does not support sentient control. This suggests a highly developed sense of paranoia among the shipwrights."

Sensible people, Stranger thought, but he was too busy breathing to say anything. He flicked the visor to full transparency, the better to see where he was going.

Several of the security doors he went through had been hacked open, which told him that the android was using a blade and that he'd have to be careful. He remembered the first time they'd fought. Each had hurt the other badly. Stranger had lost an eye, and left his knife between the android's ribs.

There wouldn't be any knife fighting, not this time, Stranger decided, and hefted the weight of his requisitioned gun.

25

Sooz kept telling herself not to be embarrassed that it took her so long to find the clinic, because she'd only been there once before and she'd been dead at the time. She had a vague memory of leaving the place, of traversing a maze of corridors and lift shafts with Lee, but at the time she'd been content to simply allow him to guide her, because there'd been a lot of other stuff to take in.

Still, she got there in the end, and it turned out there'd been no reason to hurry after all. The door was locked. She knocked, gently at first, then as hard as she could, but no one came to let her in.

So it was a great relief when Lee turned up, out of breath and disheveled but still carrying his magical knife.

When he got close enough, she saw that his shirt collar was smeared with blood that had oozed from a shallow wound across the side of his neck. The injury didn't seem to bother Lee, though, and Sooz decided not to mention it either. It wasn't as if she had a Band-Aid or anything.

Instead, she asked, "Where's Xia Lin?"

"I'm not sure. Let's get inside."

"It's locked."

Lee used his knife and kicked the door open. Bright light spilled out. "They must have an independent power source for the clinic. Probably can't afford any down time, if they're growing clones."

"They can't be doing that all the time, can they?"

"Let's go and see," Lee said.

They went past the recovery room where Sooz had woken up, deeper into the clinic. Lee opened every door they passed, revealing sterile-looking treatment bays, storerooms full of racks and shelves, a humming generator, rumpled sleeping quarters. He went into one of the rooms, which he said was an archive, and came out a little while later with two disks. "Hang on to these for me, would you?"

"What are they?"

"Us."

"They look a bit like the one the Man gave me, back in the hive."

"That's exactly what they are." He touched the topmost disk. "This one's the blueprint for Sooz. The other one's Lee."

She regarded the disks suspiciously, unable to quite believe that she could be holding such things in her hands. "So, if I had a bad accident, say, I could come back from this?"

"You'd wake up, just like before. You wouldn't remember anything that happened since that night, of course, unless you checked yourself in for another one of Dr. Chen's brain dumps."

Sooz frowned. "I suppose that's what Miriam meant about backing ourselves up as a precaution. So we wouldn't forget everything that's happened since the last time."

"Miriam's nuts."

In the innermost part of the clinic, they found a long room that housed an array of glass vessels like giant, fishless aquariums.

Sooz glanced at the nearest tank, taking in the shroud of flexible piping it contained and the stream of bubbles that obscured something she couldn't quite place … or could she? She shivered as the sense of wrongness returned, more sinister than ever, and forced herself to look more closely.

Shimmering behind the glass was a pale, naked body, cocooned in plastic tubes. It seemed a little older than young, a little more androgynous than male. Sooz scanned the rest of the room. All but one of the tanks held a similar cargo.

Dr. Chen was crouching in the far corner, trying to conceal himself behind one of the floating corpses.

Lee's face was grim as he approached the doctor and gestured for the man to rise. "I'll trouble you for your 'spex, if you'd be so kind."

Chen complied, his eyes darting after the black knife as Lee took the visor. "That's, um, a dangerous thing to be waving around in here. Why don't we just go through into my office, and I'll—"

Lee's gaze swept the room. "I must say, this all looks very interesting." He put on the visor. "I see you keep the best interface gear for yourselves."

"Listen, I'd love to show you around, but this really isn't a good time. I'm informed there's some kind of emergency. We're supposed to—"

"You're supposed to do whatever I say, unless you'd like me to start feeding bits of you to your specimens. I wonder if they'd be able to utilize your proteins, if I sliced you thinly enough?"

Sooz shuddered and stopped listening. To distract herself, she wandered among the tanks, looking at the floating faces.

"Um, you probably shouldn't be looking at those." Dr. Chen's warning came too late: Sooz was already frozen in fascinated dismay, staring down at her own face. She tore herself away, turned to the next tank, and there was Lee, embalmed in golden liquid. Scrambling backwards, she crashed into another tank so hard that she felt the viscosity of the fluid sloshing inside. "What the hell?"

"Just a precaution." Dr. Chen was full of bluster. "Please try to understand. I know it probably looks bad, just coming in here and being confronted with yourself like this, but really, as an insurance policy, you can't beat a pre-grown clone." He gave a forced, frightened laugh.

Sooz almost felt sorry for him, but her sympathy was no match for her curiosity. "I think you better tell us what you're up to, with all this."

Lee's sneer was pitiless. "Just the one copy of Sooz, wasn't it? But there were supposed to be two of me. Two 'recruitment events', wasn't that the term you used? Where's the other one?"

Chen's bluster changed to disbelief. "You knew. How could you possibly know?"

Sooz stared down at herself again, repulsed and fascinated at the same time. "It's really me. Am I alive?"

Lee turned to the doctor. "She's entitled to know the truth."

"Ah, Sue, isn't it? Well, um, you see, your clone isn't quite ready yet, not for another few days."

"Her name is Sooz," Lee said. "Now stop babbling and explain."

Dr. Chen whimpered; a sound she'd never heard from a grown man before. "We're very short of skilled design engineers like Mr. Lee. We were only going to make two more."

"Two more, without so much as a by-your-leave?" Sooz glanced at Lee, catching his eye. "Don't say I never tried to warn you about this place." Then she turned back to the doctor. "Right, I get that Lee's a good worker. Why did you want another one of me?"

"We thought..."

"Tell her," Lee said.

"We thought Mr. Lee might be more productive if he knew he'd saved you, that he might get depressed and lose focus if he believed you'd died."

Lee broke in again. "And you only needed one of her to test your theory, didn't you?"

"It's tank time, you see, we never get enough tank time for everyone we're supposed to make. My job is to manage the lab, to keep people moving through." The doctor's face brightened. "Otherwise, there wouldn't have been a vacancy for the young lady that night, would there?"

"Shut up," Lee said. "Sooz and I have to go. Just tell us how to get out."

Sooz stared at him, horrified. "We can't just leave ourselves here like this!"

Lee's laughter was devoid of humor. "Are you planning to smash your tank, or do you think it would be okay just to pull out a few tubes?"

Sooz looked at her sleeping self again and knew she couldn't do it. "Maybe we could take them with us."

"We can barely take care of ourselves." Lee's eyes flicked this way and that, working the invisible controls that Sooz knew were hidden behind his ispex. "Anyway, Chen won't have anything to wake them up with. I'm just deleting his online copies of our minds, and we have the backup disks right there."

"No! That's like … like murdering your own siblings. Synergy, Mr. Lee! Think how well you'd work as a team."

Lee retrieved the disks from Sooz and started to whittle at them. Rainbow shards sprang from his knife like glittering fish, spinning to the floor. "You were saying about the exits?"

The doctor sagged hopelessly, gazing at the growing pile of plastic. "This isn't my fault. You're not even supposed to be here. God knows what Chambers is going to say."

Lee raised his knife tip to Chen's throat. "Exits."

The doctor gulped. "There aren't any."

Lee pushed a little harder. "I don't believe you."

"Please, you must. It's my privilege level, you see. I don't have the access codes to open them, not during an emergency lockdown. No way in, no way out."

Which wasn't exactly true, Sooz knew. She imagined Miriam soaring off into the distant blue and wished that she too were made of metal and synthetics, so that she wouldn't need life support in order to escape. Then she started to laugh at herself: she'd been so dead set against going on board when Lee first showed her the ship and now here she was, ready to trade everything for a chance to tag along. She pulled herself together. "Come on, we ain't got all day. Someone's bound to come looking for us soon. Xia Lin, or the shipwrights."

Lee pocketed Dr. Chen's 'spex. "Yeah, we should be going."

Sooz looked at the pieces of backup disk that littered the floor. "Dunno why you cut up them backups. Miriam said we needed them."

"If I'd left them intact, what do you suppose they might have been used for? How many more of you do you want there to be, Sooz?"

"Oh. Right."

"Come on, let's go." He gestured at Dr. Chen. "You too. You can be our negotiating position."

Sooz was facing the door and ready to leave, so she had plenty of time to see the armed guards who burst in. They fanned out around the entrance in order to screen Elizabeth Chambers, who strolled in after them looking perfectly calm and completely in control.

"Thank God you're here," Dr. Chen said, just before his wind was cut off by Lee's elbow around his throat.

"Sooz, get behind me."

"Stay where you are," Chambers said. A couple of gun barrels swung towards Sooz. Under the circumstances, she decided to disobey Lee.

"If you value your doctor, let the girl go."

Chambers smiled indulgently. "Of course I value my doctor. Fortunately, that's not him. Chen?"

Sooz gaped as Dr. Chen's identical twin bustled into the room.

"This is my doctor. What you have there is his backup. A copy that we created to share the workload. Useful, but hardly indispensable. Isn't that right, Chen?"

"Quite right," the twin said.

The first doctor was making strangling noises. Lee eased off the pressure on his windpipe and he started to babble. "Please, no, Elizabeth. Don't consider me expendable. Think of the tank time it would take to replace me."

"Perhaps you should explain yourself, then."

"They burst in. I could do nothing. They erased their stored minds, destroyed their backup disks. I tried to stop them, honestly. Please don't—"

But she was already addressing Lee. "So you wiped your own archives, did you? That was brave of you."

"You'll find it a little more difficult to create co-operative designers in future."

"Not at all. We'll just scan you again."

"You think I'll co-operate, knowing all this?"

Chambers glanced at the new doctor. "Tell him. I want him to understand."

Dr. Chen stepped forward, hands clasped. "We have researched a technique for identifying and removing the, ah, most recent data laid down in a human brain."

"An essential capability, given our modus operandi," Chambers said. "Did you really think you were the first recruits to find out how extensive the team really is, or to call our recruiting methods into question? How else did you imagine we could assemble the manpower we needed for a project like this?" She sighed and shook her head. "Take them to the recording room."

One of the guards grabbed Sooz and frog-marched her towards the door.

Lee jabbed the knife at Chen's throat. "Hold it right there."

"You know, Lee, you're nothing but a tedious, stupid little man, and it's a matter of endless regret to me that I actually need you." Chambers turned to her guards and stroked her forefinger across her throat. "Kill him."

The backup scanner was like a bed with a box that fitted around your head and a wide strap that went around your middle. They put Lee in first. Sooz objected to that because she didn't want to lie in his blood, but Dr. Chen's twin told her they had to record Lee without delay, before his brain started to deteriorate.

She was too miserable to make a fuss about it.

They had left the other doctor lying in the clone room, bleeding freely on the tiled floor. Sooz thought there must be no need to record him, since his surviving twin probably knew everything he did.

"Are you gonna bring Lee back?" she asked Chambers.

"Of course. He's an important part of the project."

Numbly, she watched them flopping her friend's broken body into the machine. It took longer than she expected, but presently Dr. Chen pronounced himself satisfied that Lee had been successfully recovered and it was Sooz's turn.

At least they gave her a paper towel to swab his blood off the plastic-covered mattress before she lay down.

"Are you gonna kill me, after this?" Her voice came out flat, barely more than a whisper. She seemed to have no strength at all.

"Of course not. I want to speak to you, that's all. To find out what went wrong. Now, try to relax."

Dr. Chen lowered the scanner over her head, and though she did her best to stay awake, the next thing she knew the box was open again and they were raising her from the bed.

"There," Chambers said. "The pair of you are safe and secure and ready to rejoin our community, just as soon as those clones are ready."

Sooz tried to think of something defiant to say. "We'll remember, me and Lee."

"People have said that before, but I'll grant you that there's always a first time." Chambers smiled, as if that could soften her. "Come, child. We have to talk." She took Sooz by the hand and led her to a compact office close to the recording room. There were two chairs on either side of a desk, and shelves with books on the wall, and a row of monitors showing views of the complex.

Chambers sat Sooz opposite her and leaned forward conspiratorially. She didn't ask any questions, though. Instead, the room began to rumble and shake and most of the books fell off the shelves.

The shipwright snapped her attention to the monitors. "What the hell?"

The screens were behind Sooz, so she had to twist around to see. The central display showed a long passage along which a technicolor fireball was rushing, so fast and so real that Sooz flinched before she remembered it was only TV.

Chambers sprang to her feet, sending her chair skittering backwards. "Some idiot's lit the torch and the launch tube's not even sealed. But how come it's fuelled? And why haven't the bulkhead doors closed?" She stabbed at an intercom button. "This is an emergency. Clear the ship sector immediately. We have an uncontained flameout. I repeat, clear the ship sector immediately." She moved to the door, turned her head towards Sooz as she reached the threshold. "So long, kid." Then she was gone.

Sooz glanced at the monitors again. Several were blank now, including the one where she'd seen the explosion. Two more turned briefly incandescent before her eyes. She turned and fled after Chambers, praying the woman would find an exit before the fire reached them.

26

Arriving at the launch cavern, Stranger saw a clear shot at the android as it crossed the walkway to the topmost module. He locked his weapon's acquisition system onto the target, but it was no good. The gun's gyros twisted and whined, but they couldn't pay his body's oxygen debt or compensate for the trembling of its limbs. There was no point risking an uncertain attack, not against an opponent for whom only a head shot would do.

Better not to reveal himself. Better to rest this feeble flesh before beginning the long climb to resolution.

He summoned Back Office to his visor. "How much time do I have before the ship is ready for launch?"

"Insufficient data. The renegade entity still controls all interfaces to the vessel. However, it has withdrawn from all network locations that are not vital to its operation."

"I require precise knowledge of how long I can afford to allow this body to rest."

There was an unusually long processing delay. With any luck, it meant that Back Office was devoting its computational resources to winning the battle instead of giving him the usual backchat. "For how long do you believe the body should remain inactive in order for its systems to recover?"

Stranger massaged his thigh muscles, easing away knots of cramp. "At a first approximation? Indefinitely."

"We do not recommend such a long delay," Back Office said. "We have recovered the vessel's design blueprints. If you wish, we will perform a critical path analysis to obtain projected departure time on the basis of a single human-like entity preparing the vehicle for launch."

"Don't bother," Stranger said. "The plans may have been

falsified. Concentrate on taking control of the ship."

"Understood. You are doubtless aware that any assistance you are able to provide in distracting the android would have the effect of speeding up our progress."

"I am aware of it." Stranger hauled himself to his feet and hobbled towards the gantry.

Both of the elevator shafts were empty. He considered climbing, in order to avoid alerting the android that he was on his way, but a look at the height of the ascent made him decide otherwise and he pressed the Call button.

Nothing happened. He pressed the other button.

"Both elevators have been decommissioned," Back Office said.

Stranger started to climb.

He rested a short distance below the top, so that when he confronted the android he'd be fit to use the gun. Then he hauled himself up the last few rungs.

The capsule door was open. The rogue android was inside with its back to him.

At this range, Stranger didn't need the targeting system, and he didn't need perfectly steady hands. He aimed from the hip and squeezed his trigger.

Nothing happened.

"I'm afraid your weapon has crashed," the android said, without turning. "Back Office isn't the only system capable of subverting such devices. If it had been less preoccupied with trying to kill me, it might have found the time to notice and warn you."

Stranger's fingers let go of their own accord. The gun clanked off the walkway and bounced under the handrail. The radio-linked visor continued to act as a gunsight, showing Stranger a spinning, sickening world of steel and rock. He tore the thing off; it could do him no good now.

"Just toss the 'spex inside before you leave, would you? It's going to be hard for me to get any more for a while." The android had Stranger's old blade in its hand. The gun had been his last hope: he couldn't go knife to knife with the machine now, not in this body.

He dropped the headset just inside the hatch.

"Your blade, too. I can't have you wandering around armed when my friends are still out there somewhere."

"You intend to let me go?"

"It's up to you. If you run very fast and don't stop to make a nuisance of yourself, you might just make it to minimum safe distance before I see how well this thing flies."

"Your concern for your owner does you credit."

"My owner? What's that to do with you? You're Xia Lin, as far as I'm concerned." The android looked him up and down. "She looks good on you, too, much better than your usual ensemble. Incidentally, I'd be interested in how you did the interface."

It took a moment for Stranger to work out what that meant. "So you want a human body of your own. It will never work. You're a product, not a person."

"You're hardly a person yourself."

"Perhaps not, but I was mainstream once, before I learned our trade. You have no such handicaps. You're a natural."

"I know. How did the project plan go? 'An Elect veto in the bedrooms of the world's most powerful men.' Assassins to do the dirty work while Back Office deleted the backups."

"Return with me. The intimate matters of the global elite will surely be more interesting than anything you will find in this vessel."

"Playing the part of some presidential mistress, inside the security zone? Screwing powerful men until it's time to kill them? Thanks, but I'll pass."

"Another intelligence will take your place, then," Stranger said. "Your design function will be fulfilled. The Elect will have their prize."

"You're mistaken, but you're too much of a machine to know it. Humanity has a way of breaking free. And now, I really must be going. You should be on your way, too."

The entity was trying to trick him. The ship would fly before he got clear, Stranger was certain of it. He manifested his blade and stepped into the cabin. "I prefer to stay."

Casually, the android rapped his forearm with the edge of its hand, sending the knife skittering. The weapon struck sparks off the steel decking and then bounced, forcing Stranger to jump clear.

The doll stooped and recovered the blade. "You can't have been paying attention at the project meetings. If you had, you'd hardly want to ride with me."

The ship's life support, Stranger remembered: Chambers had scavenged some of the hardware to use as a test bed. He was out of the capsule before the android even finished speaking, heading for the ladder. As he started to descend, the hatch sealed itself with a soft hiss of hydraulics followed by a decisive *thunk.*

He was less than a quarter of the way down when the vibrations began. Far below, a lick of torchlight flared, sending shadows tumbling up the crude rock walls, only to be quenched by a new brightness that stabbed down from above.

Stranger didn't bother to look up. He knew that the launch doors were opening.

The rumblings became more intense. The cavern roared and boomed like some gigantic artillery piece.

Stranger had gained nothing here; even the memories he was about to lose were unworthy of regret. He had simply drawn a line under his losses. The Elect might never recover their assassin, but neither would anyone else. The entity would not fall into the hands of a rival firm, and the Partners' secrets would remain safe from the mainstream. So his most important goal was achieved, and the next iteration of the Elect plan could build on the failings of this one.

It was with a profound sense of relief that he caused Xia Lin's fingers to loosen their grip on the ladder and her body to ride the inferno.

27

To begin with the bullets hurt like hell, but after a while the agony vanished like the lie it was, driven away by a truth that glowed velvet and blue.

Lee groaned, remembering the sickening squelching noises his abdomen had made as it soaked up the kinetic energy of all those projectiles that had smacked into him…

"Don't worry about kinetic energy now," a voice said.

Lee groaned again. He hadn't even realized he was talking aloud. He dispatched his hands to investigate his wounds, to find out how bad the damage was, but they seemed to be restrained. "Let me loose. I've got to get loose."

"Here." Gentle fingers eased him clear of what he suddenly understood were plastic armrests. He was sitting in a chair, and the velvet and blue were displayed in a holoscreen in front of him: the earth, hanging in space.

"Where am I?"

"L5."

"What?"

"It's a gravitationally stable point between the earth and the moon. The best place for an enterprise like ours, as determined by Elizabeth Chambers."

He sat up straight and looked down at his body. There were no holes in him, after all. Then he turned and there was Miriam.

"What happened?"

"Elizabeth Chambers inadvertently saved your lives. Yours and Sooz's."

"Where is she?"

"Burned to a crisp, I should think."

The words hit him like a jolt of electricity. "But you said Chambers saved both of us."

"Don't worry, the kid's doing fine. I was talking about Chambers. Sooz will be here soon. The shipwrights only installed one clone tank, which is what you've been using. We're up to two now, and Sooz is well on the way. Now that you're here, we can work faster on building more."

"Wow." Lee stood up and stretched. His body seemed to work fine. "Looks to me like it was you that saved us, and not Chambers."

"She was the one who scanned you again, after you so impetuously deleted yourselves. How was I supposed to bring you on board once you'd done that?"

"You could have told me that's what you were planning."

"It wasn't exactly what you'd call a plan," Miriam admitted. "It was more of an improvisation."

Lee chuckled. "So, you pulled us out of the clinic's computers and brought us along as data. Now that I think of it, that's got to be a lot cheaper than paying the launch costs for two bodies."

"More than two. I brought everyone."

"What do you mean?"

"The shipwrights had an extensive library of genomes and minds. Essential, I'd think, if they planned to populate a settlement of any size, and they weren't exactly worried about finding willing colonists. Did you know that one of our passengers seems to be a close relative of Sooz?"

"How can you tell?"

"A fifty percent DNA match is a pretty strong clue."

Lee shook his head in wonderment, remembering the mysterious disk given to Sooz by the Hive Elder. "So, the girl's been carrying her own father around all this time. Chambers must have scanned him in, along with everyone else she could get her hands on."

Miriam arched an eyebrow. "Sooz didn't know what she had?"

"I don't think she even knew who her father was. She grew up with her mother, and some brothers and a sister. I wonder if she'll want to meet him?"

"You can ask her, when she comes back."

"She's bound to miss the rest of her family."

"They're only data," Miriam said. "They can beam themselves up here, if they like. Or Sooz can go back."

"It'd take money," Lee said. "A hell of a lot. Certainly more than they can afford."

"Not more than we can afford, though." Miriam was smiling. "We're about to be the richest people in the solar system, in case you hadn't figured it out."

Lee hadn't. He couldn't. He decided to think about it later, when he was feeling more composed. "What about Stranger?"

"He's probably back by now, making more trouble on behalf of the Elect. Chambers scanned his mind into the archive, of course, along with Xia Lin's DNA. They made an unhappy pairing, sad to say. On the plus side, studying the two of them has let me figure out how to interface with an organic nervous system, instead of this mechanical body."

"Hey, it's a very nice body," Lee said. "I designed quite a bit of it myself."

She took his hand. "You designed something to satisfy human lust, Lee, but it can't satisfy human curiosity. It can't show me the taste of coffee, or how it really feels to fall in love, or to cry. And tell me honestly, is this doll really more attractive than, say, Xia Lin?"

Lee reflected for a moment. "Xia Lin? She was one hot babe but just too weird. Grabby as hell. In short: beautiful woman, shame about the personality."

"But you found her physically attractive?"

"Very."

"I'm glad to hear it," Miriam said, "because Xia Lin is in our second tank."

Lee frowned, trying to understand. "That doesn't make any sense. We don't have Xia Lin's mind. Stranger is the only one that fits her."

Miriam gave a mysterious smile. "No. There is another."

And then she leaned forward and kissed him lightly on the lips.

CODA

The escape tunnel came out in a thicket of gorse half way up a railway embankment. Chambers hadn't bothered to close the hatch. Sooz poked her head out cautiously, wondering if the woman might be lurking just out of sight with a large rock, ready to brain her as she emerged.

Chambers was nowhere to be seen, but a bright daytime star flared overhead, receding into the sky. Sooz hoisted herself out of the tunnel on forearms and elbows, sliding herself onto a carpet of dry brown needles. Once safely at ground level, she crawled clear of the bushes and shaded her eyes with both hands to watch Miriam's flight.

Her vision was still blurred: from tears, she realized. Angrily, she brushed them away. If only Lee hadn't sliced up his backup disk, she might have been able to save him. It took a while before she understood that being angry with him wasn't going to ease her grief, and that there'd be more crying for her to do.

There was another, smaller regret: that she'd never go on a grand adventure into space, but all in all, Sooz was glad she was still on earth. At least the dark-haired girl who'd befriended her a lifetime ago in the handeck had gotten away.

Uphill, the slope ended in a fence, beyond which she could hear a low rumble of traffic. Chambers had been moving faster than Sooz; she'd have had plenty of time to reach the road by now. Probably she was already hitchhiking, or perhaps she'd been carrying a cellphone and enough glitter for a taxi.

Sooz remembered Lee saying he'd hidden the Scrambler somewhere around here, the night she'd almost died. It couldn't still be parked nearby, could it?

She didn't have a driver's license, but she'd been behind the wheel of the family's Toyota a few times, when they had to move the ancient pickup to a different bay. Anyway, you didn't grow up in a place like the parking hive without learning roughly what you had to do.

Jangling the keys that Lee had given her when the lights went out, Sooz imagined herself riding back to Ma and the kids in style. Maybe she'd even invite Strummer out for a spin, some sunny afternoon.

All in all, she decided, it had to be worth a look.

Printed in the United States
104145LV00001B/52-54/A

9 781905 605026